THE THIRTEENTH DISCIPLE

LEWIS GRASSIC GIBBON (whose real name was James Leslie Mitchell) was born in February 1901 at Hillhead of Seggat, Auchterless in the Buchan area of Aberdeenshire. When he was eight, his family moved to the Howe of the Mearns, which later became the setting for his celebrated *Scots Quair* trilogy. After pursuing a career in journalism in Glasgow, Grassic Gibbon served in both the army and the RAF before settling in Welwyn Garden City, where he died in 1935.

JACK WEBSTER was born in 1931 in the village of Maud in Aberdeenshire. At the age of sixteen he started work as a journalist with the *Turiff Advertiser*. He later moved on to the *Evening Express* and *The Press and Journal* in Aberdeen, before joining the *Scottish Daily Express* in Glasgow. He is now a popular columnist with *The Herald*. He has written books on a wide variety of subjects, including a highly-acclaimed auto-biography *Grains of Truth*. Jack Webster lives in Glasgow.

THE THIRTEENTH DISCIPLE

LEWIS GRASSIC GIBBON

Introduced by Jack Webster

EDINBURGH
B&W PUBLISHING
1995

First published 1931
This edition published 1995
by B&W Publishing, Edinburgh
Introduction © Jack Webster
ISBN 1 873631 55 3

The publisher acknowledges subsidy
from the Scottish Arts Council towards
the publication of this volume.

British Library Cataloguing in Publication Data:
A catalogue record for this book is available
from the British Library.

Cover illustration: Detail from
The Spotted Scarf
by J D Fergusson.
Reproduced by kind permission
of Lord and Lady Irvine.

Cover design by *Harry Puma & Co*

Printed by Werner Söderström

CONTENTS

INTRODUCTION

Jack Webster

The writing of Lewis Grassic Gibbon not only gave us a new and imaginative form of language but has so captivated and stirred succeeding generations as to give him a vast legion of devotees in his native Scotland and far beyond.

Alas, by the time even his early readers could grapple with the extent of his genius the man himself was gone, dead before his thirty-fourth birthday in circumstances which add their own poignancy to an extraordinary talent.

Lewis Grassic Gibbon (his real name was James Leslie Mitchell) was without doubt one of the great international writers of the 20th century, his reputation owing most of all to three remarkable novels, written in the last three years of his tragically short life, which followed the story of the memorable Chris Guthrie through her love-hate relationship with the land of her own seeding.

That story, which began with *Sunset Song*, was a reflection of Gibbon's own feelings about that land of the Mearns, to the south of Aberdeen, where he railed against the drudgery of toil yet could not escape an abiding love of his native soil and a wonder and admiration for the crofting folk who broke body and spirit in wresting a bare living from its tilth.

We followed Chris Guthrie through the First World War and on to the sequels of *Sunset Song*, which were *Cloud Howe* and *Grey Granite*, later given the trilogy title of *A Scots Quair* (a word similar to 'quire').

By his early thirties Grassic Gibbon had perfected his unique form of language, which was basically English but moulded quite intriguingly into the rhythms of the speech he knew in that rural North-east of Scotland.

Narrative was blended with italicised dialogue in such sweet harmony that, when linked to the depth of his passion and height of his imagery, it could stir a rare excitement in the reader. I must be far from alone in saying that the encounter with *Sunset Song* in my teenage years was to open my eyes to the life around me and let me view it with a new enlightenment. For the aspiring writer it was also a lesson on what could be done with words.

Like many another devotee of Grassic Gibbon, however, I savoured that experience for many a long day without having read anything else by the same author. His masterpiece, produced in the nick of time, was such a gem as to raise fears of possibly discovering that the earlier work was inferior.

Dabbling in his essays and short stories, however, brought the confidence to probe further into Grassic Gibbon's output. That was how I came upon *The Thirteenth Disciple*, now in your hands as a new edition, and warmed to the prospect of reading a novel, written under his own name of James Leslie Mitchell, which was said to be strongly autobiographical. That was how it turned out.

The factual story was that Mitchell was born on 13 February 1901 at Hillhead of Seggat, Auchterless, a croft on the edge of the Buchan area of Aberdeenshire which happened to be my own homeland. When the boy was eight his parents, James and Lilian Mitchell, moved across the North-east of Scotland to the district known as the Mearns, where the rest of his childhood was spent on the croft called Bloomfield, high on the Reisk road at Arbuthnott.

By coincidence, for a boy destined to be one of Scotland's greatest prose writers, his new abode was almost within sight of the farm which was the family home of Robert Burns's father, William, before he went south to look for work and settled in Ayrshire. How strange that two of Scotland's greatest literary lights should have owed so much to those few square miles of red clay in the Mearns.

But it was there on that fine stretch of land sweeping down from Grampian heights and undulating towards the North Sea by Bervie that Leslie Mitchell grew up with older brothers George and John, conventional lads who gave no hint of what could be expected in Leslie.

He walked the hilly road to Arbuthnott School where, as other boys would be engaged in playground rough-and-tumble, he could be found sitting on the school dyke reading a book. Later, when he cycled to school, that open book would be placed on handlebars, a habit which landed him at least once in a ditch.

By nine he had a passion for archaeology, obsessed by the nearby standing stones of ancient times, and at night he would wander out by Bloomfield croft and gaze at the stars till his father would call him in with a rebuke for wasting his time.

He had good fortune in the man who became headmaster of Arbuthnott School before the First World War and realised the exceptional talent on his hands. Alexander Gray sought to stimulate the interest and lent him the books he would not have found in his own home. By the age if thirteen he had been with Darwin through *The Origin of Species* and was following H G Wells, who later became a personal friend.

It was one of the pleasures of my inquisitive youth to ferret out Mr Gray, by then an old man but still teaching Greek at Drumtochty School, near Stonehaven, and to retrace with him some of the steps of Leslie Mitchell. We went back to Bloomfield, on to the old school at Arbuthnott where he first encountered the young genius, and finally down to the kirkyard where his remains are buried.

Back at Mr Gray's house in Stonehaven, he turned out the essay book which he had kept for forty years or more. What of this from a twelve-year-old Leslie Mitchell, expressing his wonder at the scope of the Universe?:

What an irresistible feeling of power comes when on a calm clear night you gaze up at the millions of glistening worlds and constellations which form the Milky Way. 'Tis then, and then only, that one can realise the full power of the Creator and the truth of the wild dream of the German poet. There is no beginning, yea, even as there is no end.

Turning fact into fiction, *The Thirteenth Disciple* takes in that rural beginning and higher education, in reality at Mackie Academy, Stonehaven, where he showed signs of the wayward genius and fell foul of the staff, some of whom he pitied for "gaping ignorance" and "shoddy erudition." The novel gives us a dramatic re-enactment of what more or less happened in a classroom at Mackie Academy, before he walked out with a whistle and a swagger and vowed never to return. He never did.

By sixteen he was a junior reporter with the Aberdeen Journal, lodging with the mother of fellow-reporter George MacDonald, who became a close friend and spent most of his career as the Glasgow Herald's man in Aberdeen.

The Thirteenth Disciple skirts round that early phase of journalism but picks up on the next move to Glasgow, where he joined The Scottish Farmer in 1919 at a weekly wage of £2. 5s. By now he was much involved with left-wing politics, witnessing the notorious scenes in the city's George Square that year but bringing his journalism to a premature end by falsifying expenses to help finance the politics.

It was a crime which would scarcely have been noticed in the journalism of a later date (though he did rather overdo the amount!) but it brought him the sack and a burden on his conscience which led to a suicide attempt. Back home there were rows with the cantankerous father Mitchell, who knew all along of course that this writing business would come to no good. The lad should be taking a "fee" on a farm like all decent people.

Instead, the unsettled Mitchell joined the army, managed

to pursue his interest in archaeology through a posting to the Middle East, and when that was over he joined the RAF, at much the same time as Lawrence of Arabia. All told, he managed to see sights like Cairo and the Pyramids as well as visiting Jerusalem and spending a Christmas Eve in Bethlehem. Those regimented years of the early 1920s could, however, have been more profitably spent.

In 1925 he married his former school friend Rebecca Middleton, from a neighbouring croft at Arbuthnott, who was by now a Civil Servant in London. In that same year they went by boat from London to Aberdeen for a holiday in their native Mearns.

Having won a story-writing competition in the RAF, Leslie Mitchell was now seriously trying to make a living as a writer, mainly with contributions to the Cornhill Magazine. But it was not until 1928 that he wrote his first book, *Hanno, or the Future of Exploration*, and a further two years before his first novel, *Stained Radiance* which, like many another first novel, was fairly heavy on autobiography.

It is sometimes quoted as a measure of the furious pace at which Mitchell worked that his writing career was squeezed into the last seven years of his life, during which he produced no fewer than seventeen books. That would certainly be an impressive achievement. But the astonishment is heightened further when you consider that fifteen of those books appeared in the four years from 1931 till 1934.

In his determination to make a living as a writer he found it impossible to turn down a commission. So we are left with the quandary: Did this ridiculous schedule hasten his death? Or did some premonition drive him on to make the most of his limited time? We shall never know.

What we do know is that that hectic four-year spell began with *The Thirteenth Disciple*, still only his second novel, in which he adjusted the facts of his own life to allow the hero, Malcom Maudslay, to fight in the First World War, an experience which Mitchell himself just missed. His imagination, however, didn't let him down in producing a vividly horrifying picture of trench warfare.

In rest-camp behind the lines Malcom Maudslay is playing football for his battalion team when he trips over an opponent and takes a second look at him. It is his brother Robert, a coincidence which was not so uncommon in the world wars. So the two of them sit down in a foreign barn and catch up with the news, awkward at first, in the manner of North-east folk, especially since Malcom has broken ties with father and home. But their thoughts are now far from the glaur of a foreign battlefield, back where the clover will be standing thick and bonnie. Robert glances out below the barn eaves and mutters to himself: "They'll be bringin hame the kye the noo."

They were simple, touching moments—the last before Malcom saw Robert disappear into battle in a tank, thrusting his face from the port-hole and shouting something to his brother. Malcom never saw him again.

But *The Thirteenth Disciple* goes on to deeper thoughts about the Diffusionist theory which took up much of Mitchell's attention. Roughly speaking, it is the idea that primitive man was a peace-loving and decent soul who was corrupted only by what we call civilisation, a notion which exercises the mind as Mitchell trails the reader into unfamiliar territory.

But for students of the man who latterly took on the name of Lewis Grassic Gibbon, one of the delights of reading *The Thirteenth Disciple* is to pick up the early threads of that writing style which was to bring him such fame and to detect what he was doing to develop it.

Little time was left. In February of 1932 a young Aberdeen journalist, Cuthbert Graham, who would later become his friend, followed his criticism of the next novel with these significant words:

How will Mr Mitchell develop? It is to be hoped that he will settle down to give us novels of the North-east. After all, he must know the countryside of his birth and upbringing best, and the Mearns, unlike the Wessex of Hardy or the Argyll of Neil Munro, has not been made to live in a novel, and Mr Mitchell could do it.

Mitchell did not over-care for the book review but he did react to say: "One of these days I'll write that North-east novel he talks about." Perhaps it spurred him into action because not only did he proceed to write his greatest book, *Sunset Song*, within the next few weeks but had it in print by the August of that same year. In the following two years he completed that trilogy of *A Scots Quair*, intermingled with the rest of his vast output. The distinctive style had been established.

As his biographer, Ian Munro, pointed out, by the summer of 1934 he was committed to more than a million words, including three novels, two biographical works, a 250,000-word history of the world, a massive study of world religions, a social commentary on Scotland and his autobiography.

Without the back-up of journalism required by many novelists, he was actually making a living as a writer of books, albeit a modest one. He now had a home in Welwyn Garden City with his wife, four-year-old daughter and newly-born son to support. But he was surely driving himself beyond the limit.

Those visits home to the Mearns had been uneasy affairs, his first appearance after writing *Sunset Song* being greeted by his mother, looking at him sadly, with: "Laddie, what did you want to write all that muck for? It's the speak of the place. Your father's fair affronted and I'm ashamed of you too."

Coming from his mother, that reaction left a deep hurt. For that "muck" of which she spoke would turn out to be the masterpiece which elevated him to the company of Scott and Stevenson.

On his last visit, in the summer of 1934, he brought his new motor car as a hint of material progress, but there was no pleasing old man Mitchell, who had a sarcastic comment about "getting up in the world." He took his parents for runs but ended the visit at the home of his old dominie, Alexander Gray, who had by now moved over to Echt in Aberdeenshire.

It was there on the Schoolhouse green that he completed *Grey Granite*, folding over his notebook but telling Mrs Gray that he doubted if she would think as much of it as she had done of the other two.

Cuthbert Graham accompanied him on the southward journey but soon a recurring stomach complaint was troubling him and in February 1935 he became desperately ill and was rushed to hospital in Welwyn Garden City. An operation failed to save his life and he died on 7 February, a week before his 34th birthday, the death certificate showing the cause as peritonitis following the operation for a perforated gastric ulcer.

A great talent was gone and Scotland in particular mourned an illustrious son. After cremation at Golders Green in London they took his ashes back to the Kirkyard of Arbuthnott, to that red clay soil of the Mearns to which he had given such eloquent voice.

The Scottish poetess Helen Cruickshank, who had been deeply concerned about his failing health, described the scene at the Arbuthnott graveside on a cold afternoon with a sprinkle of snow on the Grampian hilltops. She observed:

I looked at them, Leslie's people, wondering whether they and their kind would ever understand him as he understood them. His father, from a bare little farm on the Drumlithis road, had a face like Saint Andrew of Scotland. His mother's lined face worked nervously, conquering her tears. I thought of how they would go home to the farm routine; to unyoke the shelt, to milk the kye, to feed the hens, to know the balm that is released from the soil, without knowing that they knew it.

It is galling to think that Leslie Mitchell, Lewis Grassic Gibbon, could still have been with us in the 1990s. Contemporaries like George Malcolm Thomson, one of the first critics to write in appreciation of his talent, are happily still alive. Who knows to what heights he might have risen?

But that voice was silent now out there on Blawearie Braes, where his gravestone bears those memorable words from the closing passage of *Sunset Song*:

> "The kindness of friends
> the warmth of toil
> the peace of rest."

It was the anarchists of Rome and the East who originally brought about the victory of Christ. And still today, as then, they are the true fighting forces, the sole resources of the Christian hosts.

ANATOLE FRANCE

We are all things that make and pass, striving upon a hidden mission, out to the open sea.

H. G. WELLS

A FORENOTE ON ORIGINS

In compiling this book the present writer has had free access to the list of manuscripts noted below. This was granted him through the courtesy and friendship of Malcom Maudslay's heirs, who have decided to hold over publication of the full and unexpurgated texts for another twenty-five years.

(i) The *Autobiography*, nearly 250,000 words in length, begun in 1926 and abandoned in late 1929.

(ii) The *Diary*, with entries from mid-November, 1929, to the 14th of December—an impossible date—1930.

(iii) A typescript of one hundred and seventy quarto pages, without a title, but evidently portion of an autobiographical novel.

(iv) The lengthy statement of Ramon Pech, the Yucatecan guide, taken down and forwarded by Mr. Robert Morland, C.B.E., British Consul at Soconusco City.

Various interviews, conversations, and—for it is illuminating—the privately printed book of verse, *The Darkness behind the Stars*, have also been drawn on for material.

The passages enclosed in double quotation-marks ("...") are taken chiefly from the *Autobiography*, but large portions of the manuscript novel have been altered from the first to the third person and transferred, *en bloc*, and without other acknowledgment than this, to Chapters Four and Five of Book I.

Names have been fictionized in accordance with an established convention, and the fictions chosen at random. No reference is therefore intended to any living person whose actual name may chance to coincide with that of a character in this book.

J. LESLIE MITCHELL
LONDON, 1931

TO
MY DAUGHTER
RHEA SYLVIA

BOOK I

ANTE-NATAL

Through the great desert beasts
Howl at our backs by night.
A Marching Song.

CHAPTER ONE

SUICIDE AND THE HORIZON

I

One of his earliest memories was of how, at the age of five, he set out to commit suicide.

It was an afternoon in late autumn, and as he climbed the hill towards Stane Muir by the rutted farm road he could hear the whirr of the reaping machines and the wailing of the peewits. Behind him was Leekan Valley; fringed to the north with mountains, purple-blue in heather, granite-speared sentinels in misty serration. The bulking of the moor above him and the bright, quiescent sunshine vexed him a little, but his small rump still smarted with the chastisement inflicted upon its naked surface, and his determination to drown himself in the old well at the top of the road was fixed and unwavering.

He must have been about two and a half feet high at the time, his black hair rather long—his father cut it at intervals by the simple procedure of inverting an empty brose-bowl on his son's head, and then trimming round the edges with a great scissors—and his small face, intent and sober, a little grimed with tears and the adherence of remnants of the oatcakes which he had been discovered stealing. He looked back into the hollow where the farmhouse lay and consigned all its inhabitants to hell—aloud, and singing the word sobbingly, as he had heard the Irish hired lad do when sacked for nameless crimes. Then he stopped for a moment to gaze at a portentous hare which came loping over the bank at the side of the road. But the beast looked at him unfriendlily, in the fashion of hares, and he edged away to the other side of the track, and held on, his short, defiant person garmented in thick jacket and breeches, woollen stockings and

1

boots with heavy soles. He had started out without his fine new cap in his haste to drown himself.

By the time he came to the old well and pushed through the broken railings which surrounded it, the walking had so tired him that he lay down on the flat coping-stones to rest himself. He lay very flat on his stomach, and, having recovered his breath, prepared to drown himself. The coping-stone tilted under him, uncertainly, as he crept towards the well-head, and the hole yawned blackly, but with a certain dust-drizzle of sunshine which caught his attention. The tilt of the stone grew greater and then, with a sudden jerk, flung him flat on his face, so that he bruised his chin and cried a little. Disheartened, he lay for a while watching the play of changing colours through the teardrops clinging to his eyelashes.

Then he raised his head and suddenly became aware of the long wall of the autumn day, a quivering, bubble wall, resting on the hill-brow just above his head.

It was his first conscious awareness of the wonder of the horizon. He lay and stared at it and forgot his intention of drowning himself. Instead, a great resolution came upon him. He would creep up through Stane Muir and touch the Thing, perhaps throw a stone against it and see if it would crack. . . .

If you have any imagination at all you will see him crossing the road from the old well-head and crawling stealthily under the muir fence in the beginning of that pursuit which was to be his life passion. Broom and gorse flowered yellow up to the brow of the hill in great clumps, but a cattle-track wound amidst the bushes, and as he panted upwards with short, fat, eager legs he stooped and picked up a large and companionable-looking stone with which to batter in the Walls of the World. . . .

Late that afternoon his brother Robert came upon him, after much searching, several miles across the Grampians, dead weary and minus a boot left behind in an unchancy, swampy place. But the stone was still clasped to his chest and the conviction firm in his heart that beyond the next scaur, the next stretch of gorse, an incredible adventure awaited him.

2

II

Leekan Valley is in Aberdeenshire, a cleft in the Grampians mountain-block, lying roughly parallel with the North Sea. The winter howling of that three-miles distant sea must have been among the first sounds heard by Malcom. Though a valley, Leekan is at a high elevation, except at the point where a glacier has torn down its eastern wall in anxiety to provide a site for a fishing village. Neither Lowland nor Highland, it is a place without history, though the national hero of Scotland, Sir William Wallace ("whose reputed penchant for burning English castles seems only slightly less monotonous than Queen Elizabeth's craze for sleeping in them"), is supposed to have hidden in a yew-tree near the present manse during the early days of the rebellion against the southern aliens.

But if it lacks recorded drama of historic times, it is rich with the evidences of pre-history. Men as remote in time as the Magdalenians (such the staggering claim of the Reverend Ian Stevenson) have passed through Leekan, or halted there whole generations, hunting the unkindly fauna of the Scottish Quarternary. Later came Maglemoseans, wandering in dim tribes across the swampy plains of the Dogger Bank, later still the wielders of the epipalæoliths, then the men of the polished axes who reared in such profusion the Devil Stanes of Leekan and were doubtlessly amalgamated or exterminated by the later smelters of bronze. But of the last people there is no evidence, unless, despite the Reverend Ian, the miniature Stonehenge of Leekan is Bronze Age work.

Malcom was born into this ancient library of the hills at the farm of Chapel o' Seddel on Christmas Eve, 1898. He arrived a little before midnight, and inauspiciously, for a great snow-storm had come over the Grampians about five o'clock that afternoon and the doctor had to be fetched from Leekan village on horseback, ploughing through great drifts. The times and place were primitive enough in obstetrics—probably the Maglemoseans managed things quite as well—and some happenings of crude

3

surgery took place, which greatly upset the household in the matter of hot water and clean towels. However, Mrs. Maudslay passed through the business safely and in a week, according to the oral traditions of Leekan, was out of doors again, feeding chickens and being intent on the matter of a litter of pigs which had failed to flourish in the cold. Malcom himself displayed symptoms of retiring precipitately, and was hastily christened in consequence. There was never any doubt as to what his names would be, for his father's was John and his maternal grand-father's (including the unfamiliar orthography) Malcom. The Reverend Ian Stevenson, stout and genial and absent-minded, dripped water on his forehead and christened him by the names of John Malcom. The new Maudslay screamed atheistically.

"Probably I considered an infantile distrust of priests quite warranted—perhaps had caught a glimpse through the time-spirals of some Leekan witch-doctor with a flint knife performing unkindly operations on the body of a weakling child. Hell lies about us in our infancy.

"I was the youngest of four brothers and two sisters, though my father and mother had been married a bare nine years. Things were so in Leekan and maybe are so still. It was the natural lot of women to be perpetually bowed in the ungracious discomforts of pregnancy. They seemed to take this lot calmly, but I do not believe that any woman other than a half-wit has ever desired a large family. Child-bearing: it was a drearily exciting inevitability. . . . If only half the epitaphed ideal wives and mothers who predeceased their husbands in the eighteenth and nineteenth centuries had kept diaries of their inmost thoughts—what a history we might then possess of solemn marital lust guised under the protective name of fatherhood! Especially among the clergy. If only we knew the private opinions of the wife of that inane prig and poetaster, John Donne!—She bore twelve children in sixteen years, that pale, ghostly, eighteenth-century wife, and died in child-bed. The Sunday following her death Donne preached a sermon on the text 'Behold in me a man afflicted.' "

This is a fair specimen of Malcom. John Donne, roused from

his lair, is pursued with whoop and halloo for many a mile before we return to Leekan and learn that Malcom, by some chance, was the last Maudslay of his generation. That his father and mother discussed the matter and decided there would be no more children he finds inconceivable ("!"). They would have considered such conduct loathsomely indecent. They never, he is convinced, discussed sex at all—unless it was in the matter of bull-calves and how many cockerels should be killed and sold to Seddel House. In bed matters a wife did her duty and, like Brer Rabbit, said nuffin.

Robert, Thomas, and Peter were his brothers, in order of seniority and merit. Younger than these were his sisters, Lilian and Jessie. He grew up in the midst of a lamentable yet not unhappy squabble. Yet all, except Robert (of Jessie and Peter we never hear again), remained dim and faery figures in his memory: except Robert, who left it ineradicably scarred with a horrific picture—1916 and the attack on Thiepval and the head of Robert thrust gasping from the port-hole of a lurching, blundering tank. Malcom lay in a shell-hole and their eyes met, and Robert cried something, weeping, sweat and blood disfiguring his face. Then the tank swayed forward into a writhing cobra-nest of barbed wire, cleared that, and plunged and plunged into smoke and sulphur till the inferno swallowed it. . . .

Grave Robert with the brindled hair and snappy temper! He tended much to Malcom's childhood—including administration of the slapping which almost resulted in a suicide—developed a pride in him, and resented remarks about his puniness and pigmentation. The other Maudslays were red-haired, highly coloured children: they took after their father. But Malcom was like his mother, an Argyllshire woman—small and sallow, with hair so black that Leekan Valley was vaguely shocked. Black-haired children were in some fashion disreputable.

John Maudslay, a saving ploughman of Leekan stock, had farmed Chapel o' Seddel for seven years prior to Malcom's arrival. He had a nineteen-years' lease and a constant, canny feud with the laird, Mutch of Seddel House, a bloated, kindly individual who owned half the Valley, drank three-quarters of its whisky, and, in intervals of sobriety, paid rounds of visits to his tenants—principally, one gathers, for the pure love of picking quarrels with them. Except in romantic novels of claymores and stag-hunting and bonnie brier bushes, the Scottish tenant farmer keeps his immortal soul intact by markedly not raising his hat to the northern equivalent of squire: knowledgable farmers who knew their law and had fallen out with Mutch had been known to chase him off their rentings with shot-guns. John Maudslay had never gone as far as that, and Laird Mutch in the farm-kitchen of Seddel, drinking butter-milk and conversing edgedly with his father was a frequent play set for the observation of the bashful Malcom. The farmer of Chapel o' Seddel was unbearded on weekends, but throughout the week burgeoned an ever more bristly chin and throat; he was a tall man, with dingy reddish moustaches. "Rather like the picture-book vikings, my father, and oddly owlish. As probably were the vikings. I have never elsewhere encountered exactly that species of owlishness." He would nod at Mutch, gravely, his moustaches dripping butter-milk, his eyes—grey, indeterminate eyes—slightly protuberant, like those of an elderly lobster, and remark, 'Aye. Ye're richt.' Then nod again, after an interval, with his eyes glassily solemn. 'Aye. Richt.' Then wipe his moustaches with the back of his hand. 'Aye. Ye're richt there.'

He had a conversational weightiness which Mutch, who was inclined to an alcoholic sprightliness, must have found almost as damping as Malcom did in later years. He was of all things practical. Once Malcom, then about twelve years of age, induced him, in a moment of relaxation, to go out on a winter's night and look up at the stars through a small telescope acquired from the Reverend Ian Stevenson. He peered up through the lenses, fumbled clumsily with the gauges, then shook his head. It hurt his eyes. Probably he had never before looked up at the bright splendour of the frost-rimed star-fields. 'Aye. Aye. But what's the use o it, laddie? Ye'll no get on in the world through lookin at stars. Come awa in.'

From that moment Malcom hated him—single-mindedly, ruthlessly, as only an intelligent boy can hate. But in later years, looking back at that incident, somehow it was his father who seemed pitiful, heart-breakingly pathetic, and himself, crude and young and cruel, who was hateful.

III

Sometime in the Epipalæolithic, nine or ten thousand years ago, there was a colony of Azilians on the Argyllshire coast of Scotland—lost and degenerate descendants of the Old Stone heroes, with clumsy microliths and weapons of horn and bone, and a view of a wilder Atlantic from the savage coasts where the cave bear still prowled. Malcom discovered them—in books— at the age of twelve or thirteen, and wove a fantastic belief in them as short, dark, silent men, his own ancestors through his mother, who was an Argyllshire woman. That still, watchful gravity of hers impressed itself very vividly indeed on his mind, struck him as something pre-Neolithic, pre-Keltic, heritage of the days when perhaps stray mammoths might still be seen from the mouth of a cave and the crook-boned men made war against the New Stone invaders. . . . The Reverend Ian's books and telescope, the 'standing stones on the vacant, wine-red moor' (R.L.S. remained one of Malcom's heroes for life on the strength of that magic phrase alone), Leekan's winter splendour of stars and his mother's dark, impenetrable silence had even thus early moulded all the poetry of his being into the channels archæological and astronomical which it kept throughout his life.

Yet he never loved his mother, except at odd moments, when she came to his aid in matters of milk and unbuttoning, when he was very young and overcome with weariness and her hands were kind. But such occasions were few enough. Her hands were too roughened and too busy to be kind for long. Behind that immemorial gravity of hers it was difficult to know how she looked on her children: but hardly at all as intimately *her*

7

children, he came to think. She had no passionate loves and no passionate dislikes. It was impossible to believe that even in the early days she had ever regarded John Maudslay with other than a silent acquiescence.

Yet you must not think of her as bowed and apathetic. She was quick and patient and dark. She worked unceasingly, from five o'clock in the morning, when the alarum clock in the kitchen had roused John Maudslay and herself, until half-past nine at night when, as regularly as though the alarum clock had also regulated the moment, they went to bed. They slept in a large, wooden four-poster, John Maudslay next to the wall. Malcom would watch him, upon occasion, going to bed. He disrobed to his undergarments, but retained them. They were thick, woollen undergarments of an unconvincing grey. Then he would stride largely into bed, groan, pull the blankets over his head, groan and shuffle. Then he would snort deeply, lying on his back and staring at the ceiling. He usually fell asleep in that attitude.

Chapel o' Seddel was a farm of seventy-five acres. John Maudslay kept one hired man, who slept in a garret under the eaves. This hired man got up in the morning at the same time as his employer, and descended to the kitchen. Then, if it was winter, they unhooked from the roof-beams, from a medley of swathed hams which had graced the Seddel pigs throughout the previous summer, three great lanterns which burned paraffin, smokily, in cracked, five-windowed cages. With these in their hands they'd unlatch the kitchen-door, sway in a booming gust of wind coming through the passes from east Aberdeenshire, and then plod across the cattle-urinated courtyard to the stable or byre. Then would come the tending to horses and cattle, crushing of oilcake, mashing of turnips, carrying of water and treacle and straw. Meantime Mrs. Maudslay would issue from the dairy and also cross the courtyard, with such clank of milk-pails as would rouse Malcom and his brothers in the great upstairs bed where there were sometimes such anarchistic outbreaks over undue shares of blanket. There were usually three milch-cows at Chapel o' Seddel; Malcom's mother had a small, three-legged stool which she would plant amongst the soiled straw; then she would plant her head firmly against the ribs of Meg or Kate or Nancy, and begin milking. She milked with an extraordinary rapidity: it was fascinating to watch her milk while the cows stood patient, cud-chewing and borborygmatic.

At half-past seven the children were breakfasted. By then John Maudslay and the hired man had been out in the fields for over an hour, and the slow, Northern morning was spreading wanly from the eastern seaboard of the Valley, and the bitterns calling and calling, and thin pencil-points of smoke rising from all the scattered steadings of Leekan. Chapel o' Seddel lay on the western side of the glen; right athwart it, a glitter of far slate roofs on the ledge of the foothills that climbed to the sea-cliffs, were the school and schoolhouse. Three miles to the north was the manse, a mile beyond it Seddel House, and, at the tip of this crescent, Leekan Village, straggling back from its railway station. South-east, in the glacier-scaur riven through to the sea-shore, was Pitgowrie, the fishing hamlet, hardly of the Valley at all, drenched perpetually with a dreadful odour induced by the practice of kippering butties. . . . Over three hundred years before, the galleon *Santa Catarina*, struggling incautiously north-wards from the disaster of the Armada, had come within smell of Pitgowrie and had sunk like a stone, with all hands.

By eight o'clock the Seddel children were ready to set out for school. They were generally wrapped up so warmly that, short-legged, it was difficult to proceed at any pace other than a shambling trot. They would set out one by one, released with a final efficient pat and injunction. Across the Valley to Leekan school was a distance of three miles by the footpaths and probably nearer five when one took the main road. Malcom covered this distance, day in, day out, from the age of five to the age of fifteen; except for occasional illnesses. At a conservative estimate he walked fourteen thousand miles in pursuit of an elementary education.

But behind, in Chapel o' Seddel, the day's work was well advanced before the children had arrived at school, and at eleven o'clock John Maudslay and the hired man were unyoking the horses and coming back across the laired fields to the steadings. Then came more feeding of cattle. Then the three peasants themselves fed. Then by one o'clock the men were again gone to the fields, and Mrs. Maudslay was feeding poultry or pigs or making butter or jam or sewing clothes or—one and a dozen other occupations enslaving her dark silence. . . .

A grey, grey life. Dull and grey in its routine, Spring, Summer, Autumn, Winter, that life the Neolithic men brought from the south, supplanting Azilian hunger and hunting and light-hearted shiftlessness with servitude to seasons and soil and the tending of cattle. A beastly life. With memory of it and reading those Catholic writers who, for some obscure reason, champion the peasant and his state as the ideal state, Malcom is moved autobiographically to a sardonic mirth. . . . He is unprintably sceptical as to Mr. Chesterton or his chelas ever having grubbed a livelihood from hungry acres of red clay, or regarding the land and its inhabitants with any other vision than an obese Victorian astigmatism. . . . Sometimes, unkindly, he would vision Mr. Chesterton sentenced to pass three years at Chapel o' Seddel as hired man; picture of a large, distinguished presence staggering across the slimy floors of Chapel o' Seddel byre behind a barrow-load of reeking manure often cheered his dourer moments.

IV

And yet—
There were memories of those early days in Leekan of which he never wearied: memories of Spring mornings—never such mornings in the world as those, when the air was better than Benedictine and the red earth turned beneath the drive of the coulter and the horses' breath drifted in a little cloud and the peewits cried and cried; purple autumnal nightfalls, with the darkness creeping from the hills on the dim, far steadings and the fir-trees etched in ink against the looming of Stane Muir; Leekan mantled in

snow under scudding clouds, with the baa of lost sheep in the mountain-scaurs; the sound of summer rain on the roof; long tracks of kye through broom that lead to a beckoning, conquerable horizon.

V

At midnight on New Year's Eve, 1900, a great bonfire was lighted at the summit of Stane Muir. This was by permission of John Maudslay, but a result of the enthusiasm and organizing abilities of the Reverend Ian Stevenson, who had prevailed on Leekan to believe that the century ended then, and not a year previously, as some folk had thought. Great cartloads of whins and broom-roots, twigs and logs, had been hauled to the little plateau above the Devil Stanes. Leekan turned up in its hundreds and its Sunday best, with large mufflers to keep in the warmth and scores of bottles of whisky to put it there. Gallons of paraffin were emptied on the pile, and when midnight arrived by the Reverend Ian's watch, when Mutch of Seddel House—considerably at variance with the laws of gravitation and hilariously guided forward with his torch—had fired the reeking foundations, a stray, misguided Highlander with a pair of bagpipes burst into the skirling clamour of *The Cock o' the North*.

The sound roused Malcom and his brothers in the muckle bed at Chapel o' Seddel. They crept out on the cold floor and hopped and shivered by the window, two-year-old Malcom disregarded till he had plucked Robert's shirt-tails to attendance.

'Want to see! Want to see!'

He himself remembered little of this; Robert was to tell him of it later. He was elevated in friendly arms and bounced and danced ecstatically at the sight which greeted his eyes.

They were burning out the nineteenth century. The flames fled skyward in crazy architecture, built themselves into pillars golden and smoke-shot and red-streaked, then melted into a great roaring lowe against a revealed horizon. The wailing of the pipes

11

pierced now and then down through the sound of the blaze to the ears of the shivering watchers in Chapel o' Seddel.

They were burning out the nineteenth century: Victorian England, Victorian Europe, cant a religion, smugness a creed, gods in whiskers and morals in stays. . . . That fire went up with the crackling of crinolines and bustles, brothels and bethels. It screamed with the agony of murdered children in Midland factories, soughed and glimmered in a wind of such pious belching as no other century had ever seen. It flamed on a gaseous literature and an idiot art, sank and seethed and roared again with the fuel of gutter dreams and palace spites. Christianity and nationalism, socialism and individualism—they flared and broke and showered the dark hillsides with glowing embers.

And from amidst the ring of the Devil Stanes great shadows arose, faceless and formless, and went swiftly out of the light, over the mountains and into the world.

CHAPTER TWO

FOURTEEN THOUSAND MILES

I

Leekan School, as I've said, lay three miles across the Valley from Chapel o' Seddel. From the Maudslay farm the road ran straight for about a quarter of a mile and then took to crooked courses from which it never recovered. You passed by a loch, reedy and curlew-haunted and brown with stagnant water; about half-way was the ancient stone quarry from which the cromlechs of Stane Muir had been dug by the Neolithic herdsmen; climbing the other side of the Valley the path wound past the fields of a fat and choleric man with very red hair and a nose sympathetically tinted. His name was James Greig and he farmed Redleafe. His swedes were very good to eat, much better than Chapel o' Seddel's. Or so the Maudslays thought when they stole them, which they often did. It was a delight to reach through a wire fence and steal a Redleafe swede and be conscious that all the time a stout and wrathful figure probably lay concealed in a ditch further on, ready to vent vengeance. He would leap out and brandish a graip or other implement; his nose would flame danger.

'Damn you!' he'd cry. 'Damn you for ill-gettit weans!' Then he'd cuff them with a grittily-caloused hand. 'Tak that.'

They'd take it and slink past till distance lent them courage again. Then they would turn round and howl insults at him. 'Pot-Belly! Auld Pot-Bellied Jimmie!' Thomas was especially good at this; long and lean and rakish, he'd elevate his fingers to his nose. 'Auld pudden-heid!' Then experience a spasm of terror. 'Rin! here comes the auld devil!'

13

Sometimes, for he was foolish and choleric, the auld devil would pursue them again, and they'd run like hares.

Being the smallest, Malcom would lag behind and make vocal his fear. Then Robert would turn back and swear at him and grab his hand. 'Dash it! *Come* on!'

In ultimate safety beyond Greig's furthest pursuit they would turn and gesticulate their unquenched aversion. Malcom would join with the rest, putting small, sweating hands to his mouth and shouting in a thin treble. 'Po-Belly!' he'd cry. 'Puir auld Po-Belly!'

Only as they trotted on again would uneasy thoughts assail them. How were they to pass Redleafe coming home in the evening! Sure as death he'd be waiting for them.

'And just for a swede, too,' Thomas would exclaim in sorrowful amazement, forgetting his feats of finger-elevation. 'The auld B. should be locked up.'

There was a curious code of etiquette among Leekan children. It wasna decent to use the grosser swearwords before a junior like Malcom. So the swearword was reduced to a bursting initial, regretfully, and Malcom, panting, would murmur, agreeably, 'Aye, he's an auld B.'

Past the lands of the unfortunate James Greig, who was probably neither a Bulgarian heretic nor acquainted with homosexual diversions, they'd be well up the other side of the Valley, and, looking back, could see Chapel o' Seddel below its Stane Muir, brown and dour, its biggings set against a straggling background of firs. But they seldom looked back. By then they'd have about two minutes to spare and would do the last lap at racing speed.

Leekan Parish School had three teachers—a man and two women. They called the man the Dominie; there are many such curious words in the Scots dialects, pathetic reminders of the once-national worship of scholastic attainment. The Leekan cobbler was the Sutor; and of course a plate was an Ashet.

There were two playgrounds, bare asphalt stretches in front of the school. One was for girls, one for boys, and transgression by the latter into the former's territory was punished by the

14

authorities with quite amazing ferocity. Delimitation of his play-ground as a boy was Malcom's first introduction to those sex tabus brought north by the Neolithic men six thousand years before, and still sprouting, like so many foul fungi.

At nine o'clock each morning the Dominie would stand at the head of the wall dividing the two playgrounds and toll a hand-bell, irritably. He was an uncle of Mutch of Seddel House, a tall old man, and to Malcom at the age of six or seven looked much more like the uncle of God Himself. Then the children would snake-wind into the school, the doors—long sliding panels separating the three rooms would be flung open, and a great gust of chattering would arise. Then the Dominie himself would appear, shepherding in such strays as the Maudslays, and take his stand in front of the blackboard in the middle room. From this position he could command the school. A deep silence would fall. The Dominie would close his eyes and raise his clenched right fist. The children would stare at it fascinatedly. Upon its upper surface a disturbance would be observable. This was the thumb gradually rising to the perpendicular. As soon as it at-tained that position, the whole school burst into the Lord's Prayer.

This rite of the Dominie's Malcom describes in detail, with much irreverent speculating as to its origin. Then, abandoning the daily routine of Leekan School just as it promises interest, he launches into a destructive criticism of the education provided in those three rooms. Halfway through the diatribe he halts abruptly, with thought that such criticism is generally done by the tribe he detests—"professional politicians, pressmen pimps of the Sunday newspapers" and the like regrettable pustules upon the face of civilization. One gathers an idea of stuff aus-terely, if not always uninterestingly, taught. There was practi-cally no religious teaching. History was circumscribed enough, but the dates enlivened with figures like Malcolm Canmore (a fruitful source of gawkish puns), and Mary Queen of Scots, whose blood was lapped by a dog. Arithmetic was taught on a straight-forward plan, geography was no dull subject, and, being

15

Scots, they found English fascinating enough. They were told to open their mouths, to roll the letter 'r,' and to avoid the elision of aitches, otherwise they might be mistaken for Englishmen—poor, cowardly, excitable people whom Scotsmen had chased across the border again and again.

But that was the pitiful all, apart from decorative subjects. 'Natural History' consisted in snippets about the wombat, the eider duck, and the unseemly habits of the duck-billed platypus. 'Science' did not exist. Drawing was a smudging of paper with unrecognizable objects; first in popularity as model was the Dominie's hat. No music was taught. There were massed singing lessons in which no attempt was made to train voices. The children merely stood up amidst the benches and sang, and enjoyed themselves considerably.

They suffered from neither elementary Latin nor still more elementary Greek. Later in life Malcom taught himself to read Latin with a fair ease in order that, at Haeckel's urging, he might meet the over-praised Lucretius. From the latter he wandered away into the sterile mazes of Roman letters, emerging with the quite unwarranted theory that most of the Latin authors had suffered from chronic constipation. Inexplicably, he detested Rome and the Romans.

"Of all unsavoury peoples that race of bloody-minded barbarians which over-ran Italy and the Mediterranean basin seems to me the worst; of all dull and platitudinous fools endowed with a vote in the republic of letters I have still to meet a drearier than Virgil."

II

Outside school, in the morning playtime and the lunch hour, whatever supervision the children had been under ceased to exist. They burst forth into the playgrounds, whooped and ran and stirred the dust, played nameless games, played football, sneaked through the hedges to sleep in the fields, stoned the Dominie's cat, chased his hens, perched on the school boundary-wall and insulted passing carters, quarrelled, fought, became reconciled, organized slides, mass-torturings and pitched battles with lumps of turf, stole tomatoes from the Dominie's garden, smoked cigarettes and brown paper cigars and were sick.

They played the devil generally, Malcom records with appreciation.

Most of the pupils (but they called themselves scholars) came from some distance and brought sandwiches for lunch (but they called it dinner). One's social status was graded according to the contents of one's food-parcel. Poor children and the children of ploughmen brought pieces of bread and jam and were consequently pariahs; sons of small farmers, like the Maudslays of Chapel o' Seddel, brought oatcakes and butter and home-made cheese and soda-scones; they bowed in abasement and went to eat in sheltered nooks when the children of the factor, the postmaster, and the forester unrolled ham sandwiches, buns, and cream biscuits.

But, apart from feeding-times, there was little snobbery at Leekan School. Or rather, the snobbery in the boys' playground was inverted. It was lassie-like and namby-pamby and quite damnable generally to have a very clean neck or collar or boots very shiny; also, it was bad policy, for then the more ragged boys, the Mundens and the Edwards, threw stones and dirt at you. Much depended on the head boy of the moment. This office had no official recognition, but was very real in its powers. It was an informal tyranny (in the Greek sense) exercised by the strongest boy in the school. His was the organizing of the more potent hooliganisms and campaignings. He might even head a movement against dirty beasts, and clean necks would flourish; more frequently he and his hoplitai—embryo he-men—scorned the softer and preferred the more unscrubbed virtues, smoking pieces of cane, talking filth, and tormenting the lassies: the main functions of he-men throughout the ages.

Surreptitious juvenile sniggering over genital organs and the production of babies was, as elsewhere, Leekan's idea of sex education. Malcom sets out his puzzlings, his curiosities and his self-abasements in bitter detail. He was nine years of age when they began to worry him, but twenty-seven or twenty-eight when he came to them in his *Autobiography*, and his very definite opinions and prejudices obscure the facts considerably. After an unnecessary jibe at Dr. Marie Stopes' penchant for invoking the Deity as a watch-dog to ward off the smut-hounds, and a summing up of her scheme of sex education as "admirable training for Platonic pornographers" he goes on to tell of the only time he ever asked his mother's advice in the matter.

He had arrived home from school and posed her with a quite simple question, anxious to combat a theory of young Jock Edwards'. Her sallow face had flushed and her usual composure deserted her.

'You are a *dirrty* little beast.'

That was all, in her slurred Argyllshire English. Malcom had stared at her, hot-eyed, and blushed and stammered involvedly, aware of a disgusting *faux pas*. His abnormal sensitiveness festered over that repulsion. It left a permanent scar on his confidence and faith and "if I ever possessed the beginnings of an Œdipus complex, like Mark Twain's celebrated beetle on the red-hot shovel, it displayed a wild surprise and then shrivelled up."

III

In spite of Malcom's hurried christening in the far-off days when it had seemed that his stay in Leekan was likely to be short, there was at Chapel o' Seddel no 'real' religion, just as there was no art, literature, fun, high vision, hideous despair, or shocking blasphemy. In Leekan, as in almost every other parish of Scotland, the Established Church and the very kindred Free Churches had killed popular religion through extreme simplification of rite and the democratic election of priests. Few gods survive the ballot-box or the bullyings of a John Knox.

Malcom's childhood Jehovah was a dim and emasculated old man, no more frightening or inspiring than the weak and languid Christ of the Sunday School texts. They were both outside reality. The old phrases, the old hopes and the old terrors had become meaningless. No one believed in them, just as no one repudiated them. Malcom, his brothers and sisters, were sent to Sunday School; occasionally the Maudslays went to church, to be like their neighbours. But they never applied the references in the hymns, the prayers and the sermons to themselves, says Malcom. They would merely feel vaguely uncomfortable. They felt ashamed in their secular lives to hear words and phrases associated with religious observances. Malcom, at the age of five or six, had his backside smacked by his mother for uttering during play some innocent sing-song nonsense about Jesus Christ. He was smacked, not as a blasphemer, but just as if he had neglected some personal sanitary precaution. "The only occasions on which my father would invoke the Founder of Christianity with any passion were when he hit his thumb with a hammer or a horse stepped on his toes."

The Reverend Ian Stevenson, the Church of Scotland minister who had dedicated Malcom, an unwilling sacrifice, to a god who was already as little terrifying as the forgotten totems of Stane Muir, was a large, corpulent man, an enthusiastic anthropologist, an archaeologist of some note (his monograph *On Pictish Burials* still rouses amazingly unwarranted passions), member of innumerable learned societies, and one of the poorest preachers who ever graced a Reformed pulpit.

He was 'Auld Ian' to Leekan, and was mildly liked, especially at funerals, for death and burial interested him and on such occasions he ceased to be vague. It was only in the approach to his god, or his ordinary parochial duties, that he moved behind a dim, genial cloud of absent-mindedness. Leekan did not lack its semi-agnostics, crude doubters who would spit on their hands and lean across the plough-shafts and pose the Reverend Ian with intimate physiological questions on the Virgin Birth, Jonah in the whale's stomach, and suchlike mythic problems of parturition

19

and digestion. They never succeeded in angering him. He would light his pipe, lean against the other side of the plough, and launch out on a discourse on primitive symbolism from which the doubter would generally emerge with the dazed sensations of one who had been temporarily upended and immersed in a lake of pea-soup. During his twenty years in Leekan, the minister had dug up about a quarter of the Valley in pursuit of the prehistoric. Farmers would arrive at the boundaries of distant fields and stand cursing under-breath at sight of immense earth mounds uprising in the middle of a promising acre of young corn.

He had books on all subjects. He was the most widely read person Malcom was ever to meet. Three rooms at Leekan Manse scarcely sufficed to house and stack the volumes he had accumulated, and his housekeeper, a soured woman by the name of Sarah Jameson, spent her days waging an unending war against the intrusion of still more skulls, eoliths, microliths, macroliths, celts, and in flicking a ruthless duster amidst piled calculations of cranial depth, periodic ooze, and what not. Leekan gossips hinted that the Reverend Ian frequently 'slept with' his housekeeper, which struck Malcom as an exceedingly foolish thing to do when one had a big, fine bed of one's own.

It was not until the summer of that year when his own interest in the puzzling matter of mammalian reproduction had begun to flower that the minister came intimately into his ken—the occasion an afternoon in June and Malcom in search of stray ewes. He was re-crossing the Stane Muir from the hills when, in the middle of the circle of Neolithic stones, he came upon the Reverend Ian, his coat off, a spade in his hand, and much perspiration dripping from his face. He was digging vigorously in a very unpromising patch of heath. Malcom stopped and gaped at him respectfully. The minister wiped his forehead, considered the boy, and smiled vaguely.

'Ah, you're an Edwards boy, aren't you?'

Malcom was a trifle indignant, being much more clever and better-looking than any of the Edwards boys, especially the detestable Jock. (An early school-group photograph bears out the contention that his appearance was at least not lacking in interest. Amidst the gauche, healthy wonder of the group he stands, slight and dark, his nose even then with the tip slightly askew, dark green eyes still and grave in appraisal of the photographer. Probably he presented just such appearance standing and repudiating the Reverend Ian's suggestion.)

'Na, sir. I'm Malcom Maudslay.'

'Oh yes. Can you dig?'

'I'm fine at diggin,' said Malcom, simply.

The minister relinquished the spade, sat down, and lighted his pipe. 'Then try your hand at this patch.'

Malcom did. It was a tough patch. Perspiring sympathetically, he cut through the thick roots and then, as he had seen his father do, cut the sods in neat oblongs, and delved them out. All the while his mind seethed with wonder. He paused to interrogate the Reverend Ian.

'Are ye diggin a garden, sir?'

The Reverend Ian shook his head. 'No. I'm looking for the kirk-pulpit of another minister who used to hold services up here in Leekan. Up here on this hill, Malcom, in the days when the Pharaohs ruled in Egypt.'

'I ken aboot Pharaoh,' said Malcom, helpfully. 'He was drooned in the Red Sea. But that was lang syne.' He felt that he must have mis-heard. 'An—an there were savages up here then, sir?'

'Long before then, and not savages. Very like you and me. Come here and I'll show you the calculations I'm digging on now.' He brought several sheaves of scrap-paper out of his pocket. 'Let me see—no—here it is—no. Where is it now?'

Malcom went down on all fours beside him while they searched among the papers. Then the situation was explained. If the minister was correct the centre of this miniature Stonehenge had once been occupied by an altar, oriented to face the single standing cromlech to their right—the guest-house of the sun every midsummer morning, in the days of the New Stone men; while that pillar to their left was the point behind which the sun sank on the ancient day of feast and sacrifice. Not that the sun

21

would come through the wee house accurately now, or sink just exactly behind the pillar. Fraction by fraction of an inch each century cromlech and pillar had lost accuracy. 'For five or six thousand years have gone by since the priest stood where we stand and watched the sun rise over Stane Muir brae or sink behind the Dominie's school.'

The boy had listened with an eager if fragmentary understanding. Five or six thousand years. . . . He looked away from the kneeling and measuring minister, out over the Leekan Valley, hazed in sunset, haunted unendingly by the peewits. Five or six thousand years. . . .

And then, as he struggled with the elementary arithmetical equipment of his school class, suddenly, mysteriously, as he tells, he caught such shuddering glimpse of that pit of no-history as was to haunt him with its dim, hazed slopes and voices as unendingly as Leekan itself was haunted—a glimpse that in memory terrified and then fascinated, that for long years remained to him inexplicable, until he read the time-spiral speculations of Reimann and Einstein.

The sun sank rapidly. And suddenly Malcom felt afraid. He glanced scaredly at the minister. A voiceless scream struggled up into his throat. The minister had vanished. In his place a naked man squatted against the sunset lowe, his gnarled arms outstretched to the pillar, his body dipping and swaying in frenzied rhythm.

Himself—naked, kneeling, in his hands a bloody trencher. . . .

And, as they waited there, priest and shivering acolyte in an immemorial rite, the pillar blackened against the western sky and darkness came wailing down the valley of the New Stone men.

IV

But that glimpse of local limbo dimmed in a new discovery— books and the beauty of words.

How he read! He devoured all the poor few volumes at Chapel

o' Seddel—they consisted of a Bible, a *Basket of Flowers*, a tattered Burns, *A Catalogue of Sheep Dips*, and a *Life of Our Saviour*. The latter was heavily illustrated, with Christ "dressed by Clarkson and always clasping in his arms a peculiarly repulsive lamb, evidently far gone in the staggers." He would wonder what had been done when the lamb misbehaved itself, in the disconcerting fashion of lambs.

He scoured neighbouring farm-houses, borrowing books. At last he summoned up courage to make application to borrow from the Dominie's private cases. Crowningly, the Reverend Ian, with whom he had become a favourite, made him free of the manse library.

Books and books and yet more books. Marryat, Ballantyne, Henty, Stevenson. Grown-up books. Scott and Dickens, Fielding, Smollett, Thackeray. Flaubert in a horrible translation. (Oh, *Salammbo!* Matho! Spendius! Hamilcar!) The early Wells, Haggard, and Jack London, Hardy (queerly, he liked Hardy), Kipling (whom he could not abide), a stray volume of R. H. Benson's which left an unfortunate and ineradicable conviction that Roman Catholics were of necessity bores, and brainless bores to boot. . . .

But fiction palled quickly. By the time he was thirteen years of age he was reading the *Origin of Species*—and enjoying it. This was afterwards to strike him as the most inexplicable of all his early loves, "for the *Origin*, re-read, is dry stuff, dry and heavy, mental dyspepsia in tabloid." But at thirteen it was wonder. He read and understood and pondered and agreed; he procured other Darwin books and voyaged the unplumbed seas with the Beagle of heroic memory; he secured books by Huxley and Haeckel and rejoiced with them at the discomfiture of the Deity. ("That gaseous vertebrate!") He read Herbert Spencer. ("My God, I read Herbert Spencer!")

Innumerable others. He read Matthew Arnold. He read the Bible—"as literature." He tried a translation of the Qurân and gave it up, without forfeiting a life-long liking for Mohammed. He read translated sagas of Morris and Magnusson and Greek stuff in translation. He became a champion of the Norsemen as the discoverers of America. He passed to the early Arthur Keith in anthropology, Avebury in archaeology, Herschel and Proctor and Ball in astronomy. He read and read till for days the outside world faded into a shadow-play of phantasmata, till his mother worried lest his brain should soften—this was no joke, but a grave apprehension!—till John Maudslay, belching in the kitchen firelight and the aftermath of a heavy supper, would prophesy for his youngest son a dour future of poverty and unemployment as result of such wastrel ploys. . . .

("Poor father! Had he vision of myself and May Laymore that sleeting night in the wilds of Whetstone?")

V

He went out of doors the evening he finished reading that book of Ball's, and stared at the Milky Way streaming across the heavens. It was an early Spring evening. The cattle moved and clanked, cud-chewing, in the mush bedding of the byre. The smell of ploughed fields was in the air. Across Leekan Valley, clear and distinct from some ploughman's bothy, came a hoarse singing presently extinguished in guffaws. Overhead, watched by the Chapel o' Seddel boy, that amazing thing at which none stood astounded but himself.

Flat, like an enormous biscuit perhaps, Ball had said; whirling in space, with the solar system, like a spinning of dust-motes, somewhere midway: The Galaxy. . . .

A fragment of poetry—a lovely fragment—was remembered by the staring boy:

> *The gemmy bridle glittered free,*
> *Like to some branch of stars we see*
> *Hung in the golden Galaxy,*
> *The bridle-bells rang merrily——*

And then, conjured up in some misty fusion of images, he saw, across the star-floored Galaxy, the riding of an immense horse-man, helmed and armoured, the shatterer of the horizon, the conqueror of the skies, pressing forward amid the dust of suns and the moan of nebulae to the Rim of the Galaxy, out on some tremendous Adventure in the wilds of space.

The laughter across the valley rose deafeningly, like the baying of a beast. The vision vanished. Malcom stared, shook himself, and turned indoors.

VI

This curious self-education of his—in character neither nine-teenth nor twentieth, but eighteenth century: a bland disregard of that feeble creed that youth should occupy itself with being youthful—was carried on without aim or objective. "The future occasionally rose and stared in my youthful face. I would stare it back, angrily, and then cut it dead." It and its problems seemed irrelevant nuisances except in school holidays of Spring or Autumn when his father and brothers would impress on him his peculiar uselessness as a farm-labourer. He was a consummate failure as a farm-labourer, for his thoughts would not merely wander from the job in hand—manuring, hoeing, seeding, thresh-ing—they would leap from it across half the world to pithecanthropi and Greek marbles and Rome and Hannibal and Pyrrhus and Genghis Khan and Abyssal Plains and Easter Island and Red Eric and Winland: they plunged and glittered and soared again on every subject except the red clay fields of Chapel o' Seddel.

'Od, ye lazy brute!' John Maudslay would bawl, plunging along an adjacent Spring-time drill, showers of rich, reeking cattle-dung flying from his graip, Thomas and Peter in hot and competitive pursuit, Malcom with his finicking implement shat-teringly recalled from an excavation at Zimbabwe.

'By God!' he would find himself swearing, in hot-eared rear-ward regard of his kinsmen's pliant buttocks, 'I'll show you yet. . . .'

He did, immediately following a particularly unbearable Spring planting. 'Feeder classes,' to be entered through competitive examinations, and with scholarships donated to outstanding competitors, were being established in the county elementary schools. The intention was that those classes, after preparatory work of eighteen months or so, should feed into Dundon College such pupils as might win a second scholarship. Malcom came home from school one evening and startled his family.

'I've won a bursary,' he said.

'What?' said Chapel o' Seddel.

He was thirteen years and two months of age. He had passed the examination overwhelmingly in all subjects, with, in history, a 'free subject' essay which covered over forty foolscap pages. His bursary of twenty-five pounds was contingent upon his immediate entrance into Leekan School's newly-formed 'feeder class.'

'Na, na,' said John Maudslay, 'we canna spare ye. Ye'll hae to tak Peter's place when he leaves hame and gangs to Redleafe. We canna spare ye. Na.'

But this was not the last of the matter. Leekan's intelligentsia massed its battalions on Malcom's side. The Reverend Ian appeared on the scene, for once affirmative, un-vague. Malcom must be allowed to take the bursary; he was a born scholar and should be trained for the Church of Scotland ministry. While Chapel o' Seddel was shaking its head cannily over sic daft-like ideas, Dominie Riddoch crossed Leekan Valley, strongly supported the contention that Malcom was a born scholar, and made it clear that he should be trained as a schoolmaster.

John Maudslay stroked his foolish viking moustaches and looked at his wife, sitting dark and calm and efficient, hands in her lap, thin lips neatly folded. She listened variously to the Reverend Ian and to Dominie Riddoch. Then came to a decision.

'If the laddie has anything in him,' she said, in her slurred "Azilian" English, 'we will not hold him back.'

VII

So he entered the Leekan 'feeder class' and was put to studying for a further scholarship at Dundon. He fell to learning French and German and algebra and Shakespeare and other things of a like import. There were two others in the class. Both were girls. The three of them sat apart from the rest of the pupils in the Dominie's room, at two small benches, and, after having bloodied Jock Edwards' nose in a great playground fight which was attended by the whole school and cheered like an arena-combat in ancient Rome, Malcom, provedly classifiable under no circumstances of time or fate as lassielike, deliberately set about training himself on an un-Leekan-like model inspired by his books.

That dark-faced, fantastic boy was to provoke both the wistful laughter and the equally wistful derision of the autobiographer who succeeded to his body. But the self-reformer saw nothing humorous in the business. He procured a spare exercise-book, ruled it neatly with black and red lines, took it up to the circle in Stane Muir, and spent an unsmiling afternoon among the menhirs, drawing up his programme.

He must learn to walk properly, as Domina Riddoch did (the average walk in Leekan was an urgent galumph). Bathe daily—or as often as his mother and Chapel o' Seddel kitchen would allow. Always use a handkerchief (Jock Edwards did serviceable work with the sleeve of his jacket). Stop blushing when spoken to; speak English, never Scots; keep your mouth closed (all Leekan suffered from adenoids); learn to eat properly (like the Reverend Ian did that time he gave you dinner); get up every morning at four o'clock and put in an extra hour's reading.

Those were only a few of the points he was to remember in later years as having jotted down in the columns of the exercise book. Unlike the protagonists of other historic points, he set about putting them into operation at once.

Hidden in Stane Muir, he practised his clumsy legs in walking straightly, his neck in keeping his head erect, not arcing from the spine like the neck of a Neanderthaler. He kept up the practice every spare moment school, his books, and the farm would allow him and acquired an easy carriage which even the drill-sergeants of Salisbury Plain failed to destroy. He deliberately faced the blushful and uneasy—giggling girls in Leekan shops were his chief enemies—and in a couple of months could probably have carried out W. L. George's test of buying baby ribbon in a multiple shop without any other appearance than indifference. ("Everything is possible to youth, and, thanks to that blessed prig who was once myself, I can walk into a women's lavatory—as I once did in an absent-minded moment in Westminster, thereby probably establishing a record for males—and make my apologies to a startled feminine twitter and walk out unable to summon a single red corpuscle from its normal duties.") He jerked himself back to nose-breathing—agony for the untrained—every time he found himself with lips ajar, and in a short time found it possible to dispense with a handkerchief, that happy breeding-bed of bacteria, altogether.

Chapel o' Seddel, after goggle-eyed, dark and composed, or guffawing starings, gradually became accustomed to a member of the household 'tryin' to mak oot he was a gentleman' by eating without lip-smackings or gulpings, by washing himself, all over, in the kitchen, naked and composed and unashamed. ("Nakedness was as shameful a thing in Leekan as it is among the unclean Anglo-Saxons everywhere.") The Valley, as Malcom speedily found out, now looked on him as 'prood an conceited—did ye see the cratur raise his hat when he met the minister?—Thinks he's gentry.'

The Reverend Ian put it differently, remarking with a sigh after talking to a polite and unembarrassed book-borrower, 'You're growing up terribly, Malcom.'

Of the two girls in the new 'feeder class' Jean Stanley, the forester's daughter, was the elder. If Malcom was "Azilian" she was flaming Nord. Her hair was corn-yellow, her eyebrows almost white. She had eyes a china blue in tint, with unusually large pupils, and was the possessor of a lumpish, large-built

28

body budding into the questionings and cravings appropriate to her age. She had very unreliable garters and a habit, when immersed in the uneasy equations of algebra or the obtusely irregular verbs of France, of twiddling her legs and disclosing very white knees—to the intriguement of the loutish Jock Edwards of Class VI. Malcom, on the other hand, considered her knees merely indecent.

("Those shapely things—a girl's knees!")

Years afterwards he was to recognize that among the older pupils of Leekan, Jean and Jock Edwards and rest, it was himself who had been sexually underdeveloped and they who had been normal. At thirteen he regarded the practical issue of sex—he knew all about it from his readings in physiology—as a filthy business of the order of bodily evacuation, but fortunately not such a widespread necessity. It need never concern him.

"All this a result achieved by my mother and Jock Edwards in incongruous alliance. I had then no idea that all civilization is but a by-product of sex, that my book-passions, my early socialist dreamings, my self-trainings in Stane Muir, were the results of early sexual repression."

The other girl of his class, newly arrived in Leekan, was in all things the opposite of Jean. A year younger, her skin was a gypsy olive, her hair black—much blacker than Malcom's, that black which in the sun is almost blue. She had a small, thin face and straight thin nose, with eyebrows shockingly thick for one of her age. But then she was altogether shocking, being a foreigner.

She was the Dominie's niece, and, ludicrously, her Christian name was a variant of his official designation. Domina Riddoch. Her mother had been French, and since the age of three, when her father, an analytical chemist in London, had died very horribly while experimenting with certain toxic acids, she had lived at Avignon. She had come to Leekan for a little preliminary training before going on to the Dundon College and London University—she was quite definite in her intentions and ambitions; she was to be a chemist, like her father. She shocked Leekan. It was reported that she bathed daily and walked about

29

the School-house stark naked in hot weather, in spite of the startled protests of the Dominie. She had a passion for bathing—again in the nude—in Leekan River. She ate sweets in church, not decently and under-breath, but with loud, enjoying cracklings. In the girls' playground she mentioned gigglesomely awful things with the same calmness as she mentioned her dinner. She was never going to marry and have babies because 'women—dhey say it is dhe very devil.' She had considerable trouble with the hard English 'th,' laying too much stress on the 't' constituent. Leekan shook its head over her as an awfu, foreign cratur, no decent.

To the eyes of Malcom this vivid brown thing, alive to the fingertips, was merely a nuisance—in the absences of the Dominie from the schoolroom perpetually brawling and playing the devil, getting up on her desk and dancing on it, for example.

But her residence in Avignon had given her unfair advantage in matters linguistic. Malcom threading a careful way through a French passage would elicit a giggle, presently crescendoing into an unashamed laugh, regardless of the Dominie's presence. The schoolroom would hush to her breathless justification.

'But I cannot help it. Dhey are so funny. "Longkel dee Missyou Perreeshong" dhe Maudslay boy said.'

The Dominie would have no family favouritisms. His shrivelled face aureoled by its long, white hair would harden. 'Stand up, Domina Riddoch.'

She would leap to her feet, eyebrows thunderous, and extend a thin, brown hand to the tingling strokes of the strap. Then sit down, face uncovered, and burst into dry, tearless sobbing while Jean Stanley, china-blue eyes a little frightened, would stand up and stumble on through *Le Voyage de Monsieur Perrichon*.

Over the development of the affair between Jock Edwards and Jean she presided with the frank curiosity she might have devoted to the wrigglings of two interesting worms, and, intimately physiological, would question the discreetly whispering Jean.

'And you permit him . . . ? You *like* him to? But he is such a dirty peasant boy!'

It was the Spring of 1912, seed-time, and weather of such stifling warmth that the school was allowed an extra half-hour at lunch-time. Jean would wander away from her playground unostentatiously, into the nearby broom thickets, and Jock Edwards, grinning, would slouch in pursuit. The Dominie's niece would lie hidden in the bushes, and, by prearrangement with Jean, watch the whole scene with insatiable zoological zest.

But one afternoon the observer burst out of the thicket, white-faced, raced to the school, and roused the unwilling Malcom from his book on the Dominie's lawn.

'Oh, come quickly! Dhe Edwards boy and Jean—he will kill her!'

Malcom pushing into the thicket came on Jock and his inamorata mutually entangled, Jean's face red to bursting. The matter had passed beyond mere horseplay, and Malcom, considerably disgusted, planted a satisfying kick on Jock's broad and sonsy buttocks. Thereat the combatants fell apart. Jock grinned sheepishly, stuck his hands in his trousers pockets, whistled a trifle uncertainly, and swaggered out of the thicket with a notable rearward shrinking. Jean, under the unsympathetic eye of the relief force, burst into the cacophonous dismay of a scared barnyard fowl.

'He—he tried to, Dommie, he tried to—'

'Aye, and didn't you make him try to?' demanded Malcom, with a brutal lack of tact. The Dominie's niece, mopping Jean's stained face, turned on him, snapping.

'I hate you, Malcom Maudslay! Go away, er I will say dhat it was you dhat tried to do it. I will report you to dhe Dominie for assault.'

Malcom stared, and then suddenly boiled over, being in a bad temper anyway at having been parted from his book. He seized Domina by the neck, banged her head against that of the moist Jean, strewed the pair of them into the broom, and strode out of the thicket. How the Jock and Jean intrigue fared thereafter he neither knew nor cared.

"I look back on the memory and feel sick with disgust. But

not of Jock Edwards. Rather of myself. The beastliness of our upbringing! The base shames and tabus of civilization that befoul the clean desires of the healthy human animal! . . ."

But one must balk and retire behind those hesitation dots which, whether in print or in startled feminine cacophony, always so infuriated Malcom.

VIII

When he was fourteen his Leekan world suddenly staggered and swayed a little, and then acquired new colours and voices.

Firstly, he and Jean and the Dominie's niece made a journey through the mountains to Dundon, to sit for the entrance exam ination to the college there. They sat it out amid cultured and trimly-clad city folk (Dundon had a population of over three thousand) and felt like bumpkins. At least, Jean and Malcom did. The Dominie's niece looked no more foreign in Dundon than she did in Leekan. She sat in front and to the right of Malcom, her beetle-wing hair in two long plaits down her back. Paper-puzzling, he scowled at her shoulder-blades. Once she turned and smiled at him from under her sombre brows—a friendly smile, an unexpectedly friendly smile, changed, lightning-like, to a grimace as he stared uncomprehendingly. Heavy-hearted, he completed his papers, sure that he had done badly.

When the results were announced three weeks later Malcom Maudslay and Domina Riddoch headed the list and divided the honours. They were both awarded adequate scholarships—bursaries they were called—and Malcom's career at college was assured. He climbed up to the ancient circle in Stane Muir, the scene of the half-remembered vision of his childhood, and lay and dreamt amongst the bracken, under the arcing Walls of the World which he had once pursued with much faith and a battering-stone——

He turned on his side and stared at the horizon.

The Wall of the World. . . .

He had three weeks to wait before he could begin at Dundon. The hay crop was heavy and clovery that year, and consequently late in the cutting. This fact gladdened Malcom. He volunteered to burn whins on the moor and escaped from Chapel o' Seddel farmhouse each morning with a small supply of matches and a great satchel full of books, forgetting through sun-lighted hours Dundon and bursaries and dinner-time and the world and its walls as he marched with Prescott's conquistadores against the Tlascalans and Montezuma and the knightly Guatamozin. No Leekan sunshine raised the sweat under his collar: he was riding high-hearted across the stricken field of Otumba, the Aztecs squelching underfoot in bloody heaps as they clove a way to the standard of the caciques and the images of the obscene gods. . . .

And then his mother died.

It happened on a Sunday. She was feeding the chickens in the yard at the time. Robert, pipe-smoking, home for the day from the farm where he was fee'd, stood beside her. Mrs. Maudslay chirked to the chickens, bending towards them in her dark, efficient manner. Then she put her hand to her side and gave a little sigh and crumpled up at Robert's feet.

Laid on the kitchen bed, she recovered a little and asked for Malcom. Thomas searched the Stane Muir for almost half an hour before the book-reader was found and brought to look on the still, white-faced stranger who seemed, at this the end, to have some very urgent message to impart to him. John Maudslay sat beside the bed, holding her hand, but she disregarded him, peering at Malcom, her lips, with a little spume on them, twitching ineffectively. Then he saw his father's foolish head buried in the blankets beside unmoving fingers, and understood. He backed away. The door and the sunlight were near at hand. He ran.

In the fir-wood below Stane Muir he sat down, shivering. Under his arm was still clasped Prescott's *History of the Conquest of Mexico*, and the desire to continue reading it was strong upon him. He opened the book, turned back the dog-eared page, and in a moment that awful thing at Chapel o' Seddel was

33

lost and forgot in the roar of Otumba. Then, appallingly, inexplicably, he found himself lying face-downwards in the ferns, weeping and weeping as though his heart would break.

'Oie, oie, luilones!' wailed the Aztec flight.

IX

His mother was buried in Leekan churchyard on a day of sunlight and scudding white clouds. Malcom helped to lower the coffin into the grave, and was intrigued at the silkiness of the cords. Ten years later, when he saw that grave, dog roses drooped over a long smother of grass and weeds, and he stood and mixed up some vague quatrains in his mind, wondering if the rose-petals came from the same womb as himself.

John Maudslay's sister was brought from North Aberdeenshire to keep house at Chapel o' Seddel. She was small and rosy-cheeked and cheerful and forty years of age. She had quick, bright eyes, with a cold glint somewhere in them. By then the home-staying Maudslays had thinned out, through feeing to neighbouring farmers, to Thomas, Lilian, and Malcom. The first two Aunt Ellen approved of. For Malcom her dislike was manifest from the first. He returned it in due measure; he began to return it with zest, if only that he might forget his wayward, unreasonable (for he had never loved her) grief for his mother. Chapel o' Seddel was soon brisk with open feud. She stormed at the untidy heaps of books she found in every room. If Malcom left his scraps of poetry or uncompleted essays lying unguarded they were sure to be swept up and burned, impatiently, as 'dirrt.' She could not bear to see him sitting idle—reading or dreaming as his fashion was—'while yer father's oot there, workin like a slave.' She sneered at the cleanliness and fastidiousness in bodily matters which his books had taught him; he prepared himself a bath, twice every week, in the kitchen ('hae ye no shame, standin aboot there naked?'), he cleaned his fingernails and teeth—'as though ye were gentry, and yer father only a poor workin' man.'

And so forth.

In return he contradicted her every statement on general affairs, of which she was slightly less cognisant than an Easter Islander, mimicked her squeaky Northern speech, penetrated beneath that veneer of cheerfulness and good humour with which she fronted the rest of the world. She was an insatiable gossip: all the doings of Leekan Valley were speedily hers to discuss. She knew all about the girls who had stayed out late in the fields, the girls who were hurriedly sent away for all too obvious reasons; she knew which family lived beyond its means and would break at the end of the term; she'd heard things about the Reverend Ian and his housekeeper—the latter hadn't slept in her own bed for a fortnight, michty be here; she knew about Jock Edwards stealing a bicycle lamp and the police seeing his father about it; she knew—*ad nauseam*. Prim in most matters, she had yet acquired a peculiarly rakish phrase with which she would close an account of something scandalous—'It's a hell of a case!' And this she would pronounce 'hellavacase.'

To a boy at once brutal and fastidious, it seemed that she raked in filth with a poisonous liking for stench. But in after-years, when Aunt Ellen had passed from Leekan and its scandalous days and nights—no doubt to that particular hell where all folk live discreetly and unscandalously, where no juicy stories ever circulate, where all girls marry their lovers before they bed with them—he could take a clearer view. The little woman was a romantic—a romantic starved of legitimate romance. Books were beyond her, art was not even a name, music was mouthorgans and melodeons. Only the ethically unsavoury was left to provide her with colour and excitement and the light that never was.

X

Through his own last years in Leekan that light would fall, blindingly, unexpectedly, startlingly, like sudden swordfalls of sunshine in forest-clearings.

His father's foolish face, tired and sagging to weariness in the upspringing flame-glow of a lighted lamp—once, at such glimpse, he stared at his father appalled, heartwrung. He had never known he was as tired as that.

Pitgowrie Road on a Saturday night and two drunken plough-men fighting with bare fists, in the quietude of the evening, the blood pouring from their faces, their heavy feet stamping, their shadows, gigantic, elongated, swaying far across the western fields. He had passed them by, barely looking at them, yet with the crack of each blow seeming to pound on his own heart.

An old tramp in the pouring rain, his swollen feet bulging from tattered boots, his dull, hopeless eyes lighting up hardly at all at sight of a boy, white-faced, sick at heart with pity, bringing him a pile of provisions raided from Aunt Ellen's larder.

A booming sleet-storm from the Grampians driving before it a herd of lost and frightened deer. In the beating of the wind-gusts he had watched the sight from his bedroom window one November morning, and felt for the beasts no pity at all but only a wild exultation in the pitilessness of the storm.

A stifling forenoon in early Autumn, the footpath by Leekan River, and Domina Riddoch standing nude, poised above the river, smiling down at her naked self, her body like a single vivid brush-stroke of pearl and rose against the green background of wild beech. She had started at the sound of his approach and he had faltered in his stride. Then, miraculously, they had smiled at each other, friendlily, and he had gone by in silence, with that glimpse of the morning beauty of a girl his forever. . . .

And somewhere, beyond the archway of the horizon, synthesis and explanation of these things—pity and cruelty and the heart-ache of wonder—awaiting him: these, and the fantastic acceptance of fantastic challenge that rose in him unbidden each night the stars lit their torches over Leekan.

XI

Daily the three Leekan pupils—Malcom, Jean, and the Dominie's niece—made the railway journey through the mountains to Dundon. College life was in full swing. They caught the eight o'clock train in the morning, returning to Leekan at half-past six in the evening. Often they were the only passengers on the train, but even when this happened Malcom seldom travelled in the same carriage as the girls. Being polite and abstaining from his book bored him. At Leekan Station, coming back, Jean would set out to tramp her three miles in one direction, while Domina and Malcom walked a mile or so in company and then parted to climb opposite sides of the valley. On this walk Malcom did not stop reading his book, unless darkness compelled him. He had grown so expert in the lie of the land that he could walk reading for mile on mile, along the banks of ditches, up steep inclines, over the rickety footbridge of Leekan River. Generally he was only vaguely conscious of the girl's existence. She would walk behind him silent and full of thought, finding great entertainment in his last-moment avoidance of this and that boulder and projecting root. Deep in Captain Scott's Polar expeditions he would stride largely ahead, often unheeding or unaware of her pert good night as he turned leftwards through the late Autumn evenings of 1913.

Winter brought a curtailment of Malcom's reading ploys, and a slight increase of friendliness between him and Domina as they groped together along unchancy footpaths and over the rotting footbridge in the evening murk. Then came the snowing night when the Dominie's niece, who had gone to college unaccompanied—neither Jean nor Malcom had braved the day's storm—failed to return.

At nine o'clock the Dominie himself, legging'd and much be-belted in a shepherd's plaid, knocked at the kitchen door of Chapel o' Seddel, thinking his straying niece might have taken refuge there. Snow was falling, whirling thickly about him and the tiny circle of effulgence from the lantern he carried. Malcom pulled on his boots and went out to join in the search. They tramped the bypaths down to the spot where the homecoming Chapel o' Seddel and Schoolhouse bursars usually parted, and from there they set to searching the fields, pausing every now and then to shout. The snow whirled faster and faster upon them and a half-gale arose. Malcom ceased to call the Dominie 'sir,' and helped to drag him out of gulfing snow-wreaths, and was himself so dragged. They lost the paths again and again, and regained them, and came to the footbridge. Three rungs in the middle were missing. Below, the water raced dark and evil. And at that sight the Dominie swore aloud, cursing the night and the barbarous valley so that Malcom was startled and then amused and then startled again at the thought of that dark pertness torn gasping away into the darkness of the water.

'We'll turn back, John,' cried the Dominie, 'up the school-house track. The lassie must have taken shelter somewhere.'

'Mebbe,' Malcom shouted sulkily, considerably put out even then at the reminder that his official name was John.

So they turned back. But the snowstorm was so dense that not a light was to be seen in all the valley. They might have been walking a deserted world. They lost the bypath again and strug-gled amidst entangling fences neither climbable nor escapable. Then they floundered across a stretch of ground which squelched soggily underfoot. By that the boy knew where they were.

'This is Dreaichie's moss,' he called out. 'Dreaichie's cotter-house is at the end of it.'

They stopped and shielded their faces and presently saw a glimmer through the snowfall. Somehow, stumbling, recovering, slipping on caked boot-soles, they made that glimmer and searched for a door which seemed to be non-existent. Then the Dominie knocked thunderously, footsteps sounded, and Mrs. Craigan's sonsy face projected from the dim passage of her butt and ben.

'Od, the Dominie! Come awa in. Yer lassie's here.'

In they went, stamping the snow from their feet. A door opened to the cheerful glow of the kitchen, discovering a large fire and Domina seated in front of it in her shift, head down-bent and drying her hair with a towel. The rest of her intimate garments, arranged on chairs, steamed cloudily.

'My man—he's awa looking for sheep noo— found her near the brig.'

'Hello, uncle, my dear! Did you think I was drowned? Oh—!' Sound of hasty rearranging while Malcom inspected the dresser-sideboard. Then a laugh:

'It's all right now, Malcom. I've got dhem on.'

'Ye're an awfu kimmer,' said Mrs. Craigan, flushing a scandalized red. 'Ye'll hae a cup o tea, Dominie?'

'This is very good of you, Mrs. Craigan.'

'Havers. Sit doon. Sit doon, young Seddel.'

Malcom sat down, politely avoiding scrutiny of the unembarrassed Domina's detailed toilet. By the time the search-party had drunk its tea, the refugee was fully clad again. The snowstorm whoomed outside and now and then a monster gust shook the unstable kitchen door. The Dominie re-belted his shepherd's plaid.

'We must set out again, Mrs. Craigan. It may get worse later on, and the road is fairly plain with my lantern.'

'A weel, Dominie. But will ye be a'right? Mebbe ye'd better tak young Seddel wi ye. My man'll step ower to the Chapel an tell them where he's gane.'

So it was settled. The three wrapped themselves up and stepped out into the breath-catching storming of the night. The Dominie, battered by several hours' searching, was weak and shaky; his niece seemed to flutter like a leaf at each gust that caught them. They kept a path between hedges and so for a time were sheltered, but presently, as they began to climb the Leekan brae, the storm tore at their faces and garments as with the teeth of mad dogs. The lantern light went out. The boy and girl had been struggling along on either side of the Dominie, but now Malcom took the middle position.

'Haud on to me,' he cried, abandoning his book-acquired accentuations, 'I ken the road.'

And he did, for the hill to the Schoolhouse fronted Chapel o'

Seddel across the valley, and often he'd marked the long, terraced brae which shelved upwards towards the mile-distant school buildings: it had been the work of ancient men, that terrace, perhaps burgeoning green in corn and barley five thousand years before. They reached it. The Dominie held to Malcom firmly and stumbled heavily. Domina was on Malcom's right. He put her hand into his pocket for greater warmth, and heard her shout something unintelligible, probably thanks which the wind shattered on her lips. Then he became aware that she was doing what he himself wanted to do. She was singing—singing *Up in the Mornin*.

He joined in. They swayed upwards through a lull, singing and daft and young, dragging the dazed Dominie with them. Then the wind came racing and snarling over the Aberdeenshire mountains again, and they rested in the lee of a drift, and the Dominie's niece said, 'Oh hell, it wasn't much use drying my knickers.' Blushing, Malcom dragged the others to their feet; and they faced the storm for a last effort.

All that night it snowed. Trains came as far as Dundon and then stopped. Sheep were smothered on the moors. By morning the drifts covered the roofs of low-lying shielings. Then it set in to freeze.

But while the worst of the great snowstorm raged Malcom lay happit and safe and fast asleep in the guest room of the schoolhouse, wrapped in a voluminous nightgown of the Dominie's. The howling of the wind awoke him once and he listened to the whoom and pause and blatter, then turned over and went to sleep again, resolving to eschew both M.A. and B.Sc. and become an explorer ultimately perishing remotely and romantically in the dark places of the earth. And long afterwards news of his end would be brought to the Dominie's niece, and she would weep, remembering him.

CHAPTER THREE

THE WALLS OF THE WORLD

I

"In the momentous summer of 1914 I was sixteen years of age, five feet five inches in height, one hundred and ten pounds in weight, small-boned, dolichocephalic, with coarse black electric hair. I greatly enjoyed brushing my hair because of the sparkling of the 'electricity.' I had, I remember, a smooth dark face with grey-green eyes; in fact, but that the smoothness is gone, I probably looked very much as I do at the present moment. Among hairless, bald-cheeked contemporaries I found myself under the disgusting necessity of shaving from my face twice a week the by-products of sexual maturity."

His mind had matured as rapidly as his body, and "at *its* by-products my teachers in the Dundon College could only stutter and take refuge behind the blessed word 'precocity.' "

He had perhaps a better concept of world history ("real world history, I believed it, though saturated with the Fraser-Avebury outlook") than anyone in Dundon: they gawked contemptuously at anything outside Europe and Asia Minor. In the dim kingdoms of eoliths, palæoliths, neoliths he could doubtlessly have routed professors, not singly, but in battalions. Unfortunately, pre-history was not a 'subject.' Dundon concentrated on dates—exact dates. You might know very well that Aegospotami preceded the Battle of Mondynes; you might even be able to explain what those battles were about, and to offer reasoned criticisms of both Konon and Duncan; but in the Dundon College, if you did not know the exact dates you were damned. Malcom was damned.

41

Dundon, an owlishly patriotic institution—no human being has such acute resemblances to a boiled owl as the patriotic Scotsman—dealt largely in Scottish history, and Scottish history, within historical times, bored Malcom profoundly. He could not conceive a more unattractive set of kings than the Scots from Bruce to James VI. They seemed to him heavy, bunchy men, with uneasy minds and bad digestions; he discovered from one of the less orthodox history books that the much-admired Red Fox had acquired his sobriquet not through choleric appearance or handsome sunburn but a congenital tendency to erupt into pimples. He insisted on informing Dundon of his discovery.

In English classes though he could write a better essay or short story than the average pupil, he held a low place because of his inability to dissect Shakespeare and kindred bores into their constituent squeaks, and label each squeak accurately. De-squeaked, he found them nuisances. All the business of grammatical parsing and analysis remained for him an abiding mystery—a singularly uninviting mystery. "I am still uncertain as to the difference between a simile and a metaphor. I have written a book of verse that has given a little pleasure to various odd people, but the relation of an iambic pentameter to an anapest—if there is a relation—remains hid from me. On the other hand, the relation between grammarians and the decay-bacteria in a corpse have always been perfectly clear. In Dundon they tested your appreciation of Tennyson's *Ulysses* by your ability to explain whether the dark, broad seas gloomed of themselves or were gloomed over by the approaching dusk hinted at six lines previously. As my mind refused to picture Ulysses himself holding up his embarkation the while he worked out this matter, I refused to work it out myself."

In laboratory work, he could produce quite satisfying smells and discolorations, but "in language masters I seemed to produce almost exactly the same results." In French he had discovered Anatole France in the original and a host of rules with which the Master's acquaintance appeared to be as limited as his own. Indiscreetly, he preferred M. France to the rules of that writer's

42

mother tongue, and revelled in the bitter wit and tragedy of *Les Dieux ont soif* instead of hunting subjunctives in the malarial jungle of *Le Chat Maigre*. Falling in with an accidental textbook on Spanish, he found a perverse pleasure in devoting to it hours which should have gone to French or German.

He could never look back on Dundon but that he saw it as a temple-stronghold of that gross and colossal stupidity—the English tradition of education, the cowardly de-lousing, castrating, and segregating of knowledge into underground pigpens, each tended by a discreetly inoculated overseer. Knowledge (he abandons the pigs)—"in Dundon its jewel-lights scintillated from a dozen untidy heaps piled pell-mell at the ends of a dozen unaerated tunnels. Down those one was supposed to crawl, uttering mumbo-jumbo incantations, knocking one's head against the roof, urged on to sprightliness by hidden tin-tacks strewn in the darkness. And when at length you neared a pile, with its guardian-priest dancing a reverential fandango round it, you saw that the jewels, far from being rude excavations, were made of the very finest paste."

Malcom must have made a singularly exasperating pupil, sceptical, enquiring, ungaping; unboylike. He was twice solemnly reprimanded for 'disloyalty' in 'free subject' essays—a tradition of Dundon English classes. The promoted Orkney fisher-louts and Kincardineshire ploughmen who made up the teaching staff detested him.

He had class acquaintances, but no particular friends. A complete absence of pocket-money prevented him joining in college sports, even had he wanted to. After the great snowstorm he saw little of either Jean Stanley or Domina Riddoch: they had found lodgings in Dundon itself, and Malcom alone made the daily journey up from Leekan, sometimes returning at night in a train with no other passenger than his joyously book-reading self. His place sank steadily in every class; college quarterly reports caused John Maudslay to goggle uncomprehendingly. But Malcom, as indifferent to the opinions of his teachers as he was forgetful of the prowling carnivores of the examinations, squatted under the Walls of the World, immersed in dreams of their conquest.

For, led to them through a strange love for the limpid, childish verse of William Morris, he had discovered the socialists and their gigantic, amorphous literature. Here were people who, like himself, had shuddered in sick horror at sight of the dehumanized and wandering crucified; people who also had known the challenge of the winters' stars and seen solution of all the earth's bitter cruelties in a gigantic expedition against the World's Walls, though they seemed vaguely in dispute over plan of campaign. He discovered with them a splendid, romantic hope which coloured his days and nights; he had no vision of his sardonic self fifteen years in the future.

"William Morris led me into the jungle and without apparent qualms abandoned me to a voracious fauna. They poured from the forest paths of Dundon Free Library and the Reverend Ian's bookshelves. Best of them I remember Lafargue ('The Right to be Lazy' was great stuff), Dan de Leon, Hyndman (a patriarchal Jew with a mission of economic circumcision), Blatchford (booming treacly and a little self-conscious over his sergeant's stripes), Kark Liebknecht (still one of my heroes: one of the world's great heroes), Shaw, the incomprehensible Marx, and, haloed in mystic clouds of fantasy and ferocity, Mr. H. G. Wells. Mr. Wells it was who, scattering feline Shavian and amphibian Blatchfordian, finally ran me to earth near the drinking pools, sprinkled me liberally with a scientific Epsoms salts, and devoured me at a gulp. At odd moments I still suffer from the bleaching effects of my intra-Wellsian immersion."

IIa

He was just finishing *New Worlds for Old* when the War broke out and—event far more portentous—Sammy Dreep came to Dundon as the Rector of its college.

He was long to remember that very bright autumn day when, in the accepted phrase and like a poison-laden pustule, War broke out. It was holiday time and he cycled down to Leekan village and bought a newspaper and brought back to Chapel o' Seddel the news that War had been declared on Germany. On the way home he met his brother Robert, by then foreman at the neighbouring farm of Hillside, driving a box-cart. Malcom dismounted and showed him the news.

'Daft B's,' said Robert, with no shadow of Thiepval blackening the bright moor road where his horse had halted, panting under the heavy load of artificial manure, its breath rising in a gusty steam. Malcom, in deference to the Communist Manifesto of 1846, attempted to mask his excitement with belated socialistic reflections.

'Germany is after our markets,' he said.

'What! the Leekan cattle-mart?' demanded Robert, and chirked to his horse, and drove on. Malcom, grinning, stared after him down the bright valley.

"My shame at the warlike thrills the news had brought me was needless. All over Europe at that very moment the socialist leaders of my books were ululating hosannas round the bright artillery tompions of the militarists. All, except Karl Liebknecht. In England a few disappointed politicians declaimed and continued to declaim a few nonsensical anti-war platitudes, but the majority of the Labourists, aitchless and obliging, and ceasing to stress the *pit* in capitalist, flung themselves into war-work and salaried positions with an hysteric abandon. And the literati—! We've forgotten, you and I in the years between, who manned the publicity sections of the war departments and poured out that nauseating stream of propaganda filth—we've forgotten, till a stray paragraph identifies some clamouring pacifist of the third decade. Somehow, this shameful memory clouds across that other, dimming the bright Leekan road and the face of my brother Robert."

Mr. Irvine Tring Bell, M.A., arrived at Dundon in late September to take the place of the enlisting Rector. Some Glaswegian wit had further christened him Sammy Dreep—a name which preceded his arrival by at least a week.

It was a singularly appropriate name. He was a tall, thin man with a shuffling gait and a constant and apparently incurable sniff. He had a narrow head and a face suggestive of a sheep in the possession of an unsatisfactory liver. Aware of his unfortunate appearance he went on a constant sniffling crusade against imagined disrespect. Taking over classes in Senior English, he discovered it in Malcom's 'free essays.' Malcom, who had taken no part in the class-tormenting of the unfortunate Rector, found himself quite meaninglessly singled out for Rectorial persecution.

It was the kind of thing his unflustered, unboylike coolness of demeanour had hitherto kept at bay in all the classrooms of the Dundon College. But his lack of clod-hopper shuffling and awkwardness merely aggravated Sammy Dreep the more. Malcom, once roused, joined battle quickly enough, exchanging sneer for sneer, spoiling the Rector's best rhetorical passages from the classics with the uplifted brows of sardonic doubt, very much at advantage in the possession of cool hands and cheeks and a devilishly assumed innocence. It grew to be a familiar entertainment in class 3B, this baiting and counter-baiting. The Rector's eyes would constantly turn on Malcom, and his colour mount. The blood would spread across his thin parchment face like ink spilt on stained linen.

'Now, Maudslay, if you'll be so kind as to give us your opinions on——' whatever was the subject of the lesson hour. He would neigh out such clumsy sarcasms, and Malcom, upheld by the devil, would sit and smile at him. The climax came one afternoon with a reading of *Henry V*. Sammy Dreep was expatiating on the oration 'Once more into the breach' when his eyes encountered Malcom's and he stopped.

'But our friend Maudslay is bored. No doubt he will stand up and give us something better.'

Malcom thought for a moment and in that moment was on his feet.

'Certainly, sir.' His heart was beating high in his chest but the first ring of his own voice in the silenced room steadied him.

> *'We mix from many lands,*
> *We march from very far,*
> *In hearts and lips and hands*
> *Our staffs and weapons are,*
> *The light we walk in darkens*
> *Sun and moon and star——'*

It must have made an amusing tableau. He recited as many of the lovely verses—three of them—as he could remember, bowed politely, and sat down. The unfortunate Sammy Dreep sniffled, the mottled glow high in his face.

'Ah, Swinburne. The perverts' poet. A revolutionist, are you, Maudslay?'

'A socialist, sir.'

'Oh. Well, your friends, who murdered my brother a week ago' (his brother had been an officer in the Gordon Highlanders) 'are coming nearer every day. Perhaps you would like to study German exclusively in future?'

The only socialist periodical procurable in Dundon was *Justice* (afterwards, in the yearbooks, to urge its pathetic claim to fame—'though Socialist, was pro-Ally during the War') and through its influence Malcom imagined himself a National Socialist, as patriotic as anybody. Suddenly he found his carefully-trained temper boiling through the flood-gates of his control. All his disgust and contempt for Dundon, its gaping ignorances and shoddy erudition, exploded shockingly.

'You damned sniffling fool, if you don't know the difference between a socialist and a pro-German——'

Sammy Dreep was on his feet, neighing. 'Leave the Room!'

Malcom picked up his books, stood up, strode to the door,

whistling, opened the door very carefully and left it negligently ajar behind him. As he went down the corridor he heard the Rector's voice calling 'Maudslay!' but he paid no heed. He walked out of the college gates and never again entered them.

III

Thereafter he passed two weeks in a carefully-garrisoned hell. He did not return to college, and Sammy Dreep's Rectorial letter duly arrived. Reading it, John Maudslay blinked his foolish eyes. 'Michty be here! Sic a disgrace!' Then looked across the dinner table at Auntie Ellen. 'It'll be the speak o the parish.'

Malcom forestalled her. 'It's a hellavacase,' he said, tilting his chair back and digging his hands deep in his trousers pockets. She flushed and shrilled at him while Thomas fumbled uncomfortably at his plate, and Lilian, spoon-poising, stared open-mouthed. But both regarded Malcom as an unnecessarily-pampered member of the family and neither had any great sympathy for him.

'They'll laugh at ye noo, richt enough,' said Auntie Ellen, addressing her brother,—'a coorse brute that insultit his teacher and stuck up for the Germans.'

'Och, I canna eat,' said John Maudslay. He pushed away his plate, foolishly dramatic. Then, addressing Malcom directly, 'Foo did ye do it, laddie? Could ye no think o the disgrace to yer fouk?'

Malcom was to remember sitting and looking at him with a contemptuous dislike. He was foolish, broken, cowardly. His poor eyes had a glassily unintelligent gleam. Good God, would he never stop whining?

"Poor father! Even while I hated I remember the twinge of sympathy and compassion I had for him. I was the Maudslay whom he'd never understood, the boy who was to do great things, become a schoolmaster or even a minister. He'd grown to accept my inability to be agreeable, my inability to listen to him, my inability to do farmwork as things linked with my ability to achieve scholastic distinction. And I'd failed and disgraced him."

John Maudslay had a feeble, patriarchal spurt of anger.

'Ye'll get oot o this as soon as ye can get a fee. D'ye hear? I'll no hae ye bidin at hame, livin aff yer fouk, nae use to onybody. Ye can get a fee.'

'You can go to hell,' said Malcom, and rose up and left the kitchen. Most of that day he spent in the room which he had come to claim as his own—the same room from which he'd watched the nineteenth century in conflagration. No one disturbed him, no one called him to meals. But he hardly noticed, being busied putting into execution the plans he had elaborated on his last train journey down from Dundon. In the evening he went to Leekan village and posted the letters he had written.

For twelve days his ostracism continued. Spite his self-taught Spartanisms the silences of Chapel o' Seddel drove him almost frantic. He spent most of the time out of doors, up amid the Druid stones of the moor, lying flat on the heather with a primer of Pitman's shorthand in front of him. Below, he could see the last of the harvest being carted home and built in great stacks in the farmyard. His father was an expert builder of stacks: he was recognized as an expert all over the Valley. In intervals of memorizing phonograms and watching those stacks Malcom would turn to his favourite dreaming of the vanished New Stone men of Leekan, wondering if any of them had ever sat here above the Valley and longed to escape from it with such passionate desire as himself.

On Sunday he went to Leekan kirk. The Reverend Ian had gone to England on a month's vacation and to preside over the annual meeting of the Hanno Society, as Malcom learnt long afterwards. In his place a young man of bulbous throat and glinting spectacles won Malcom's appreciation because of the speed at which he spoke. It was exactly the right speed and the youngest Maudslay covered the blank pages of two Bibles and a hymn-book with a shorthand report of the sermon. Coming out of the kirk—no other Maudslay had attended it—he found that he had become an object of interest to the Valley. Greig of Redleafe accosted him.

'Ye'll be lookin for a fee noo, young Maudslay?'

Malcom became aware of a circle of Greig's cronies, in their Sunday blacks, their red, weather-lined faces creased to hopeful smirks. Suddenly his coolness deserted him, he ceased to think of a cutting retort. This peasant malignancy routed even his English.

'Na,' he said, a little breathlessly, and walked away. And then, because he was only a laddie, and wouldn't be able to do much even though he did overhear, a voice remarked 'Ill-gettit young B.'

He made for home in a boyish passion of anger which he knew was boyish and foolish, which caused him to clench his hands and sob through his teeth. In the gusty jeering of clowns he had seen his own soul stand naked for a moment, shivering and lonely and frighteningly young.

IV

But on Monday the postman brought him two letters. One was from Glasgow, one from Edinburgh, both from editors of daily newspapers. Edinburgh offered him employment as a cub reporter at a salary of thirty-five shillings a week. Glasgow outbid this offer by half a sovereign. He did not give Edinburgh a second thought.

He had written five letters altogether, to various newspapers, and had been certain that some would reply. His youthful optimism was justified. Wartime thinning of staffs had already begun.

"I remember my letters were extraordinarily well written: I was respectfully humorous; I enthused over a reporter's calling, yet not gapingly or too amateurishly; I set forth my abilities in languages and shorthand without too much ostentation; and I made no mention of the fact that I was a socialist and had been accused of pro-German tendencies. Some of the ingredients may be out of date, but I offer the recipe to any journalistic aspirant who may care to use it."

Two days later, with six pounds borrowed from Robert in his pocket, he left Leekan Valley and did not see it again till after the passing of ten crowded years, nor ever again see either his father or Aunt Ellen.

V

He landed in Glasgow—that strange, deplorable city which has neither sweetness nor pride, the vomit of a cataleptic commercialism—in the midst of a characteristically Glaswegian downpour of rain: rain compounded of soot and other ingredients in steadily lessening proportions. After damp searchings to and fro throughout a moist and uncertain afternoon he at length found lodgings in Franklin Street, on one of the Glasgow hills. His room was in a house at the highest point of the arc, and at night he could look across half Glasgow and see the belch and glare of all Clydeside. The landlady stressed this advantage, though not unduly, tastes differing in such matters. She was a motherly woman, fat and good-natured, with small and beautiful eyes and a face pitted with smallpox. She became markedly respectful when told her lodger was a journalist. Then she showed him up to his room, climbing in a fat and contented vanguard waddle the innumerable stairs, and Malcom admired it diffidently, unaware that within two years it was to be the scene of his second attempt at suicide.

It was a large house, that house in Franklin Street, which bedded and breakfasted Malcom. For many a day its inhabitants puzzled him at odd and idle moments. It appeared to be let out in flatlets, but the male tenantry changed with bewildering rapidity. Fat men, decrepit men, young men, gaudy men passed and repassed on the evening stairs. All of them were agreeably jovial, however, and would wink at Malcom or raise friendly eyebrows.

He had been there nearly a year before he realized the house was a kind of brothel, and the male tenants mostly clients. Only himself and one other were bona fide lodgers, their rooms let for purposes of camouflage. But they were exceedingly cheap rooms, very clean and neat. Neither that first night when, strayed 'Azilian' boy that he was, he sat and watched Clydeside's lights, nor afterwards was his custom solicited by the torpid young Circes of Franklin Street. He came, indeed, to nodding acquaintance with one or two of them, cigaretted mezzo-blondes whose names he never learnt.

He was only sixteen years of age, though he looked eighteen at least. As he undressed in the unfamiliar room he and his reflection took stock of each other, solemnly, in the looking-glass. Then he saw his reflection smile and after a little smiled himself, in response, and turned out the light.

Next morning, his stomach full of bawdy-house bacon and eggs, the new Homburg firmly planted on his head, he rode down to Sauchiehall Street on one of those Glasgow trams that whoop round corners at speeds that are hair-raising. The overnight rain had cleared away, and Glasgow was stirring to life under the light-shot smoke-screen which is her daylight. Sitting in the tram, he was aware that his country boots were grotesquely thick and heavy, and that wing-tip collars had apparently gone out of fashion. (Later, he was to cultivate that wing-tip collar as a reportorial idiosyncrasy.)

The offices of the *Daily Tribune* were in one of the innumerable lanes debouching from Sauchiehall Street. They occupied a three-storied building. On the ground floor the accountant section laboured under the direction of Mr. Cleuk, a man with a white moustache and a singularly self-libellous nose ornamented near the left nostril with a hirsute Cromwellian wart. The second floor housed the editor, the sub-editors, and others of a like kidney. Under the roof was the reporters' room, long and bare, with tables dotted here and there, and a space enclosed in glass walls—the sanctum of the chief reporter. The photographer, who was also the artist, occupied a cubby-hole in a passage leading towards the rear of the building, where the printing machines thudded.

Though its new reporter was unaware of the fact, the *Daily Tribune* was on its last legs. Swayingly, it kept those legs till the Armistice, and then fell like a second Mars. It was a Conservative sheet, a kind of ineffective Scots *Morning Post*. Northcliffism had hardly touched it; it still exhibited pages guiltless of all but the essential cross-headings; it had no women's page; its leaders were long and Latin-strewed; it printed on an extraordinarily coarse paper even for wartime. Though a supporter of Church and State, it was edited—had been edited for twenty years—by a crude peasant Highlander, one John MacFarlane, who was in politics a Gladstonian Liberal and in religion a member of the Free Church of Scotland.

Malcom's portrait of MacFarlane might be a lapse into all-too-frequent caricature but for its evident sincerity. "He was a man with a mind so narrow, said the reporters, that some day he would fall over it and cut his throat. He was obsessed by belief in an insane Gaelic-Judaic God, a Keltic Moloch who had withdrawn his patronage from the Jews and bestown it on such Scotsmen as the irreverent dubbed Wee Frees. This God was not only a jealous God, he was a prying sneak-thief, a Peeping Tom and a queasy stomach. He could not abide the use of the word Sunday, this God, and through his chosen instrument in journalism, and that instrument John MacFarlane, He held an incongruous Sabbath in print. Drink and tobacco and the beautiful and intimate things of women's bodies were loathed by this God; but gatherings of horny-handed and insanitary islesmen and highlanders who prayed for the damnation of all that was clean and vivid and joyous in life 'bucked him no end,' to quote the jargon of the reporters' room. Men have never bowed in worship before a grotesquer deity than dominated MacFarlane; beside Him, Kinich Ahau and Itzamna were benevolent gods."

How MacFarlane managed to reconcile with his faith much that he was forced to print Malcom never knew; but he did reconcile it. Nor was he any conscious hypocrite. He believed utterly in himself and his own righteousness; he was unflinchingly honest and just; excepting his own God he hated all tyrants; except the basenesses of his own creed he hated all cruelties and shams. Behind the steel-rimmed spectacles riding awedly the bridge of his high, thin nose, he regarded the world with a vision liker to that of a Hebrew prophet than probably anyone else alive in the world.

Behind those spectacles he regarded Malcom's collected politeness frowningly at their very first interview. Then he dictated a passage as a shorthand test, found the transcription satisfactory, delivered a short lecture on the high responsibilities of the journalistic calling, and finally dismissed Malcom with an invitation to tea on the following Sabbath—if Mr. Rollo, the chief reporter, could spare him.

The new reporter climbed up the grimy, uncarpeted stairs to introduce himself to Mr. Rollo, who sat in his glass case at that early hour with the air of an incompletely resurrected museum mummy. He grinned at Malcom, wearily unmirthful.

'B'God, a loikes em yong myself, but how old are you?'

'Sixteen.'

The chief reporter thrust a ledger towards him for the filling-in of his address. 'Um. I suppose you'll want Sunday afternoon free, like all new arrivals?'

'God forbid,' said Malcom, thus winning his way to the heart of the chief reporter, who reverenced neither God, MacFarlane, nor the Glasgow *Tribune*.

VI

So he began life as a reporter and learnt the meaning of copy and stick and caps and quotes and many things that are here altogether unquotable. He found his way to the machine-room and watched the machines hounding forth thousands of *Tribunes* to the outside world; he introduced himself to Mr. Cleuk, and heard his funny story about a woman in a bath-room; he learnt to avoid the editor on the stairs, and to hail all policemen in a jovial manner; he bought a slouch hat and a fountain pen, and had large inner pockets made in his jacket.

"I was to fall out of journalism as an over-heavy brick falls through a rotting ceiling. It is a trade to which I have no intention of returning: I have long ceased to find interest in garbage. Even in those early days I remember a passive disbelief that such life could ever be permanently mine. . . .But it was a lucky chance, nevertheless, which saved me from drudgery at the age of sixteen and sent me out with fountain pen and notebook, and probably such multitude of irreverent curiosities as was never before let loose on the streets of Glasgow."

The *Tribune* imposed certain routine duties on each reporter. Most junior of those was the daily round of the quays and harbours and shipyards, and to this Malcom was assigned. For the first two days a reporter who was joining the Army took him round and introduced him. Thereafter he was free of miles of offices and warehouses and garnered acquaintance with nodding anonymity in the gross. He grew to know the types and makes of ships, to speculate which boat had newly come from Rio or New York, which was settling under the derricks with steel cargo for the Mediterranean. He heard innumerable stories of fights at sea with unauthentic German raiders. He was passing a quay one morning when a soldier in khaki and full harness jumped into the water and tried to drown himself. He drank his first and last pint of beer in a harbour tavern, discovered an extraordinarily sensitive stomach, went out of doors to a sheltered spot, and was quietly sick. He hunted copy up the gangways of Levantine traders and Belfast cargo boats. New factual hosts in myriads assaulted his senses. He was out on his adventure against the World's Walls.

As always, he inspired either instantaneous affection or instant dislike. Captain Romley of No. 12 Harbour Office appears to have liked him, and one would like to know more of the captain. But Malcom leaves him a figure hardly tinted and but slightly limned. Romley's inner office was a sanctum to which only a few of the harbour frequenters were admitted; Malcom, news-hunting, was accidentally admitted on his first visit, stormed at, and bidden to stay.

There, in company with a Norwegian shipping agent, Herr Jorgensen, blond and grey-garmented, wearing short brown boots and a short brown beard, a retired foreman of the ship-yards who believed in Schopenhauer and was minus an arm, superannuated whaler captains and others of like ilk, he would sit many an hour on Captain Romley's desk, swinging his legs and listening to the stories: mostly lies, and very good, solemn and satisfying, so that Malcom remembering them in after years would sometimes weep for mirth. There seems to have been singularly little of the bawdiness Malcom was afterwards to associate with the squatting place laughters of the convivial male.

Meantime, he wrote and wrote. His first efforts were reli-giously rejected. He buried himself in the office files, acquiring the technique of the paragraph, the art of writing journalese—Glaswegian journalese, pomposity and impudence carefully blended. He eschewed the splitting of that infinitive which the English verb does not possess, producing in consequence those unfortunate, latinist-blessed sentences amid which the adverbs mouth and mow like persecuted epileptics. "My style, I'm conscious, has never recovered from those Glasgow days. It remains always a little uncertain, a little florid and uneasy. Even throughout this plain record of things felt, seen, and believed I hear resound an occasional reportorial sickening thud."

But he began to find his paragraphs, sadly mangled by the sub-editors, sprouting in remote columns of the *Tribune*. Journalistically, he was launched.

Within a month Leekan and the schoolboy impertinences of the Dundon college seemed remote indeed in the memory of the dark young man who would return to his room in Franklin Street at one or two in the morning and yawningly undress while across the dusky miles of roofs the furnaces flamed and whoomed as Glasgow hammered out the ships for that desperate necessity already foreseen.

VII

Late one afternoon in November he strolled into Captain Romley's office and found the harbour-master alone. It was a newsless day, and, after the usual exchange of war-time rumours and surmises, Malcom was about to leave when the Captain asked him to take a note over to Herr Jorgensen's place. The new reporter had not been there before, but the shipping agent might have publishable scandal or gossip of a neutral tinge. Malcom took the envelope and walked over the swinging bridge to the indicated quay through a crispness of air successfully defying the Glasgow smoke. In the middle of the bridge he stopped to light a cigarette and look down the shining lanes of water going eastward into a mirage of funnel-stacks and haze. He found Herr Jorgensen's office on the second floor of a small, prim building, knocked, went in, and discovered Rita Johnson.

She had been sitting on the office rug, in front of the fire, regarding the flames pensively ("I know so well she must have been regarding them pensively!") and her face was flushed and her skirts in disorder at the abruptness of his entry. She became professionally attentive.

'Yes?'

'A note for Herr Jorgensen.'

'Oh. He's out; but he may be back any minute. Like to wait?' She moved a chair towards the fire.

'Please,' he said, though he had no particular reason for waiting. He sat down and looked at her. She fiddled with her typewriter, turned towards the fire, and turned away again. Then their eyes met and they both laughed. They seemed to share some amazing, secret jest.

'I know who you are, I think. You're Mr. Maudslay, the *Tribune's* new reporter, aren't you?'

He nodded, producing an unnecessary card. She frowned at it, but pleasedly.

'And I haven't one to give you.' Then her eyes sparkled. 'But I will in a minute.' She reached for a monstrous sheet of card-

57

board and inserted it in her typewriter. He sat and stared at her dancing fingers.

He could never describe Rita adequately. She was in the longish skirts of 1914, but wore a pretty white blouse which showed her neck and throat down to an intriguing secrecy: a veiled wonder, indeed, of breasts like Sapphic apples and a body like a canto from Swinburne. She had fair brows and blue eyes such blue as is the sea's in Summer, sometimes greyish and smoky, sometimes deep and dark. Try as he might in after years he could never remember the colour of her hair. Perhaps it was some tawny shade. She had a little twist to her mouth, so that she smiled with a crookedness that surprised and fascinated. Her fingernails curved to fine points, like Chinese fingernails.

These the faint limnings for likeness of that Rita whom he was to know to the uttermost secrets of body and soul. She was a year older than he was. She was English, and came from Cheshire—"Chester, I think." He never knew if her father or mother was alive. She shared a small flat with another girl, Edith Standish. She had a purity of thought and act and demeanour so real and yet so intangible, so divorced from life and morals, that he was to remember her as a child might remember a fairy—a jest of the atoms, a chance of the tides, miraculously garbed in mortality. She had a fairy wonder in things, a fairy coolness and kindliness. Even that passion she was to burgeon was somehow to seem unhuman, a lost chord from the pipes of Elfland.

However much else of import he was to forget, always, and with an amazing clarity, he could recall the firelight dancing in that room and Rita's pointed fingernails flashing above the typewriter keys. Then she whipped the card out of the roller and turned to him with mischief in her eyes. Doing so, her elbow knocked against the table and the card fluttered to the floor. She got off her chair and knelt and reached after it: she knelt like a boy, and the firelight pirouetted a fairy dance on the hair that was perhaps some tawny colour. He stood up with some idea of assisting, and she rose into his arms.

She rose up into them, literally, flushed and warm, and suddenly closed her eyes and sneezed, minutely, like a child. She did not struggle and he never knew how she came to be there. The wonder of it was like the sound of blown bugles. Then he saw her eyes kindle and kindle with a kind of urgent fear, and in that moment he kissed her.

Her lips resisted him for a moment, then opened, softly, terribly, unbelievably, as though it was the Spring he kissed and was kissed by in return. So, for a moment, then she had wrenched herself away, breathless, her eyes shining with laughter. She held out the typed cardboard.

'My card,' she said, with the little lights flickering like flame-blown tapers in her eyes.

VIII

He went home to Franklin Street earlier than usual that night. But Lucretius had lost savour. He dropped his book and went to his favourite position at the window and clasped his knees and stared across Glasgow. He rose and turned out the light. And then, as he tells, as he stood there dreaming the vague, clean, cloudy lusts of youth, a sound in the street below caught his attention. It was a beggar, an old man, singing in a dull, cracked voice, his face uplifted under the dreary gasjet of a street lamp.

Malcom stared down at him, shivering, the girl of Herr Jorgensen's office forgotten. All his life the people of the abyss, the cheated of the sunlight, were so to haunt his happiest moments and dreamings. These, the eternally crucified, who are not of Demos, who challenge in mindless hopelessness every scheme of reform or revolution.

The old man heard a window wrenched up, and stopped his singing, then bent and groped at his feet as a handful of a dreamer's scanty change rained about him in the dimness.

IX

Chance was to abet his revulsion from memory of the incident in Herr Jorgensen's office. Next morning, consulting the ledger on the chief reporter's desk, he found himself taken off quay-patrol and put on police-courts, hospitals, fires. He sat in grimy chambers with juniors of other Glasgow papers from ten in the morning till sometimes late in the afternoon, watching case after case come up, and yawning, and stealing out into draughty corridors to smoke surreptitious cigarettes. Police-court procedure and minor crime and punishment palled on him rapidly, except when sentence of the lash was passed on some youthful offender. Then he would sit with fingernails dug in his palms and torture in his heart. Such sentences roused him to a passion of hate and pity: they so roused him all his life. He would sit and watch some Glasgow Bailie, some chemist or baker, "a thing with a mean little bleached soul stung to a sadistic glow," pass sentence on shivering boys who probably, many a time, suffered the consequences far less in actuality than the white-faced junior on the reporters' bench did in imagination.

Three others occupied the reporters' bench with Malcom. One Morris, a billiard-player, a cheerful and warty young man, had the reputation of a better acquaintance with the street-walkers of Glasgow than any man alive. Girls on a charge of 'soliciting,' entering the courtroom—some desperate and forlorn, some upheld by a poor, tawdry defiance—would glance round the unfriendly place and suddenly brighten at sight of Morris. Sometimes they would smile at him, sometimes bow. Malcom was to remember one hailing him, ' 'Lo, boy!' and the shocked faces the Bailie and clerk turned towards the reporters' bench. 'Blast her,' said Morris and stared at the ceiling.

In the afternoons Malcom went the round of the hospitals, looking for interesting accidents. Once he came on a large and satisfying fire, complete with firemen, brass helmets, miles of hose, and a hysterical crowd watching two work-girls being rescued from an upper storey. The whole procedure of the rescue struck him as profoundly funny and unnecessary, seeing the girls had merely to walk across a flat roof to a neighbouring building in order to attain safety. Morris went back to his paper and wrote half a column of sob-stuff. To the *Tribune's* representative there appeared to be other possibilities in the happening. He wrote a malicious account which found a place among the war news on the front page of next morning's issue, and led to innumerable telephone-calls and protests. MacFarlane, while reprimanding Malcom and the sub-editors for the flippancy of the account, chose to approve generally, and defied the fire brigade authorities.

Once, at eleven o'clock at night, he heard from a constable coming off duty of a particularly grimy murder in the Gorbals, which is Glasgow's Soho and Stepney in one. He risked hiring a taxi and made it wait for him outside the odoriferous warren of courts leading to the house. A police-sergeant admitted him, doubtfully, and he heard the story and looked at the victim, a woman lying on a heap of sacking, her throat cut from ear to ear by a jagged razor—and hurried back to the *Tribune* offices and, abruptly and disastrously, was sick on the floor of the reporters' room.

It was his first and last scoop. He passed from general to specialised work. He was climbing. Great gaps were appearing in the ranks of the *Tribune's* staff. Two reporters had joined the Army. Two suddenly deserted and went elsewhere to fill vacancies at higher salaries than the *Tribune's* directors could abide. The paper catered largely for agricultural interests, and one of the deserters was the assistant of Grayman, the overworked and irritable agricultural editor. Grayman demanded Malcom as replacement; previously he'd talked the matter over with Malcom, and the latter had agreed willingly enough.

So, surprisingly, did MacFarlane. With his salary raised to three pounds a week, Malcom transferred his professional interests to railway journeys and marts and fairs and cattle-shows all over Scotland. Once, at a sale in Aberdeen, he encountered a Leekan acquaintance in the bulky shape of Greig of Redleafe— a Greig who addressed him as Mr. Maudslay, for he wanted the

Tribune to make mention of his prize Shorthorn. Once he crossed to Belfast, that lesser and baser Glasgow. Once—the night of his seventeenth birthday—he journeyed south to Reading for the great stock sale of the 27th December. He began to learn more of prize stock and agricultural method than the average farmer ever learns. He became accustomed to being drawn aside confidentially and pressed to accept ten-shilling notes in return for the much-prized 'mention'. He grew bored of life in hotels and in handing over long telegrams in post-offices with the magic word 'Press.'

It was early 1915. But the War touched him hardly at all—the dark, rather silent agricultural junior who had still to make a single friend in Glasgow, whose reserves in smoke-room story-telling, whose blank uninterest in cards and billiards in frowsy northern hotels possibly won him no great popularity in his profession. "Billiards is a passion of the Fourth Estate." But Grayman confessed him a success. "And I was a success. You see, I had no reportorial traditions of hedging, tabu, or kowtow. What I wanted to know I asked—a thing so unusual with a reporter that I was often mistaken for a young gentleman of leisure with agricultural interests."

And then he met Rita again.

X

It was four o'clock in the afternoon of a day in mid-January. Snow was falling outside Glasgow Central Station. Malcom had just returned from a long, cold journey up to a horse-show in Oban. He stamped out on the pavement and stopped to beat his frozen hands together, thereby obstructing the passing of a girl. Then he became aware that the obstructed persisted in suffering obstruction.

' 'Ve you forgotten me?' she said.

Her throat was swathed in a fur, and her left hand, a small, gloved hand, was at her throat, patting the fur. Her cheeks were pink in the coldness, her nose was white as only a fairy's could be in such weather. He looked at her solemnly.

'There are two more tapers in your eyes.'

She laughed, the lashes drooping over the smoky-grey eyes ingenuously. 'It's the weather. Saves me carrying a Primus stove, you know.' She regarded him with lighted curiosity. 'You've got a moustache.'

The War had brought about an amazing out-cropping and in-trimming of moustaches. At the moment the football moustache prevailed—so-called because there was supposed to be a maximum of eleven hairs on either side: usually a generous estimate. This was the growth which Malcom had achieved. He records that he felt no shyness at all, only gladness. He put his arm through Rita's.

'Come and have tea with me.'

'Love to.' She was as simple as himself. 'There's a nice place near the Picture Galleries.'

They sat in that nice place near a heartsome fire and Rita poured tea with a solemn ceremony. They talked a little and looked at each other much, without embarrassment, in happy appraisal.

"I have never seen in literature, that poor cracked mirror of life, reflections of such characters as ourselves. Are all seventeen-year-old boys and girls of these post-War years as our cretinaceous fictionists depict them? Either awkward, insanitary beings, under parental control, addicted to games and sweets and lumpish calf-loves entirely sexless, or else moribund perverts immersed in pleasures Lesbian and Gomorrahn under the able tutelage of clerical schoolmasters? Are there no frank young people who want to talk together and kiss together and sleep together, and is my ineradicable conviction that sixteen is the ideal mating age merely an amoral obsession?

"I doubt it, though I've little means of putting the question to test, here in this room above the River, surrounded by my Maya codices, divorced from all acquaintance with the very young, unless it be the intrusive Steven. If it be true all my philosophy of change and envisagement of the European War's main function in history goes glimmering. If it be true Rita and I were spiritual parents of the spiritually stillborn. For we did not play at being grown-up: we presumed we were grown up, however falsely we presumed it, and the fact that after that meeting I looked back on the memory of it with an obscene shame and disgust does not alter a jot my conviction of our representative normality.

"We sat and talked and admired each other and allowed our tea to get cold and ordered more and talked again. Perhaps I did most of the talking."

It must have been a fairly typical Maudslayan talk.

He lighted her cigarette and they went out into the snow—snow which changed into a rattling downpour of hail before they gained the pavement. Rita laughed and caught his hand and together they raced up broad steps into shelter. Malcom shook the hail-stones from his Homburg and looked about him. They were in the Picture Galleries.

'Like pictures?'

She shook her head, a fairy Philistine. 'Not very much. They're tiring. I've seen them all before.'

He turned round and looked at the hail-storm through the glass-panelled door. Then reconsidered the entrance-hall.

'Some statues under the light over there. Let's look at them.'

They walked over and stood below the pedestals. Above them towered not portrait statues, but plaster-casts of nude antiques—an Aphrodite, the usual discus-thrower, a headless Nike Pteros and some others. The Leekan barbarian had never seen their like; he drew a deep breath. Behind the statues rose a painted wall donated as fitting background by some Glaswegian æsthete.

Malcom walked round the Aphrodite in frowning wonder. Then had a sudden thought and looked from the statue to his companion.

She flushed, sweetly, more tapers kindling in her eyes. She nodded.

'Yes, very like her. So my tailor says.'

XI

But from the mind-picture of Rita standing so he shivered away next morning, and for many a morning thereafter, in much the same spirit as he closed his ears to the genial smut of the reporters' room. With a sick distaste he would turn from it, all unaware that the key to his irrational shame was the memory of a thin-lipped peasant woman accusing her questioning nine-year-old son of 'dirtiness.' He saw as little of the wondering Rita as he politely could.

Moreover, and his work apart, other things clamoured for his attention. After extensive research among the war-shattered fragments of the British Socialist Party he had joined a seceding wing, the Left Communist Group of Glasgow. That was in January. In mid-February, such the power of his youthful enthusiasm and sincerity, he found himself elected the Group 'co-secretary.' The other secretary was the white-bearded Anton Meierkhold, then a Professor of Russian Literature and now an exile in Siberia from the Sovyets. The Group was aggressively anti-war and anti-constitutional, and Malcom, crusader against both the challenge of the stars and that savage cruelty which sent old men to beg their bread in the streets, went to the logical extreme of his knighthood. He was far from the 'National Socialist' patriotism of Dundon.

The Group soon made it plain that as a journalist he held a strategic position in the Army of the Revolution, and it says much for his conviction that the world of real news is never even skimmed by the press that for over ten months he betrayed *Tribune* secrets with set and deliberate intention, helped to engineer the great shipyard strike of that year, and was politically and objectionably active without being once suspected by either his own or any other Glasgow daily. He assisted Meierkhold in the editing of the Group journal, a libellous and obscene and exceedingly active and bitter weekly which was twice suppressed and its plant smashed in police raids. "A raiding policeman was my first glimpse of how vigorously the machine-hating serf still flourishes."

Caught in one of those raids Malcom, with the incalculable luck of the fanatic, was suspected of nothing more than reportorial acumen on behalf of the *Tribune*. . . .

"It is all very remote. Like most decent young people I hated cruelty and pain and poverty, loathed these things and believed they could be made to pass from the earth. Socialism could do it, and to help in the task I was prepared, very logically, to inflict pain and cruelty on myself and on the whole human race, just as a surgeon inflicts pain by cauterization. And afterwards, afterwards, on a decent earth, there was to be a tremendous planning of a tremendous Something. . . .

"That was in 1915, you must remember. Socialism was still a thing for which young men were prepared to die. I myself had still to meet and hate in his undraped savagery the contemptible, pitiful Demos, had still to watch from this Chelsea room the collapse of the entire socialist philosophy and the monstrous outburst of putrescent heresies upon its decaying corpse. I'd still to witness the shameful flunkeyism of a Labour Government in office, its clownish leaders grotesque in court dress and kowtow at the shrines of a fungoid tradition and a moribund commercialism the while the Cheated of the Sunlight starved in their hovels. I'd still to hear that commercialism's leaders, those microcephalous morons whose visionless incompetence has made chaos of the economic world, hymned and hailed by the Wellsians as the promised Messiahs. I'd still to learn of the murder of a Liebknecht by an Ebert or to read of a dreary old man's rejoicings over the blood-spattered bludgeons of Fascism; I'd still to realize that that misty Something which I and Metaxa and Domina call the Adventure is entirely beyond the imagination of the orthodox socialist—that neither the Adventure nor salvage of the Abyss lies with either the socialists or any orthodox politico-religiosity."

The Group chairman was an engineer from the shipyards, an orthodox Marxian who believed that Marxians should breed like rabbits and encourage the rest of the proletariat to do the same. Thus, in congestion, overcrowding and unemployment

66

conditions would become so terrible that revolt would be inevitable. Then the capitalist system would be overthrown and the workers take control and the capitalists with their whores and harlots set to working in mines and puddle-pools.

He had a large, damp wife who breeded vigorously and whom he frequently beat. This was his vision and this was his life.

The Group treasurer was an evicted schoolmaster, an enthusiastic and ambitious and robust young conscientious objector. He had not repudiated his Christianity: he was a sincere and earnest and muscular young Christian, impervious to all arguments on behalf of the materialist conception of history, for he would prove that God had always been on the side of the working man, that Isaiah was an early Engels, Christ a practical revolutionist, St. Paul a more enthusiastic socialist than Proudhon. But their teachings had been corrupted. . . . His muscularity and sincerity developing a dignified *embonpoint*, he was afterwards to rat to the Labour Party, the comforts of an Under-Secretaryship, and a belief in the inevitability of gradualness.

Meierkhold was a sentimentalist, a gentle soul as much out of place in the Left Communist Group of Glasgow as he was later to prove in the blood and iron government of Stalin. He suffered agonies from the War. Each recorded battle, each list of casualties made him wince as from a personal hurt. 'Akh God, this carnage!' he would say, and cover his face with his hands and then in self-defence grope back into dreams with his beloved Kropotkin, to picturing a future earth of grain and flowers, a paradise of the leisured craftsman and the happy peasant, without sin or blood. . . .

These three were representative socialists. Probably, indeed, they were the flower of the Group, and to Malcom, oddly romantic realist that he was, they were presently to seem as sincere and selfish and utterly silly as three Neolithic shamans plotting the perpetuity of desirable Neolithicisms in the Druid's Circle of Stane Muir.

XII

And then the Spring came.

Late in March Grayson, the agricultural editor, was seduced from his allegiance to the *Tribune* and went to Edinburgh to take over the editorship of a farmers' weekly. Thereon MacFarlane sent for Malcom, lectured him dourly, and ended up by offering him Grayson's post at a salary of £6 a week. This was a rise of three pounds and even Malcom was a little staggered, though he seems to have had no doubt of his ability to carry out the work. Neither, apparently, had MacFarlane, though the times and circumstances must have been exceptional enough when they allowed of a boy of seventeen becoming agricultural editor of a daily newspaper. It was arranged that local correspondents should largely carry out the duties he had performed as Grayson's assistant.

But the Spring came up even to Franklin Street, and Malcom began to remember Rita again. He had not seen her for over a month. Once since their meeting at the Picture Galleries he had taken her to a theatre on a press ticket, once to a dance where she had introduced him to her friend, Edith Standish, and then herself vanished and failed to re-appear, to the relief of his inhibited next-morning self. But now there were nights in bed when he turned, sleepless and sleepless because of that wind which came down from the northern lochs to Franklin Street and shook the window-curtains, when the ancient shames of Leekan Valley were no protection, when the foulest of the reporters' room stories sang through his mind like epics and he craved for Rita with an unclean cruelty of craving altogether inexplicable by any extension of the materialist conception of history. . . . "From such strange cess-pools, no simple animal desire rooted in clean earth, I suppose all our loves have flowered since the ancient primitive promiscuity withered away before the restraints and tabus of civilization."

In his first free evening—a Saturday evening— he called round at the little flat shared by Rita and Edith. But he was not to see her even then. He found Edith alone, and packing. 'I'm leaving here tomorrow,' she said.

'Sunday? What for?'

'Going into training as a nurse. Rita's at Chester for the weekend—somebody ill. Hold that trunk open, like a dear.'

He held it open, though probably not at all like a dear, bade Edith goodbye, and came away. It was a very still Spring evening over-watched by a sickle moon. He came through a Glasgow park littered with amorous couples, the men mostly in khaki, the women's bodies as gigglingly garbed as their voices. Near a man-deserted hedge he stood and listened to the sleepy cheeping of a bird, and was oddly comforted thereby. But there were still the long hours of darkness to come.

He could not sleep. He lay and strained to hear in the night silence—distant, furtive laughter and soft rustlings, sounds which had never troubled him before the coming of that Spring. He stuffed his fingers in his ears to keep them out, hating as he glimpsed him—the slavering beast which rose and gloated and lusted in the jungle-undergrowths of his soul.

Why not go out into the corridor and knock at a door and get one of the house-prostitutes? asked the beast, with grinning brows.

And a voice answered him very truly out of the gulf of the years. 'Because I'm *not* a dirty beast.'

On the Monday and Tuesday he was away in Perth, but on the Wednesday returned early in the afternoon, went to the *Tribune*, wrote up his copy, had early tea, and set out for Herr Jorgensen's office. April rain pelted him in the streets, and for a while he sheltered in a doorway watching the lightning flashing over the moored shipping in the harbours.

He found Rita locking the office door, and when he saw her suffered such shock as brought back the knight and banished the beast into unthinkable thickets. Her face was pale and weary, though she smiled her crooked smile at him and put a small, froggy hand in his. She looked the tiredest person he had seen for weeks, and very young.

He said so, holding her hand in that curious, unadolescent friendliness her actual presence always inspired.

'Tired? I came back only yesterday, and . . . somebody dead who was good to me.' She bit her lips and looked away from him, then smiled again with that sweet kindness that was as much part of her as her crooked mouth, that hatred of troubling others with her vexations. 'And I'm old. Oh, I'll be old as ever tomorrow!'

'Tomorrow?'

'I'm eighteen tomorrow. Edith and I were going to hold a party—you were to be invited. But that's quashed with her going to London.'

It was his opportunity, albeit it was now the knight who planned. 'I've a complete free day tomorrow. Come to a matinee with me. Bernard Shaw's *Pygmalion* is on. We can have tea afterwards at some place and you can go home to bed early again.' She came just neatly a little below him in height. He looked down into the smoky depths of her eyes and wandered a little. 'All the lights have gone out, all except one.'

'I kept you just one. . . . Love to see Shaw and have tea: I'm shaw I will. . . .'

She stood on the steps above him at parting, and ruffled his hair, tiredly, with fairy fingers, when he took off his hat.

' 'Morrow afternoon.' Then yawned with the sleep which had been denied her. 'So'y. So sleepy.' She knuckled her eyes and smiled drowsily. ' 'Night.'

He awoke next morning into a Spring dawn still and fervid, with Glasgow smokeless and the sunlight upon her streets. He dressed and went out. At one o'clock he came back and put on the new suit of flannels he had bought. He had also bought new shoes: the first good shoes he had ever possessed. Then he filled his case with cigarettes, frowned at his nose in the mirror, called a taxi and went round to Rita's flat. She came out at the sound of the taxi, a Rita he had never seen before, in a wisp of green dress and brown shoes and stockings and an odd little hat, shaped like a jockey's cap, which made her look like an earnest boy. At the neck of the green dress was pinned one of the roses he had sent that morning.

'But all this must cost such a lot. Sure you can afford it?'

'Easily.' He sat in the taxi beside her and told her of his £6 a week, and then said something else of which he had thought overnight, and, saying it, realized he was being ridiculous. For some reason memory of the Aphrodite of the Picture Galleries flashed across his mind. It was like trying to tempt her from her pedestal with the offer of a bun. 'I could afford to marry now.'

She leant back opposite him, and closed her eyes and then opened them again to uncover a multitude of hurrying lights below the grey veils. 'Oh, Malcom! Sounds awfully old even for eighteen. Dull and old and awful.' She considered him happily. 'Look a dear boy, except——' She leant forward and patted his tie into satisfactory shape. 'Better.'

It was the first Shaw play he had ever seen. They sat and looked at it, and Rita, kind thing, gurgled obligingly over the Shavian 'bloody.' In a surprisingly short time they found themselves out in the afternoon air again. She shook her head over another expensive taxi, and they walked through radiant streets to Ranald's Restaurant. High on the American roof-garden Malcom led Rita to a table and found her a wicker chair and piled it high with cushions. She lay back in it and looked at Glasgow and at him, and was suddenly grave and wistful under the peak of her jockey hat.

'I love being fussed over. How did you know?'

'You're very fussable,' he said. Then was startled. 'What's wrong?'

There were tears in her eyes. She smiled through them, adorable, a fairy remembering mortality. 'Nothing. Being silly. Only— Oh! I wish. . . . What was it Joshua said when he wanted the sun to stay in the sky?'

He sought back through Leekan days of the Bible 'as litera- ture' and found it. '"*Sun, stand thou still upon Gibeon; and thou, Moon, in the Valley of Ajalon.*"'

'You have a beautiful voice. Did you know? Oh, look! There's the sunset already.'

They sat at tea and watched the sun set over Clydeside, with Rita's curve of cheek and peak of hat a silhouette growing duskier and duskier to the eyes of Malcom against that remotely threatening sky. They sat there with glowing cigarette-tips when the darkness had come down and the lights of Glasgow were all around them. Then Malcom surprised Rita in a dim yawn, and took her away.

Outside her hall door she stopped a moment and was silent and shadowy. Then slipped her hand in his.

'Come up and I'll make you some coffee.'

In the darkness of the second landing he stood and fumbled with her key, and she laughed a little, and her hand came over his, and the door opened. They were in the little flat. The door closed softly behind them.

He searched for the electric switch, and, searching, met her fingers again. She did not move.

'Rita,' he whispered; and then 'Rita.'

He found his fingers taken from the switch. Suddenly she laughed, clearly, joyously, making ridiculous that whisper of his.

'Oh Malcom dear! . . . so much?'

He held her for a moment in his arms, kissing her.

He found himself alone.

XIII

And so, in a little while, she came to him.

XIV

Sometime, very early in the morning, he awoke. Beside him slept the stranger who was his. One shoulder was bared, but as he adjusted the quilt he found it warm and dimpled. He pulled back the quilt again and kissed her there, and lay listening for a little to her even breathing.

Then he became aware that the room was flooded with a silver glow. He reached out his hand to the window and drew aside the curtain.

Over the Valley of Ajalon stood the Moon.

CHAPTER FOUR

THE MOON IN AJALON

I

They would sit and look at each other in a shameless, delighted possessiveness. It was to Malcom as though he had never known hunger or thirst before, or (he—the student of physiology!) the sensitiveness of his fingertips, the miracle of blood, the texture of human skin. There was neither shrinking nor cruelty in all the play and interplay of desire between those two young lovers. Physically, they were as perfectly matched as, mentally, they were utterly dissimilar.

For even at the quivering edge of keen delight they were both conscious how alien each to the other was. Malcom, like all true sagamen, had fallen in love with a fairy. Their minds were of different texture, their interests so wide apart that they were not even incompatible. They remained strangers—kindly strangers, courteous strangers, strangers adoring each other with utter passion. And they never developed the least intimacy.

He would come upon her, pensive and pyjamaed, squatting on the rug in front of the bedroom fire, hands clasped behind her head. He would kneel beside her and kiss that dimpled place on her shoulder. She'd smile, still pensively, and lean against him.

'Thinking of?' She'd turn her darkened eyes upon him, and he'd see himself, unthinkably remote, in their depths. 'Oh. Just things.'

They were things outside his sympathy or comprehension. As irreligious as himself in the sense that she never bothered about the sex-codes of ancient Levantines, deified or sanctified—or perhaps thought of them only as remote snarlings of impotent

74

age—she had yet a passionate love of 'Church things': organ music, incense, the triumphal chanting of the risen sacrifice, all the sensuous beauty created by eunuchization of the ancient cannibal rituals. "*The Hound of Heaven* was probably her favourite poem; she liked my abhorred John Donne, loved the mistier Keats. She had read a little, but deeply, and along bypaths of literature which seemed to me to end in meaningless swamps of verbiage. And all this—her music, her reading, her intellectual appraisements and envisagements of Life—she stood a little apart from, sweet and kindly, as though her fingers merely played with those things the while she listened for the far, keening horns of another universe sweep by along the Walls of the World. . . ."

So he would attempt, long afterwards, a stumbling poet, to net in words the memory of her elusive quality. She evoked in him a passion that was not all passion; sometimes it was an aching humility to try and understand those gossamer delights of her mind, a tenderness numb and numbing because it was oddly foreboding. He was young enough and deeply enough in love to believe in the possibility of ultimate, perfect understanding. And in response he would find her, faery-puzzling, attempting to comprehend those boring and irrelevant things to which he evidently attached so much importance—politics, history, socialism.

Sometimes, remote behind those smoky veils in her eyes, he would catch a look of puzzlement or swiftly suppressed resolve. She was shutting the door on things bubbling over with interest, but incomprehensible to him.

But those were only occasional ghostly suspicions and depressions. They were happy in a golden happiness, wistful, solemn, absurd. Unconscious the achievement, she created for Malcom wonder in a thousand commonplace things having no direct connection with the fact that she slept in his arms. A book left open by her was an amazing discovery; her clothes, piled on a chair—they gave you a little shock when you touched them— it was astounding to know that they had been intimately worn by her; the place where she had sat in a chair—it was a nest he could not bear to sit in himself, when he noticed it; a piece of morning toast with a neat semi-circle bitten in it, abandoned on a plate (she would discover the clock and office-time with an ever-recurring dismay, and swallow hasty coffee, and kiss him, and fly, doorbanging, longstriding like a boy, in pursuit of an early bus)—he could never prevail on himself to dispose of such scraps. She found this out and teased him, but there were scores of such absurd obsessions undiscovered by her, unknown to himself till his conscious mind would give a sudden jolt of surprise at his own conduct. . . .

They played the oddest pranks in that Summer Glasgow. Rita taught him dancing, and, long hours after midnight in some hall or restaurant, they would come out into a darkness softer than velvet and make a mutual discovery: too early to go home. So they would tramp the streets to Clydebank, into the red-smeared glow of the great shipyards, and peer into roaring furnaces and the blue whirr of pounding machinery; or wander the quays and count the ship-lights in the harbours; or gain admittance to Herr Jorgensen's deserted office and brew and drink amazingly bad tea for no particular reason but the fun of it; once, down at those same quays, they were challenged by a sentry who displayed towards Rita a hoarse familiarity until Malcom threatened to punch his head, whereat he retired behind Cockney luridity and a bayonet; once they heard screams and came upon a man lying in a stream of blood which gushed from his neck; they fled.

One Saturday afternoon they went out in the pelting rain, mounted to the top of a bus, and rode far to the confines of Glasgow, drenched and exultant in the tidal breaking of the rain upon their faces. The driver ultimately turned his bus round and brought them back, two solitary passengers who refused to ride inside and whom he probably considered either lunatics or spies: Glasgow was spy-crazed at the moment.

And once, returning from a picnic in a remote village, they missed the last train and bus and tram, and tramped and tramped for hours, and sat on occasional doorsteps, comforting each other. It was the period of the month when Rita suffered for her incarnation as a mortal woman; in the last stages that walk must have been sheer agony to her. But she kept up a pretence of gaiety, which was more than Malcom did. His blisters had reduced him to a sulphurous silence. And then, still two miles or more from home, they came to a fortunate coffee-stall, and a stall-keeper who gave them both coffee and Rita a chair and mild remonstrances. Long years afterwards her lover would still see her, sitting in that chair, her small face very pale in the glare of the stall naphtha burner, her small body twisting uneasily. The last few hundred yards were an incredible adventure. Malcom sank into an armchair and sprawled exhausted; and recovered to find Rita attempting to unlace his shoes. It roused him to the only anger he ever felt against her.

'Don't be a fool,' he said, and pushed her away, roughly. She sank back, not looking at him, with her small face averted, and he was overwhelmingly conscious of a cad sitting in his chair. He knelt on the floor beside her, shoeless and ridiculous.

'Oh, Rita. I'm sorry. Let me——' He began to fumble with the straps of *her* shoes, raised his head, caught her look, and suddenly they forgot their tiredness, swamped under in wave on wave of hysteric laughter. They laughed and laughed, clinging to each other. Rita gurgled over hastly-grabbed morning shoes for days afterwards; Malcom, seated and bored behind the judges at some distant agricultural show, would find himself grinning at his shoes, fatuously.

Queerly, she—who was nothing of a social rebel, had no new theories of conduct—shrank from the thought of marrying her lover. Malcom had proposed it once, certain of wringing an astounded, affronted consent from his nominal guardian in Chapel o' Seddel. Rita, in her vest, slim as a boy, stretching fingertips to ceiling and to toes in evening exercise, stopped and flung back her hair from her face, standing half-poised, like a threatened bird.

'But why?' All the tapers had gone out.

He considered. There was a score of arguments. And he did

not believe in one of them. He shook his head.

'You're the immoralest of fairies. . . . I don't know.'

She touched her pink toes, limberly, and flashed upwards again, all the tapers re-lit.

'Neither do I.'

II

Malcom had no intimate friends in Glasgow. His colleagues of the Left Communist Group were the merest acquaintances, as were the people of the *Tribune*. Since the departure of Edith Standish, Rita was equally happily placed. Nevertheless, he induced her to rent a new flat—an unfurnished ground-floor flat in a building which he could enter and leave without observation from any other tenant.

They furnished this flat sketchily and hilariously; Malcom had a bearded Morris on the mantel-shelf and a bookcase filled with books on archeology and history—not one on agricultural journalism. Rita enjoyed herself in the purchase and plastering of outrageous wallpapers. They bought wicker chairs and black cushions and spent nearly a whole weekend on their knees, polishing the floors of the bedroom and living-room, for they could not afford carpets. The floors of the miniature bathroom and kitchen they covered with an unsatisfactory linoleum which gave off a permanent, turpiney stench. The coal-cellar was under the stairs leading to the first-floor flat, a trap of a place falling away into the crumbling foundations of the house. The coal emptied into it, unless this was done with care, would jettison away under the floorwork of the flat, and be unprocurable except through sketchy jabbings with a long-handled broom.

'This damn place is dangerous,' Malcom would fume, a soiled troglodyte in the depths with a coal-bucket. 'If one fell down here in the dark it would mean suffocation on top of a broken leg.'

Rita, candle-poising, would peer down, like a fairy inspecting hell. 'If one fell down there one would be daft.' Then gurgle. 'You *do* want a bath, darling.'

They shared the expenses of the flat in strict ratio to their salaries. Rita still stayed on at Herr Jorgensen's and altered her everyday life hardly at all. Malcom kept on his room in Franklin Street. He went there infrequently, to collect Chapel o' Seddel letters; sometimes he slept there when he returned after midnight from journeyings outside Glasgow: the bawdy-house understood he spent most of his life outside Glasgow. Once or twice political refugees of the Group or kindred associations 'on the run' used his room; he loaned it for one night to a gloomy and austere Sinn Feiner, who, to judge by the evidences left behind, had none of Malcom's fastidiousness in the matter of bed-women.

The Group's co-secretary was developing fastidiousness in other matters. He attended fewer and fewer of the Executive meetings, excusing himself on the plea of business. To Meierkhold only did he confess himself.

'No, of course, it's not business, Professor. It's just—oh, I don't know.'

'It is just,' said the old Russian, 'that you are not a socialist.' He shook his head and leant back tiredly in his chair. 'And perhaps there is no more socialism left. We have followed something wrongly, and our dream is smirched, though I am too old to change now. Perhaps this trickery, this strike-making——'

Malcom had a pang of wonder if this new political self of his was merely a result of Rita. 'No, it's not that. All things are allowable, any means is—if the socialism we aim for is what I used to believe it. . . . But is it? Once, years ago, when I was a boy——'

His white-bearded co-secretary nodded. 'Yes, when you were a boy?'

'I was about five. I went up over our moor at home one day, and saw the horizon. I thought it the Wall of the World, I thought if I could get near enough I'd be able to break through to something tremendously exciting behind. I chased it all that afternoon with a stone. Later, I read Ball and the astronomers and made a tremendous discovery: that thing beyond the horizon was the Galaxy, the universe we focus, and we'd go out and conquer it yet.' He fumbled for words. There was something else, some abyssal, haunting, forgotten thing on which he had built his vision. He found his ideas tongueless fœti. 'Socialism—I thought it was a planning for that, somehow.'

'Akh God, it is the Satanists, not the socialists, to whom you belong. And even among them——'

The Professor looked at him wonderingly, kindly. 'Per ardua ad astra. Young men shall see visions. This sky-storming, it is poetry, dream of a struggle more remote from human purpose than any dream.'

'It is a dream worth following.'

Meierkhold nodded. 'As you will follow it—if you remember—alone. . . . And there are beasts that wait for lonely men.'

III

The summer of 1915 passed over Glasgow in days of glassy heat. War news ebbed and flowed in waves of pessimism and hysteric hope. Recruiting slumped. The patriotic Glaswegian female took to parading the streets and decorating with white feathers the unpatriotic, ununiformed male. Malcom evaded their attentions with a cool agility, and Rita-wards hurrying from a sale in Perth, was distant witness of the famous incident which so shattered the morale of the campaign: the leader of a bevy of summer-frocked feather-bearers suddenly snatched off her feet by a disgusted Highlander, her scantily draped person bared for chastisement, and loud, public and careful smacking administered by a trench-grimed hand, to the delight of a traffic-blocked Sauchiehall Street.

That night Malcom took Rita to one of the infrequent Left Group dances, where she was a puzzled favourite and danced with partners who discoursed industrial unionism and passive resistance to one who had slightly less interest in revolutionary ethic than a cat has in the differential calculus. 'Queer people,' said Rita, meeting Malcom, 'all except Professor Meier-something.' The Professor had discoursed on Orthodox Church music with a refreshing intelligibility.

But towards the end of that dance she fainted and had to be taken home in a taxi, a Rita whispering apologies and leaning against him, the tiredest of fairies. He undressed her and put her to bed and marvelled at a sudden shyness, almost terror, peeping from the smoky-grey eyes. It was gone in a moment, but he thought it fear of himself. A little chilled, he told her he would sleep in the living-room. He put out the light and kissed her good night and went through to the sofa with a blanket.

But he could not sleep. He had never felt more wakeful. He prowled the darkness for a little, softly, found matches, and sat in a chair at the window, smoking. And then, suddenly, as from the bottom of a well, he saw the stars again.

He had not seen them for months. He had been too busy living—living with Rita. He dropped his cigarette, staring at those old friends, old enemies of Leekan days.

> The august, inhospitable Night,
> Glittering, magnificently unperturbed. . . .

Right athwart his vision hung the Great Bear, fanged, the undying beast which guards the skies. He kindled to that ancient challenge. By God, however had he forgot them?

He dropped his head in his hands, shutting out the starlight. He listened for a sound from the bedroom. Nothing. He sat and thought.

Study? Nothing for months. Socialism? Lost somehow: nothing to do with the Great Bear and his challenge. He found himself unable to think clearly and with any coherence. He fought his own mind with a kind of desperation—a mind erupting innumerable irrelevances, spraying into reminiscence of ecstasy and delight, uncontrollable, flabby. Christ! As though his head was full of yeast!

And all this was because of Rita.

Not only his mind, but his body clamoured against him. He fought them off—he, the essential Malcom Maudslay, smothered for months. Of course it was true. But what was it he had lost, who was this essential Malcom Maudslay? He groped down lightless corridors of thought. Nothing to help him there, no reason, no clue. Then he raised his head from his hands and saw his hands bathed in starlight. He looked at the sky and drew a deep breath, and *knew* with a mystic certainty.

There was the clue. . . .

He must break with Rita.

There was a long, dazed silence in his mind after he had told himself this. He heard the clock on the mantel-shelf ticking loudly. Morning was coming, wheeling up through the ensaffroned east. He felt a horrible loneliness. Then he saw that the stars were paling. The Great Bear faded from a violent challenge that made his blood leap into a dream and a whimsy. What had he been drowsing about? Break with Rita?

He heard her breathing then, in that pallor of the morning. His resolvings, meaningless, faded and went out with the Pole Star. He moved his numb feet, rubbed them to warmth. . . . Rita? God, what had he been dreaming about?

He began to think of her in a passion of contrition,—her sweetness, her kindliness, her faery gaiety. Close at hand, all of it. Real as that amazing dimple in her shoulder, where there was always a little shadow lurking.

What a fool he had been—those damned stars! He crouched rigid in the dawnlight while a hundred singers in his heart, a poet in every cell of his body, began to tell him of all the gifts that Rita had given him—the simple, splendid things, all the delights of touch and consummation and physical exaltation, all the gracious loveliness of lust. Passion and purity, chryselephantine, splendid, unwritten and unportrayed, she had given him.

It lightened. Day. But he still sat dreaming. By God! Some day he would write a novel, the world's first real love-story. 'I thee with my body worship.' What a book, *what* a book one could make of it, with the essence of every love-story—the sex act—

stripped of shame and reticence! With neither the wordy pawings of the pornographer, the scared brutalities of the realist, the romantic's firelight and curtains——

Interpolation

I am transcribing that novel of Malcom's now, and, looking back over its pages, I see that I am neither the realist nor the romantic—both so despised. I am the pornographer. I have called in moonlight and bare shoulders. I have not described the naked Rita, unexpected and unbelievable, in his arms that first time. I recourse to chapter-endings and hesitation dots. For I at least, however little Malcom, am a child of my age—as much so, perhaps, as the snuffling elderly smut-hounds of the literary press, and all prudent considerations apart. To us of the early half of the twentieth century the detailed sex-act is still impossible in all literature but the pseudo-scientific. We are, all of us, still too young and nasty-minded. The sniggerings of the Victorian mental water-closets are still unescapable. Behind shields of phrase and phantasy, ludicrous and pitiful as Nahuatl virgins dreading fertilization, we hide our faces from the sun.

IV

He attended a meeting of the Group Executive one Saturday afternoon in late October, fell out with the chairman, and was accused of 'reformism.' The shipwright thumped the table in a manner oddly reminiscent of Sammy Dreep, and Malcom, enragingly, sat and smiled at him. But he felt almost sick, and with a desperate desire to get out into the fresh air. God, it was for this—this social spite and meaningless chatter of strikes and tactics which still left men hungry and misery an unapproached reality—for this he had thought any weapon justifiable, any means honourable. He found his thoughts, in a manner all too common, jerking away from the situation, refusing to face it.

Outside, Meierkhold drew him aside and protested against him paying the fares of two delegates to a London conference— one of the innumerable abortive pifistac conferences. 'Akh God, you are a young man and it is much money. We take all your money.'

'I have plenty left, Professor.'

The old Russian smiled his tired smile. 'A capitalist, akh God!' Then peered into Malcom's face and muttered to himself. 'It is well. It is well. I am a fool.'

Malcom left him and took a bus to Rita's flat. It was windy weather. The sky flickered like a film with scudding clouds. He had not seen Rita for three days, and found her, wrapped in her overcoat, in front of a glowing fire.

'Thought you'd come today.' Her arms round his neck, she yet turned aside her face from his. 'Don't kiss me, please. I've a cold and my lips are all cracked.' She laughed and pushed him away, 'like my head.'

'Eh?'

She stood up and hugged him, then laughed again. Against him he felt her quiver like a violin-string. 'Oh, nothing. I'm all on edge today. Let's go for a walk—out into the country, where there's grass and trees. Coming?' She leant back in his arms, face upturned, while he went through the usual ritual of counting the tapers in her eyes.

'There's one more than usual,' he discovered. Then, after a surprised interlude, held her away and teased her, a little breath- less himself. 'I thought your lips were too cracked for kissing?'

They rode out to the country by tram and bus, beyond the confines of Glasgow, and walked through fields with fading grass and shivering hedges. Brown leaves scuttered through the air, limped from tussock to tussock. Underfoot they squelched in heaps. Behind the flying clouds was an angry lowe of sky, and the wind whistled through the tree-boughs. Malcom was con- scious of a numbing astonishment.

'I never noticed Summer was past,' he said.

Rita laughed. She caught his hands. She began to sing, holding his hands, looking into his eyes, her face wrung in an absurd caricature of emotion.

'*The swallows are making them ready to fly,*
Wheeling out on a windy sky:
Good-bye, summer, good-bye,
Good-bye——'

He laughed with her at the lugubrious Tosti. The gale coming down the Clyde boomed gustily. And then he saw a horrible thing. Rita was weeping. No pretence. She had dropped his hands. Weeping and still singing. He stared dumbfounded, not knowing this play, and at his look the desperation in her eyes changed to mere misery.

'Oh, Malcom! Summer's past. Remember that night and the moon in Ajalon? Remember? All the swallows gone, and I'm going to have a baby.'

He said nothing. He could not say anything. An icy finger reached through his skull, wrenched something loose in his brain, and withdrew. He fumbled for his cigarette-case. He could not find his pocket.

'I'm going to have a baby, Malcom.'

He nodded. It was too much for his finicky stomach. He felt sick.

V

She was going to have a baby. She had known it since that night in August when she had fainted at the Group dance. It would soon begin to show.

They were back in the flat again, the world locked out with the autumn wind. His arms were round her. She knelt at his feet in the firelight. Sometimes she was seized with a fit of shivering and his arms would tighten, and she would raise a terror-quivering face and laugh at herself.

'And you're glad—really glad? Then I'll be. Oh, Malcom, if I weren't such a coward!'

He had never seen such courage. 'God, you're the best and bravest thing ever,' he said, indistinctly, and at that her hands came up to touch his face.

'Why, Malcom, dear, you've been——' She raised herself, slim as a boy still, and bent over him, and spoke without any quaver now, but solemnly, with an accent of relieved discovery. 'Do you know, my lips are much better now? . . .'

He heard the Glasgow clock-towers strike twelve, strike one, strike two, strike three as he lay in the darkness. His left arm was under Rita's neck. It had grown cramped, but he did not move it in case she also should wake. She was close against him, lying straight from shoulder to ankle, as her custom was. He could feel her breast-nipples against his chest, making soft indentations. Once she moved and seemed to choke, she sobbed for a moment in her sleep. Her hand came out and found his thigh. She grew quiet again.

Three o'clock. His brain was an arena of sand. Round it kept limping, wearily, a dusty pedestrian of a thought: 'But however did it happen?'

They had talked together and puzzled over this before going to bed. The useless question plagued him, pretending an importance it did not possess. It had happened. That was enough.

The question limped up. 'But how?'

From the first—excepting that first night of all—Rita had used the crude contraceptives of her time, inventions of that strange idiot genius, Science, who has so little leisure for these things, being in a slavering haste to dispose of surplus populations with better and better eleven-inch guns. She had used these clumsy fumblements in the utmost faith, and Malcom had gone in light-hearted certainty of her safety. Not until long afterwards was he to realize how pathetic and misplaced was their confidence. In that night when he lay listening to the clanging Glasgow hours, his mind kept denying the possibility of the happening, over and over again. And then he records a very vile thought which came to him while he lay by the sleeping Rita. Perhaps he was not the father of her baby at all. . . .

The base thing whispered, mowed, and then fled at his fury. Oh Christ, you swine. For a moment he seethed with loathing for himself, and, though he did not move, Rita's arm came up and went round his neck. Still sleeping, she kissed him. At that unconscious absolution he bit his lips till blood, warm and saline, trickled in between his teeth. He drew Rita closer, closed his eyes in determination to sleep, and instantly began to think again.

'Now we'll get married.'

They would get married—nail their lives to the same board because of this intruder in Rita's body. They, who otherwise would never have married. They had not a thought in common. They were lovers, and lovers only: that had grown an unacknowledged certainty with them. He looked down a horrifying vista of prison-walled years, saw, with sudden clearness, how in the ordinary course of events they would ultimately have parted. A little bitter regret, tears, and many good memories. Kindly strangers always. . . . That night of stars—it had been the beginning of the end of their time as lovers but for the fact that it had also been the beginning of Rita's secret, terrifying knowledge.

Rita a mother. . . .

Thousands of Ritas there must be. He had never realized it before. Women for whom motherhood was the equivalent of human sacrifice, marriage a bestial trap; women spiritually and physically tortured by rack and hoist in the name of an insane convention. . . .

He wrenched back his reluctant attention to a horrifying picture: Rita grown thin and drab and careful, awaiting his uncertain returns, Rita with an undesired and unimaginable baby, Rita with all her romantic mysticism foregone in order that she might . . . wear a ring and act the part of a licensed bed-woman——

God! What a long time it was till morning.

They decided they would be married in the first week of December. Meantime the great Reading Stock Sale, earlier that year, drew near, and on the 15th of November, Malcom set out by night train for England. He went in a sleet-storm and returned in a fall of snow, seven days later. Outside the Central Station where, eleven months before, he had met Rita for the second time, he ran against Mr. Rollo, the *Tribune's* chief reporter, muffled, hairless, sardonic.

'B'God, our Agricultural Correspondent, straight from the byres.' He grinned at Malcom incuriously and glanced at the station clock. 'Had a good time among the pigs? 'Scuse me, got to scoot. Taking the missus to a show. Boy home from France. Oh——'

'Eh?'

'MacFarlane wants to see you soon's you're back. Better write up your copy first, though. Jehovah can wait: the *Tribune* can't. 'Night.'

He ran. Malcom took a taxi to the office, climbed to the reporters' room, and found it deserted, as was usual at that time in the evening. He sat down at his desk, brought out his notes, and wrote from six o'clock until nearly seven. He was just finishing as MacFarlane, tall and bowed and heavy-footed, came in.

'Mr. Maudslay? I gave instructions you were to come to me as soon as you came back.'

'Thought I'd do my copy first.'

'Have you finished it?'

'Yes.'

'Take it to the sub-editors, then come direct to my room.'

When he had gone Malcom poked the fire carefully, picked up his copy, lighted a cigarette, and went down the stairs. In the glass panel of the sub-editors' door he saw his face, composed and cool. He glanced at his wrists and found them perfectly steady. He was glad of that. He was conscious of nothing more than a certain headachy alertness.

Then he went in to MacFarlane.

The *Tribune's* editor sat at his desk. Impaled on a wire file in front of him was a sheaf of papers. He peered at Malcom over his steel-rimmed glasses. Sitting so, his shoulders hunched in his black coat, he looked like a condor.

'Sit down.'

Malcom sat down. With a little tightening about his heart he had recognized the papers.

MacFarlane coughed. Malcom waited, politely, alertly, a little sick.

He knew what was about to happen. He had been very simple indeed, when he started on his career as a Communist bandit, not to foresee the possibility of a counter-check. . . .

VIa

He must have missed a preamble of several minutes' duration. He had been thinking of Rita.

'. . . from checking your expenses' accounts, I find you have forged bills for more than £60. You have not even forged them. You have been a small and contemptible thief, altering original figures with an ink-eraser and substituting others. Your father in Aberdeenshire has a reputation for honesty, but . . . laddie, you've disgraced the woman who bore you. If you ever have children of your own, if you ever learn honesty and speak to them honestly, I'm sorry for you. It'll be fine for you to say "Your father was once a contemptible thief who betrayed his trust and stole money from his employers." '

The editor stopped and glanced across the table. Probably Malcom's face was very white. MacFarlane had a twinge of pity.

'You may smoke if you like.'

Malcom was never to forget the kindliness of that. He nodded. 'Thank you.' He lit a cigarette, and then, the gaze through the

89

steel-rimmed glasses still upon him, raised his head.

MacFarlane was leaning towards him almost appealingly.

'What did ye do it for? Laddie, you're the best of my staff, you've no look of a thief, you've ruined a brilliant career. What did ye want with this sixty pounds?'

(Sixty pounds? Had it come to all that? Delegates' fares, printers' bills for the Left Group weekly, bail for a 'victim' who had promptly vanished to Ireland, financing the Group chairman in a threatened libel action—God, the Group chairman!)

'I can't tell you—sir.'

MacFarlane dropped his eyes and sank back into his seat and the wing-like shoulders of his coat. Looking at him, Malcom was conscious, even at that moment, of such feeling of pity as his father had once evoked under almost similar circumstances. . . . Poor ranting anachronism!

He found himself on his feet, listening to his sentence.

'Don't come back to the office, but don't attempt to leave Glasgow. I've got your address in Franklin Street. When I've seen the directors I'll let you know what action they intend to take. For the sake of your father——'

VIb

He was out in the snow. He was in Sauchiehall Street. He was being accosted by a young woman whom he had never seen before—an obtrusive young woman, one of a giggling group. He heard himself impatiently answering a snivellingly accusing Glaswegian whine of queries. He was conscious of the young woman's steps receding, of receding gigglings. He was glancing at the thing stuck in the lapel of his coat.

It was a white feather.

He hung up his coat and hat in the dark passage and opened the living-room door.

'Rita.'

She was not there, but a fire burned cheerfully in the grate. Her miniature comb lay on the mantelshelf. He crossed to the fireplace. He combed his hair. The firelight splashed bright arabesques on the walls, on the cushioned chairs. Something white lay in one of the chairs. He picked it up and held it towards the light of the fire. It was a baby's half-knit vest. He laid it down and groped for the switch of the electric light, then stood looking round the bright room. A book lay face-downwards on the table. He picked that up too, and looked at the title. It was one of his own books, Morris's *Signs of Change*. A coal fell out of the grate, startling him.

'Rita,' he called again.

She must have gone out. But a scissors and a ball of wool lay near the unfinished vest. He went into the bedroom and looked at the wardrobe. Her coats were all there, very neatly hung. One of her dresses shimmered. He touched it and it swayed, emitting a faint perfume.

On the double-pillowed bed lay a suit of his pyjamas. On the dressing-table an upended powder-puff stood to peer in the mirror.

'Rita!'

He went into the kitchen. A kettle hummed on a low flame of the gas-stove. He picked it up. It was almost empty. The kitchen clock ticked absorbedly.

'*Rita!*' Then he stopped, startled at the sobbing sound in his own throat. He peered round the kitchen. Hiding somewhere. A gust of irritation came on him, but he stood very still. Presently he would hear her breathing.

What was that?

Sift . . . . Sift . . . . Sift . . . a whisper. Then he saw through the window the ghostly whorling of the snow. He was listening to the flakes stroking the glass. He turned and blundered against the kitchen door and felt for the passage switch. His fingers on it, he began a sobbing argument with himself.

'You blasted fool. Don't look round. You fool. *You mustn't look round.*'

He looked round.

The door of the coal-cellar hung slightly ajar.

VIII

He never knew how she had died. Perhaps she had slipped on the linoleum outside the cellar entrance and fallen down. Probably she had landed on her feet, a little breathless, a little shaken, hearing the door above swing to in the draught. It would then have been too dark for her to see. She must have felt round the walls, twisting her small body in an effort to reach the upper floor with her fingers. Perhaps she may even, reaching on tip-toe, have touched the opening. And then, alone in that darkness and suffocation, something happened. Something within her snapped like a parting thread and her mouth was suddenly filled with blood. She must have fallen then and rolled a little, and perhaps died very quickly. . . .

He had lifted her up out of the cellar and carried her into the bedroom, before he was aware that he had done so, while his mind still protested the insanity of looking at that cellar door. Also, he must have done other things, his thoughts static, his brain petrified at a dreadful moment lost far back in the evening. He must have washed the stains from her face and hands, and the blood from her lips. He must have undressed her and placed her in the bed. He must have combed her hair and closed her eyes. He must have folded her clothes and hung them on the chair by the bedside. All those things he must have done, because about midnight he awoke to find them done and himself shivering because of the perspiration soaking through from his back and loins into his underclothing.

He felt cold and unemotional. He sat down in the living-room to think, and found his decision already made, without thinking. He rose up and began to search the flat, burning all papers and letters having his name on them. None of his books was marked and he had few clothes in the place. As he went to and fro in the bedroom the shrouded figure under the sheet vexed him a little. He found himself sobbing once and turning towards it. But he pulled himself up savagely and completed the business in hand. There'd be no sadistic coroner to beslaver her memory with his queries and views. The charwoman would find her in the morning. There would be no trace of himself, and it would have every appearance of natural death.

It was time that he went. Now he saw something that he had done mistakenly. She should not have the sheet over her face. He folded it back.

CHAPTER FIVE

SALISBURY PLAIN

I

In spite of his definite purpose he must have wandered Glasgow for hours during that snowing night. Towards five o'clock in the morning he found himself again in Sauchiehall Street, staring vaguely at the offices of the *Tribune*. An hour later, his clothes soaked by the fine sleet which had set in, he came to the house in Franklin Street, climbed to his room, locked the door, and sat down in a chair. Thereafter came another long blank. He either fainted or fell asleep immediately, for it was four o'clock in the afternoon before he came to himself, cramped and cold, with a white sun shining across the snow-covered roofs.

He rose and made some tea and woke up again to find the tea cold and untasted and the night coming down. Frost set in that night. It grew colder and colder. He sat in the darkness, huddled in his clothes, dozing and awakening and falling again into a shivering doze.

But somewhere near midnight he aroused himself to his original intent. The house had stilled of its scufflings and creakings. He lighted one of the two gas-brackets which stood on either side of the mantelshelf and drew the curtains across the window. He opened his writing-desk and brought out great stacks of the Left Group weekly. Then, with a penknife as tool, he set about stopping up every crack and opening which allowed ingress of air to the room. In a little he had plugged paper all round the door and window-frames. He closed the damper of the fireplace, stuffed it with wads of paper, sealed it across with sheets of paper. By the time he stopped he was again drenched with sweat and already the air in the room seemed to have grown stuffy.

Then he undressed carefully, put on his pyjamas, switched out the light, waited two minutes by the luminous dial of his watch, and then turned both gas-taps full on. For a little he stood by them, listening to the hiss of the escaping gas, then lay down in bed and closed his eyes and fell asleep without another thought.

II

He awoke in a stifling darkness. The blood beat through his head—*thlim, thlim, thlim.* With an effort he raised his left arm and saw the face of his wristwatch through aching eyes. It was four o'clock.

He got out of bed and staggered and coughed as his head impinged on a deeper stratum of gas. His throat and the roof of his mouth felt coated with a disgusting slime. He clung to the bedrail and shivered and vomited. In the wall glimmered two pallid rectangles and at sight of them a frantic desire assailed him. Stumbling against unseen furniture, he reached one of the windows, unhasped it, and flung it open. A wave of winter air, cold and pringling, as though stalactited with frost, poured into the room. Far on the western horizon wavered the unceasing fires of the foundries.

He sat in the window-seat holding his aching head till the throbbing died down a little. Momentarily it grew lighter. The furnace-fires paled and behind him, flinging a ghostly radiance into the western sky, the morning was coming. He stared at it, he says, as though it had been the first morning of the world. Then, attacked by a fit of sneezing, he lowered the window a little, groped for and found his pocket electric torch, and inspected the gas-brackets.

No gas was emerging. The supply had run out: probably it had run out half an hour after he turned on the taps.

He sat down on the bed, helpless in hysteric laughter. He had bungled dying as he had bungled living. . . . Then the fit of

95

laughter passed. Still mentally numbed, but with a curious wonder upon him, he held up his fingers and looked at them and moved them. He took off his pyjamas and stood naked, passing his hands over his body, feeling the cold silk of skin and the faint pringle of hair with a detached amazement. God, he was alive. He was still alive.

Naked, shivering, weeping, he crept to the window and watched the impossible morning coming again. . . .

A rumour of hideous happenings awoke remote in his memory, startling a multitude of fears to shout of one pressing desire: he must get away, he must leave Glasgow.

Already there was a stir in the house. He sluiced himself with ice-cold water from the bedroom ewer, towelled himself to warmth and dryness, then dressed. He flung the windows wide open, withdrew the paddings from fireplace and doorway, and lighted a fire which gloomed dangerously through the room for a moment. This fire he set to feeding with clothes and books and papers. In an hour there was left to him only the suit he wore, his overcoat, hat, and shoes, about three pounds ten shillings in notes and silver, and his birth certificate. He had even smashed his empty suitcases and burned them.

Then he sat down at the writing-desk and with an ink-eraser and water-diluted ink to match the pale fluid used by the Leekan Registrar, altered the date of his birth from the 24th December, 1898, to the 24th December, 1897.

Two hours later he walked out of Glasgow and his life there like one awakening and passing out of a dream. For some reason he found himself avoiding the railway stations. He went as far south as the tram-lines would take him and then set out to walk. He tramped the slush-felted roads throughout the remainder of the daylight, leaving Glasgow far behind, and never, except in memory, were any associations with that life to impinge on him again.

"I have never known what happened in Rita's flat when they found her there, nor what coroner's enquiries, if any, were made. I have always been very fuzzy over the powers and potentialities

96

of coroners.

"Nor do I know if Meierkhold or others of the Left Group ever attempted to seek me out, nor what decision MacFarlane and the directors of the *Tribune* came to in my case. I never heard of them again.

"I do not know to this day whether I am a still-unpunished criminal in the matter of Rita: is my unsuccessful attempt at suicide still punishable? I think that the chances are I would have been arrested for murder—and probably convicted—had I gone to the nearest police station with my news of finding Rita's body in the coal-cellar. If such a thing were to happen to me again I should probably behave exactly as I did then. In such circumstances I am like the average intelligent man in these years of civilization's debacle—though unlike him in that I confess to it. I would no more trust myself to the mercy and understanding of the rat-brained clowns who staff our policeforces than I would smear myself with cub-smell and submit it to the investigations of a tiger.

"In my attempt at suicide I was in a pathological condition probably common enough to most young suicides—dazed, and yet seeing with a lunatic clearness not only the immediate tragedy and cruelty of the moment but the untheological insanity of the universe. I turned on the gas-taps on a Malcom Maudslay too sane to live. Even now I cannot see but that under certain conditions self-killing may be the only logical course left to one.

"I have been sufficient of the herd-beast to accuse that eighteen-year-old self of mine of callous cowardice. But that has been done without reflection—as is meet for a herd-beast—and in any case it is to accuse a self which had temporarily ceased to exist. Rita's death had beaten from his horse, maimed, mutilated, and mentally paralysed the pathetic young prig who had imagined himself to be Malcom Maudslay. The thing that fled southwards out of Glasgow was the scared human reality—an alien, dazed Azilian in flight from the incomprehensible treacheries and tragedies of a Neolithic squatting-place."

97

III

Late that afternoon he came to Coatbridge and made for the railway station. Three days later, on the 28th of November, 1915, he walked into a recruiting office in Carlisle, enlisted in the Norsex Regiment, and was sent to Salisbury Plain.

IV

His medical enlistment papers, seen by him long afterwards, described him as 'mentally torpid.'

In those first weeks at Bulford he lived and moved under a shadowy treaty made with himself. He did not think. He rose and dressed himself and took his rifle and tramped the parade-grounds and sweated at fatigues. He sat in windy huts and ate from a tin with a greasy spoon. He spent his evenings polishing his equipment or lying back in a chair at the Y.M.C.A. 'hostel.' He read great quantities of novels; he read multitudes of maga-zines and cheap periodicals from cover to cover; he read as one takes a narcotic. He must have appeared an abnormally stupid and biddable recruit.

Often, in the Glasgow days, he had decided that in the event of the coming of conscription he would refuse to serve—refuse to serve in the Army in any capacity.

That decision never haunted him at Bulford. It belonged to a life and philosophy so fantastically unreal that they never trou-bled him except at night.

But his nights were horrible. He dreamt horribly, though in mornings he would remember little more than a nebulous horror. His hut companions were less reticent than his memory. They told him he moaned in his sleep. He soon found himself the subject of numerous crude jokes. In a fortnight he was the butt of the barrack-room. Humorists opined that he had deserted a girl who was going to have a baby. He found himself listening with a strange, aching inability to think or feel.

"Probably I required the attentions of an alienist. Instead, I received those of Sergeant Morgan."

Sergeant Morgan, in charge of the hut, a Welshman, an Old Army soldier, a malingerer and snarling half-wit in the Old Army tradition, found Malcom a god-send. In addition to numerous other duties in the hut the new recruit found himself detailed to clean the Sergeant's side-arms and equipment, to make up his bed and fold his blankets, to fetch and carry generally. The rest of the hut applauded.

'Where iss that puggled bastard?' Sergeant Morgan would shout, poking his stained face through the endrapement of blankets which formed his 'bunk' in the least draughty corner of the hut. 'Here now—clean thosse bloody boots—juldi!'

Sergeant Morgan had been in India—a country exclusively peopled by bastards not only puggled but black, and only to be stirred to activity by the liberal application of boots and shouted juldi's—with the Old Army. Malcom would find himself clumping down between the boards and trestles to pick up the boots. A card-playing group would thrust out a foot as he went back towards his own bed. He would trip and stumble in a dark silence.

Morgan's assistant tormentor was Wilsom, a butcher from Poplar, an officer's servant and a reputed boxer. He was the typical private soldier in outward observances to civilians and his superiors—cheerful, aitchless, obliging with a cow-lick of hair over his forehead and a ready 'Yussir.' In the barrack-room he abandoned this rôle like a garment that chafed, and displayed himself as an atavistic little pervert who found a strange, mouth-drooling pleasure in blood and suffering. He would examine the various cuts and bruises acquired by the hut in wet-canteen melees with a gloating enthusiasm. The man in the bed next to Malcom developed huge boils in his neck; Wilsom insisted on hearing details of the extirpation of the pus.

He baited Malcom with zest and without provocation. The new recruit would discover portions of his equipment slung far up across the rafters of the hut, or his trestles flung out of the window, or his blankets filled with cinders. The hut would watch him make each discovery and would roar its simple appreciation.

"Until, inexplicably messianic, the coming of an evening in early January. It is like remembering having wandered in a tormented mist and then stepping out sharply and suddenly, into frost and the ring of the sea. I found myself running and panting across the waste of mud between the canteen and the barrack-hut with a single idea etched in fire inside my skull; I must settle up with Wilsom."

The hut was crowded, busied with blanco and metal-polish. Wilsom, at the far end, was bending over the straps of his pack. At sound of Malcom's entrance he glanced up, grinned, and relaxed for a little cheerful baiting.

'Ello, chaps, ere's the puggle-wallah!' Malcom walked towards him. 'Christ, fergotten where is bleedin bed is!'

Next moment Malcom hit him.

The flimsy timber framework of the hut shook as Wilsom crashed against the wall, lost his feet, and slithered to the floor. Before he could rise, Malcom was on him. Twice he found himself pulping the obscene little face with blows which numbed his arm. Then he was tearing open the greasy Army shirt to get at the Cockney's throat. . . .

The hut-inmates yelled and flung themselves at the struggling two on the floor. Malcom found his left hand trodden on. He loosed it, caught an ankle, and brought the treader thunderously on top of a nearby bed. A man clawed at his tunic, and then, as Malcom kicked him intimately, doubled up with a groan. Malcom scrambled to his knees, his feet, and suddenly found himself engaging half a dozen opponents at the same time. A neck snapped as though dislocated in the only scientific blow he succeeded in getting home. A moment later he tripped and was on the floor again, held down by half a dozen of the scared and panting Norsex Regiment.

'Ere, Christ, cut it aht!'

'Nah then!'

The reply of their captive must have surprised them. He ceased

100

to struggle. He spoke unexcitedly.

'You bastards, if you don't let me up now—when I do get up I'll take you on one by one, and—' he was lurid and physiological in the terms of their own vocabulary. They released him. He got to his feet, brushed himself, and walked to his bed in the midst of a dead silence, leaving the half-strangled Wilsom to gurgle and retch under unsympathetic ministrations.

That night, for the first time since his arrival in Bulford, he slept dreamlessly. Next morning Sergeant Morgan, hastening out to mess, glanced at him curiously, and made no mention of the fact, as he usually did, that Maudslay would have to bloody well hurry up. The man in the next bed—he of the boils—pushed over his tin of metal-polish helpfully.

'Christ, chum, seen Wilsom's dial this morning? He'll think he's at home in the old butcher's shop. . . . Goin on leave tomorrow?'

'No. Why should I?'

'Well, Christmas, y'know.'

Christmas. It was Christmas Eve. He was eighteen years of age.

V

So, absurdly resurrected from the dark pits of his imagination in an outburst of animal fury against his tormentors of the barrack-hut, he found himself again. No new self, but his old self came back—robbed of illusions he had believed divine certitudes, swifter, starker, harder than of yore, but essentially still the dreaming boy of Stane Muir. He began to think again—intensely, vividly, as though the tools of his brain had been reground and polished by an unnoticed craftsman. He would halt on his January sentry-beats at night and discover his stars again, would forget time and place, Bulford, his uniform, his rifle, everything, in fantastic explorations of the Galaxy. Lying in bed after Lights Out he re-discovered another delight of boyhood—the making

101

of purposeless mental pictures to the drumming music of the rain on the hut roof: tramps on lonely roads, trudging derelicts of the squelching darkness; destroyers at sea; the crumbling night of the mud-lavaed trenches in France.

And he discovered something entirely new: the endless variety of sexless sensation of which his body was capable. Hunger and cold and tiredness and belly-satiety, pleasure of rest and glow of sinew-straining toil—he had never before known any of those things to their utmost extremes. He found he could draw ecstasy, lingeringly, from a re-lighted cigarette end, could lie a last moment in bed while réveillé shrilled down the morning and know that last moment the quintessence of enjoyment.

There were other new things. As though his ears had been suddenly unsealed of deafness, he discovered the barrack-room— a barrack-room which left him severely alone, a barrack-room with a sergeant who had impressed into his service as batman no other than the unfortunate Wilsom himself.

Every war book he was ever to read was to take refuge behind a shamed and feeble humour in describing the barrack-room and its argot. It was an argot that plumbed the depths of obscenity for adjectives yet fetched from out those dripping depths only a few poor squirming inanities. It was an argot curiously sexual. One had the idea of an unclean beast, head on shoulder, regarding its own body and genital organs with a slavering amazement. With this diseased vocabulary went a lewd curiosity in all matters sexual, in sex-perversion, in sodomy, in incest, in rape.

He bought a pipe and coloured it and sat on his bed and listened and found himself being educated. In Glasgow days he had merely been the lone Old Stone Age wanderer, astray and unresting with dream-blinded eyes; the people of the Left Group, his only intimates, had been only political intimates; he had known practically nothing of their social lives; he had never belonged to any club or association of men for purposes of recreation; he began to realize that he knew nothing of men.

"I had believed the common man simple and just and op-pressed. I had believed that were the 'capitalists' torn from his

102

shoulders he would build the World Republic—a fair and glorious state where all would live vividly and read William Morris, where all would be interested in stars and sunspots and Azilians, where in time there would be neither disease nor death nor scandal nor futility. . . . I would lie on my trestles and grin at the remembrance while I coloured my pipe. Common Man as Man Dominant—a world of unending barrack-rooms, on unending Friday nights, thronged with the unending insanitary, deafened with shouts and yawps and comic songs, belching with laughter over the comicality of the sexual processes. . . .

"I think I can date the birth of a sense of humour from the evening I spent in outlining that democratic Utopia."

VI

He had the cowardly flesh of most men whose active life has been mental only. To reflect calmly on the fact that now, his normal self again, he might any moment be called upon to reassert himself in the barrack hut was to be conscious that he would probably prove as astoundingly white-livered as Sergeant Morgan and his associates had originally rated him. He faced the fact with characteristic lack of emotion. Essential courage had nothing to do with the matter. It was merely that his body had not been trained in either public houses or public schools to withstand 'punishment.'

The obvious remedy was patronage of the camp gymnasium in his spare hours. A bribed and mollified Wilsom undertook to teach him 'self-defence,' and for half an hour every evening, until he learned the necessary tricks, Malcom allowed himself to be smitten to and fro over the ring. This was hardly training in the accepted sense of the word, and it was obvious that Wilsom was taking advantage of a heaven-sent opportunity.

'Nah—old thet!' he would pant, and Malcom, spitting blood, would reel against the ropes. The loafing gymnasium staff, surrounding the ring for this entertainment, would guffaw or grunt in sympathy with the report of the blow. "Those grunts begot the strangest arguments in my brain the while I would face up to Wilsom again. I began to see boxing and such-like athletics for what they were in the lives of spectators—sadism at second hand. Excreted from the socialist stomach, I began to see the War itself as no struggle of capitalist states eager for fresh markets, but an international outburst of sadism. And why not? Blood-lust was our heritage. It was not two hundred thousand years since the ancestral Eoanthropus of the Sussex river-beds had tortured a prisoner in some dark rock-shelter and licked the blood from living wounds."

But this horrible theory, carried to the barrack-square and the rifle ranges, broke down. That he should march and wheel in formations useless since the abandonment of open warfare, that he should be painfully and painstakingly taught the correct angle of salute and the proper fashion in which to address a regimental quartermaster-sergeant—this was obviously no planning of beast-like cruelty, it was the fuddled maunderings of simian dotage. Hardly even that. It was not vertebrate conduct at all. It was like finding himself member of an insane and impossible ant-hill on which the ants, threatened by the descent of a gigantic and exterminating boot, paraded to and fro on their hind legs, their antennae held in complicated positions, or solemnly and portentously waving those useful members at one another. . . .

"You who escaped that cosmic jest can have no idea of the feeble tenacity and ferocity of the military mind. Tenacious and ferocious it was, but feebly so, uncertainly so. Faced with a war of chemists and physicists, its borborygmatic distresses and mental rump-scratchings would have moved the Javan ape-man to sympathetic tears. . . . It still saw no necessity for a man to be respect-worthy before he was respected by regulation. It was unable to believe that all rankers were not of necessity aitchless and not by nature sots. It had never been planned for the consideration of sociological and scientific intricacies; its ultimate, prideful achievement was the co-ordination of parade-ground baboon-snarlings.

"But, feeble though it was, I came to realize how feeble was the individual to resist its dotardism. With the very fewest of exceptions, such as Metaxa and myself, the civilian enlistments assimilated tradition and method without question and almost without demur. The grumblings and occasional riotings were against chance happenings and injustices. The system no one indicted: they submitted to it or took refuge from it in humorous guyings.

". . . church and religion, its bond-slaves of the Sunday parades, were too farcical in their bondage not to suffer worst from the humorist in the ranks. I shall always remember a crowded Presbyterian church in Salisbury, a helpless mottle-faced minister, the tune of 'Oh God, our help in ages past' being played on the organ, and a hundred or so mixed details uplifting their voices in the satisfying parody of some anonymous genius:

> " *'There was a man who had two sons,*
> *And these two sons were brothers;*
> *John Andrew was the name of one,*
> *And Andrew John the other's.*
>
> *'Now these two sons, they bought a horse*
> *And it was long and thin:*
> *They took it to the river's edge*
> *And chucked the bastard in.*
>
> *'Now these two sons they had a wife*
> *And she was double jointed. . . .'*

"And so forth. I found the adventures of the great Twin Brethren highly diverting. . . .

But the system offered greater consolations than a certain licence to guy. It offered—in place of hard thinking and stiff, undiscriminating examinations—'honours.' It gave out ribbons and chevrons and warrants and commissions and unhoped-for authorities. It gave to the bright collier the opportunity, with a corporal's stripes on his arms, to bully objectionable people who

105

had clean skins and straight limbs. It gave to the bulbous-throated bank-clerk, the Fleet Street hack and the chinless Harrow boy a cross-belt, a khaki collar and tie, an opportunity to refer to 'my batman.' (Unbelievable pride, the ownership of a batman!) Promise of promotion was a permanent urge to the energetic in the ranks—not in order that they might become more efficient soldiers but as means to escaping the festering no-life of the barrack-hut, to attaining a clean bed and wearable uniform and escaping fatigues and medical inspections."

Those medical inspections! They would parade by companies outside the medical officer's hut, and lower their nether garments, and take off their tunics and shirts, and stand in shivering, jesting rows the while the medical officer, an unbelievably old and comic medical officer with bleary eyes and a disbelief in anaesthetics, inspected them. And those medical inspections were not medical inspections in any comprehensive sense; they were merely inspected to discover if they had developed syphilis or scabies or lice or the like. . . .

VII

"If I write of things vile, it is because vileness has many incarnations. There may come another war and we be called again to train and suffer insanely, to crawl and creep in syphilitic ditches, to stagger through the hell of a dawn barrage, to hear a drunken and fuddled commander give orders equivalent to massacre. Dirty little men may again peer at and punch our naked bodies and beslime our naked souls. We may again be asked to crowd in the festering moral-reek of the barrack-room, may again be asked to applaud the militaristic ape floundering and snarling in a waste of rotting corpses."

VIII

And then, in late February of 1916, Sergeant Major John Metaxa, drunkard, vagabond, scholar, explorer, whom Malcom was to love more than any man he ever met, who was to be his principal interest and influence through two long years, came to the battalion. He came to it unexpectedly, from the shattered remnant of his unit in France, and was specially assigned to the task of drilling the Norsex enlistments in methods of warfare more modern than those approved by Cromwell. He began his work in the depot by demanding a special office and clerk of his own.

The office was found him within an hour of his arrival, and on the next parade Malcom was told to fall out and report to him. It was a grey Spring afternoon, as he was long to remember, a Russian rather than an English afternoon, as he made his way amid the welter of hutments to a door which displayed the freshly-chalked inscription 'Sergeant-Major (Training Staff).'

He entered and stood at attention. Metaxa looked up from his table and they stared at each other. . . .

The love of a man for a man has small place in English literature. Men in our books do not love, they like each other, they are fond of each other, are pals and pards and chums and what not, in the queer, rickety jargon of the second and third decades. Our books find a pleasure, a bumptiously embarrassed pleasure, in the inability of Englishmen to love. The word is tabu—perhaps because of classical homosexual associations. But without any doubt those two loved each other at first glance. Malcom had no feeling of meeting a stranger and they twinkled to a mutual smile as he clicked his heels.

'Sergeant-Major Metaxa? I'm your new clerk.'

'Good God. Sit down. What's your age?'

'Nineteen, sir.'

'When did you make that up?'

'Three days before I enlisted, sir.'

'Thought so. Never mind the "sir." Sit down.' He yawned,

being wearied with travelling, and began to search among the papers on his desk. 'Here, want a cigarette?'

IX

He was thirty-nine years of age, slightly over middle height and slightly under middle girth, with fair brown hair and the whitest skin Malcom ever saw. He had a low, broad forehead, misty blue eyes, a finely chiselled nose, and the mouth and chin of a girl. His voice would sometimes rise into music and sonorousness, sometimes degenerate into the oddest sing-song. On the parade-ground he had a startling siren-whoop of penetration that made addressed and unaddressed alike start with a nervous guilt. He had a habit, even on the most rigidly official occasions, of stroking his nose, meditatively, as though he considered it an extraordinarily good nose.

He was the bastard son of an American irrigation official and a Cairene Greek. He had been an architect—a Prix de Rome who had helped to design the mud skyscrapers of Palais de Koubbah—and had deserted his profession at the age of thirty-three in consequence of some unnamed and apparently unnameable catastrophe. Kinghorn was going south to the exploration of Rossland. His ship passed through the Suez. At Port Said it was boarded by Metaxa, demanding employment. The dazed and genial Kinghorn, after some protests that there were not even Eskimos in the Antarctic for whom Metaxa could design igloos, accepted the Græco-American as a supernumerary. At the ter-mination of the Kinghorn Expedition, Metaxa had gone to Papua with the Portmaine Investigation Mission as geologist. Thence after he had passed a year in Kamchatka, six months in the Gobi, and four months in struggling through the mountains of Indo-China, in company with Knut Hammsen, to the safety of a French river-post. In July of 1914 he had been a fugitive amidst the Wahhabi villages of the Great Dahna, the last survivor of the ill-fated Meyrin-Beard Expedition. He was a naturalized

Englishman.

Eighteen months had seen the transformation of the explorer-geologist into an extraordinarily brilliant and bad sergeant-major. Training in gunnery, in bombing, in bayonet-fighting he entered into with zest—'the zest of a lunatic at large cheered on by his doctors and nurses.' He was not only a valuable training expert who had refused a commission, but, in the spirit of an antiquarian investigating the scratchings of the sub-human, had made himself completely at home in *King's Regulations* and the *Manual of Military Law*, mean, sordid, ill-tempered, and ill-written volumes constantly being swamped under with sheaves of clownish 'amendments.' Metaxa remained unswamped, threading the bog-paths of this printed drivel like a skilled fenman.

He had a devilish facility in treating his superior officers with an astounded deference which reduced the young and overbearing to hot-eared flusterment and the elderly and cautious to an invariable formula: 'You'll know what to do in the matter, sergeant-major.' His treatment of the men varied with his mood. He hated Regulars—especially Regular N.C.O.'s. At the instigation of Malcom he proceeded to make the life of Sergeant Morgan such a burden as even a black bastard of India might have groaned under. Quite equally he disliked the enlistments from the towns—the cheerful, ragtime-singing individuals who were unashamed of calling themselves 'Tommies.' Cockney chirpiness could infuriate Metaxa. But the dull, plodding, anxious ploughmen, the nervous worried boys, all those whom the orgy of beastliness had overtaken and mentally murdered, were his protégés. He indulged in unlimited favouritism, though it was a graded favouritism that never reached anywhere near intimacy, except in the case of Malcom.

He stamped into his office one afternoon in mid-March to find his clerk deep in a book and with his heels elevated on the stove.

'Hell, Malcom, you might at least keep the fire going—missing drills and parades and reading—Oh, God of Battles, reading Guizot!—while I amass seemly cannon-fodder for Krupp.' He poked the fire irritably, drew up a chair and sprawled in it tiredly, while Malcom flung his book into the coal-bin and stretched and yawned in the fug of the hut. Metaxa surveyed the bin-assigned Guizot, reading aloud its title. '*History of Civilization.* . . . Why the devil read such muck?'

Malcom re-aligned his jaws. 'Why not?'

'Because it's nonsense. Twaddle. Tripe. All this evolutionary stuff.'

'Eh?'

Metaxa grinned, his handsome face oddly un-military under the peak of his hat. 'Just that. Oh, not the biological part—our descent from the dear old ground-apes of the Miocene. But the belief that civilization is civilizing—it's a dream of apeptic pedants in the British Museum Reading Room. . . . Civilizing! Lord Christ, I wish I had them at bayonet-practice!'

'But for civilization it'd be practice with tooth and claw. After all, we climb. Even our beastliness is infinitely less beastly than the primitives.'

'Climb be damned. Beasts? There was never such beastliness in the Old Stone Age as there is in Europe now. Primitives? You've never met them except in the splurgings of some senile Haeckelian. I have. Lost tribes in Siberia. People down Papua way. Old Stone Age still, without metals or priests or gods or kings. Kindly and care-free, like clean children. With children's angers and children's loves. Quick, intelligent, lovable animals. The modern picture of the primitive as a raving ghoul is—raving nonsense.'

'But—savages, head-hunters, cannibals?'

Metaxa shrugged. 'They're not primitives. They're the scum and backwash of surrounding civilizations—though they don't murder by proxy.'

Malcom stared into the fire. 'But, God—if that's the case all the last ten thousand years has just been training in hate and murder and beastliness—beastliness that no beast every knew. . . . Hell, it makes nonsense of history. Ten thousand years of civilization no more than——'

The Greek yawned and jammed his be-putteed legs against the

wall. ' "Emptiness and pain, and love it was the best of them, and sleep worth all the rest of them.". . . Civilization's no climb to a dawn. It's mankind lost in a pitch-black corridor.'

X

Civilization no progress from the beast, but a mind-tumour and a disease. The last of Malcom's book-learnt illusions took flight before that one of many pitiless expositions.

From the first the attraction of these two was mutual, an eager and unescapable attraction, a love at once jealous and tolerant. In him Malcom found at once the intellectual stimulus that cleared his mind alike of barrack-room loathings and Glaswegian memories. And midway some argument or discussion Metaxa would break off to tell of his own loneliness before they met.

'If you could know what it's been, those eighteen months since 1914. Not the mucky horrors, but the talklessness! Not a soul who'd ever heard of Siegfried or Tubal Cain or was interested in the morals of haddocks or the length of the Cainozoic. . . .'

They were lovers vocal enough. Perhaps few of the great lovers, the magnificent loves, have been wordless. Heraclitus and his poet talked the sun from the sky; Metaxa and Malcom sometimes talked the moon into morning in that little hut of an office, credited the while by the depot with multifarious clerical activities. Memories of Metaxa seated at his table, a parade state or a nominal roll grasped and forgotten in his hand, being hourlong and vehemently unaffectionate towards all properly constituted authority whatsoever—he was a philosophic anarchist—haunted Malcom for long years, most wistful and absurd memories.

Yet there were curious gaps in their intimacy. Malcom had told his own story in detail, but of Metaxa's pre-war life he learned little, except with regard to his years as explorer. And the Greek seldom or never spoke of France or what he had endured there: Malcom would meet the reality soon enough.

Meantime, excused most parades and drills, Malcom kept himself fit in the gymnasium, mostly at boxing, with stray members of the gymnasium staff for sparring partners. He had set himself with a dour determination to master the technique of the curious and imbecile 'art.' In the usual evening bout, a week after Metaxa's arrival, Wilsom found himself being carried out of the ring after five minutes' sparring with his unsportsmanlike pupil. A fortnight later the depot heavyweight, a hirsute and obscene ex-drayman who had patronisingly offered to show Malcom some 'real scrapping,' suffered the same fate. Technically Malcom was not heavyweight, but night after night he engaged a stream of aspirants to the depot championship.

Metaxa came several times to watch those bouts, to address Malcom as Private Maudslay, sonorously, and to make approving and sergeant-major-like noises in general. Then, in the privacy of their office or his room, he would brood on the matter. 'A clear eye and something in your wrists does it. You're no boxer. Peasant wrists and a philosophy of contempt. And you're not a clean fighter—heard the complaints last night? You just skim disqualification: you don't play the game.'

'Quite right. I've stopped playing games. No intention of playing the game. Why the hell should I? I didn't compile the ritual of the dirty Bulford blood-worshippers.'

Indeed, it was with shrinking flesh that he drove himself into each fight. Nevertheless, he found himself in the inter-depot tournament shortly afterwards carrying off the heavyweight 'purse'—an ornate wristwatch. Next morning Metaxa leant back in his chair and shouted with laughter as he looked at his clerk's bruised lips. 'Shades of Shelley and Karl Marx! Especially Karl. . . . You're brutalizing the Proletariat.'

'Blast the proletariat. Can't you quash this route-march to-night?'

Metaxa grew serious. 'Not even for you. You'll be glad of it— over there.'

In the mud and rain of that moist Spring the new battalions of the New Army trained endlessly, intensively all over Salisbury

Plain. Even as Metaxa's shamelessly favoured clerk Malcom did not escape his entire share in marching, entrenching, and musketry. The same steady eye and the same savage contempt for the business in hand which had provided him with a wrist-watch made him a first-class shot, and he was marked down accordingly on Metaxa's careful lists.

He was marked down as a sniper 'over there.'

XI

By some dubious means Metaxa acquired a second-hand motor-cycle and sidecar; it had certainly been a War Department vehicle originally and he and Malcom spent all one afternoon in erasing the broad arrow from the engine. Then the camp limits ceased to confine them. Malcom would meet the depot sergeant-major half a mile or so outside the lines, climb into the sidecar, and be whirled away to Bristol, to Salisbury, to Devizes. They spent their spare afternoons and Sundays on the road, assuming to the eyes of the officious officer or military policeman the appearance of a warrant officer and orderly on urgent duty. Metaxa, without any protest at all from Malcom, financed each expedition; the War Office, unaware of its generosity, provided the petrol.

One Sunday afternoon in early June, dipping up and down the hill roads, they breasted a long slope and Malcom shouted and stood up. On the brow of the opposite hill great menhirs, black and wonderful, marched against the sky.

'Stonehenge,' said Metaxa.

They parked the sidecar and cycle, paid a shilling at a cubby-hole, and went and inspected Stonehenge. Malcom spent a happy half-hour in talking and speculating and attempting to verify the orientation of the 'altar.' To Metaxa the great stones conveyed little or nothing of the spirit of their builders; it required at least the elements of sculptural adornment to interest him in the remains of any vanished people. In the wonderlands of the Lower Bronze Age he was the pupil and Malcom the professor. He wandered round the menhirs, poking them with his stick.

'Cut out those stones and brought them a distance of at least seventy miles? Bloody fools.' He looked round the vacant summer moors hazing into the Wiltshire hills. 'They were always halfwits in Wiltshire.'

Malcom lay down on the warm grass, threw away his shapeless khaki cap, and closed his eyes. Metaxa wandered the inner circle of stones and then came near again.

Remote with the Bronze Age sun-worshippers, Malcom heard the scrape of boots on the altar-stone. Birds were crying over the fields. It was very warm. Malcom loosened his collar and dozed.

'I remember in June two years ago. . . .'

The voice of Metaxa ebbing and flowing in drowsy sing-song, aroused him.

'Eh?'

'June morning in England, and I—I was a fugitive in South Arabia. Meyrin was the last they'd killed. They gutted him with a jambiyah, and tied up salt and sand in his entrails. I lay and watched them from a nullah.'

'Ugh.'

'Very. And then I'd crept and crawled and stumbled northeastwards for days—nights rather—across the Mesaleekh. Nejd, you know. Cultivated strips and villages after a bit, but all in the hands of the Wahhabis. I'd been living on water-melons and samh shoots and some pigeons I killed one night in a cote. I'd slept through the days in irrigation ditches, in sand-holes, in the tombs of saints; once in a byre full of goats—I saw, smelt, dreamt, and tasted goat for days afterwards. But that morning. You have never seen its like. Neither had I. Not a Mesaleekh morning at all, but moist and wistful and young. I stood in it, filthy and sand-caked, and sobbed, and suddenly had a vision of England—God knows why, for I hadn't seen it for years. Not the real England at all, of course, but Blake's green and pleasant land, where women were white and kindly and purchasable and no men hunted the roads with superannuated Mausers. A vision. I followed it.

'Exactly that. Walked upright and unconcealed. The craziest thing. Went through a village, I remember, with the women and children lining the doorways and staring at me, and the men coming running with spears and then stopping and staring at me also, and letting me pass. Walked dead eastwards till nightfall and then heard the sound of the sea. No delusion. Sea it was—wildest, treeless coast, and there, just below me, a boat that had pulled in for water from a Muscat trading sloop. . . .

'Six weeks it took me to get home to Southampton. The day after I landed war was declared, and I remembered the England of that vision in the hell of the Mesaleekh and enlisted inside forty-eight hours.'

His auditor on the grass stirred. 'Yes, and——?'

'And now, of course, I'm Sergeant-Major Metaxa, D.C.M., twice wounded—once by one of my own N.C.O.'s, who was suitably court-martialled and shot—once mentioned in dispatches, and an expert in bombing and Military Law.'

He laughed. There was such sudden bitterness in his laughter as made Malcom fumble away from the subject. 'How'll it all end?' He sat up and looked at Metaxa and Stonehenge. 'This War mess?'

'God knows.'

A blackbird was whistling down the hillside below Stonehenge. Malcom stared in the direction of that sound. He hardly knew that he spoke. 'And you and me. . . .'

Metaxa laughed again. 'What does it matter? There is *no* you or me. Read Berkeley. Read the scientists. Most likely we'll be killed over there. And it doesn't matter, because—already we don't exist. Only a temporary grouping of atoms endowed with a conceit called personality. . . . Christ!'

Something snapped in his hands. It was the stem of his pipe. He was staring, white-faced, at the summer day.

'You and me, Malcom! We're going out there—again. . . . Why should we, why the hell should we? Were there ever such damned fools? Why go to any such place? Why the hell do the Germans keep pouring into France and the Russians into Galicia?

They don't want to, any more than we do. They want to live at ease and eat and drink and make love. . . . Yet we're going, they're going. . . .'

'Saviours of civilization. Read Mr. Asquith.'

'Saviours from what? Oh, some day men'll see war for the blasted idiocy it is, whatever the priests and patriots say. We'll not manure the French fields with bloody pulp for nothing. Somehow it'll count. . . . Poor lost and snivelling brutes from the caves of Mas d'Azil! . . . And over there in this sunshine there's that slavering beastliness blotting out the sky . . . .'

Malcom had nothing to say to that. Metaxa the satirist, Metaxa the humorist, Metaxa the academic anarchist—he had met them all, but never before this tortured romantic. He did not look at him, but ached for him, helplessly. Presently, in a shrill, queer voice, the Greek began to speak again.

'And yet—there's meaning in it somewhere—our blind adventure in civilization's corridor of darkness. Upwards after all, perhaps. Somewhere in the starless ways of the mountain tunnels there's light. . . . God, was there ever such hero as Man! Think of him, Malcom! Struggling and falling and stumbling onward amidst pits and traps and the ravings of his bestialized kin. Blinded and maimed with the lies of the priests and godmen, astray after will-o'-the-wisps in a thousand stinking culs-de-sac—and yet, he climbs! There's meaning—somewhere—in his blind adventure up the mountain pass. Somewhere beyond this Defile of the Beast in which we stumble and weep, somewhere beyond your Walls of the World, there's the flame of a splendid Light. . . . '

They looked at each other, the younger man with his savage cynicism of disillusion routed to a queer silence. Metaxa stared unseeingly at the broken pipe in his hands, and then dropped the fragments into his pocket and stood up.

'Time to go back,' he said.

'What's this place?' demanded Metaxa, speeding through the streets at a rate which made the policeman on point duty wheel to look at their number. But the obscurantist mud plastered on the plate still adhered.

Malcom peered at a signpost. 'Sunninghill, Egham, to come. This is Winchfield.'

'The hell it is.' The ancient engine moaned as the Sergeant-Major flicked the antiquated controls. The sidecar rocked. Malcom snuggled down behind the celluloid screen and pulled his great-coat over his knees. Dim fences and farms rose and whipped past on the scudding road. It was seven o'clock in the evening.

In less than forty-eight hours they were leaving for France. All passes had been cancelled, all men on leave recalled. But at five o'clock a waiter from the Sergeants' Mess had brought a note from Metaxa. 'Meet me outside Bulford on the London road in half an hour. Show and supper in London.'

Metaxa also was for France. He had 'wangled' a return to France when he might have stayed on at the depot. It was an insane act that he did not discuss. There was no need.

'London by eight o'clock' he had said as he picked up his clerk and since then they had hardly spoken, except when Malcom leaned out now and then and called directions from the sign-posts. Goggled, Metaxa hung on the handle-bars and heeded only to the road.

Amesbury, Andover, Whitchurch, Oakley, Basingstoke they passed, and the light grew less, though the sun waited for them and lighted their way through corridors of tremulous hedges. Past long, gloaming-stilled fields they swept, through drowsing villages; once, for mile on mile, at some loop-way, under an arch of trees: a great, green, whispering tunnel. Malcom sat and stared at the fields and all the night-shadowed security of England like one in a dream.

God! and in forty-eight hours. . . .

"I cannot hope to tell of the vague and terrible wonder that came to grip my heart then—wonder that those English fields and hedges should stand on the verge of sleep and not know the thing that I knew: I might never see them again."

In London at last, sitting beside Metaxa in the stalls of a theatre, he covered his eyes with his hands and began to laugh hysterically. The Greek shook him concernedly.

'Steady on, Malcom. What's wrong?'

'All this—it doesn't exist. You said so. A dream. Lights and music. That girl's hair—look at it. Clean hands and shirts. Those bare shoulders. Dresses. That stuff they've just sprayed to cool the place. Christ, they can't exist—when there's that thing over in France.'

He struggled to rise, but Metaxa's hand pressed him down. 'Don't I know it? But dream them, dream them like hell! Aren't they worth the dreaming? The hair of that girl you pointed out— it's a greater miracle than the nebula in blasted Andromeda.' He stopped to jump up and cheered a lame act till his applause was contagious, then urged a reluctant stalls to its feet as the orchestra burst into the strains of a popular song which usually chilled his blood and made his spine crawl in distaste. 'Come on. All of you.'

They stood and sang—all of them, as he had commanded— and drowned the voice of the paid singer on the stage. Malcom heard Metaxa's voice, minus its sing-song, ringing out the feeble lines as though they contained a greater profundity than any philosophy on earth:

> *'There's a silver lining*
> *Through the dark clouds shining;*
> *Turn the dark clouds inside out*
> *Till the boys come home——'*

'To get *their* damn pockets turned inside out in place of the clouds. Still—sing up, Malcom! Morituiri te salutant!'

Presently the entire theatre, crammed with men in khaki awaiting their summons 'over there,' took Metaxa to its heart as unofficial stage-manager. In the intervals he stood up and called out numbers to the perspiring conductor: *Tipperary, The Long Trail, Annie Laurie,* finally, and daringly, *Nearer to Thee.* The actors came out on the boards and joined in the hymn prompted by the atheist Greek.

'Poor primitives in the Defile! Sing up, Malcom! There's no Leader or Light—but let's pretend!'

At the end of the show a note was brought him from the stage. Would he join in a supper?

He did, taking Malcom with him. They sat in a crowded restaurant, under the flare of bright lights, in the din of an unending dance-band. They were a party of fourteen or so, women, girls, and men, some in uniform and some not. Malcom sat next a maudlin Lieutenant-Colonel who for a time addressed him as 'chappie' and then became inextricably involved, as he admitted, in trying to synchronize his eyes. Metaxa he saw at intervals, at the other side of the table, seated between two girls and making love to both with apparently the greatest success. Every now and then the Greek would rise with one or the other of them and spin away amidst the tables, and then return to some half-finished and never-finished course and the replenishing of his glass. All glasses were constantly replenished, in spite of the law. The Lieutenant-Colonel—he was a very young Lieutenant-Colonel—became audible, hiccoughing a declaration. The supper was 'on' him. Nobody disputed his claim.

Least of all Malcom. He had discovered the girl on his left— a girl of whom he was to remember little except the extreme hoarseness of her voice and certain other unnecessary physiological details. She insisted on calling him 'Joe' and on laughing immoderately at every remark he made. "She was probably mildly drunk by then. I was."

He found himself dancing with her on one occasion, and on another passing through the swing-doors at the end of the restaurant-hall. She whispered to a discreet attendant. They went up a flight of stairs, but did not enter a room. The girl drew Malcom into a curtained window-recess with a long, cushioned seat. Remotely over the River a searchlight flickered in the sky.

119

They began to touch each other with urgent hands.

She bit his lips as they lay together so painfully that he took her by the throat and shook her. She fawned on him with a Lesbian abandon. Suddenly the near darkness became alive with tiny noises. Something on her bared breast had snapped and was showering the floor with tiny pellets. It was a rosary.

He crawled and searched in the darkness of the alcove, fatuously intent on retrieving the scattered beads. The girl adjusted her dress and powdered her nose by the dim reflection of the searchlight. Then she got down on the floor and joined in the search and forgot her intention in solicitously powdering Malcom's bitten lips. As they came out of the alcove together his heavy Army boot crunched to fragments the brittle Christ of the rosary.

Going downstairs, they encountered Metaxa ascending, a girl on each arm. In the restaurant the hoarse-voiced girl was snatched from Malcom's side, out of his life, and away in the arms of a naval officer. Yawning every now and then, ear-achingly, he made his way to the table of the theatre-party.

It was deserted but for a single girl—one he had not noticed before, with her back to him and seated, strangely enough, in the chair he himself had occupied.

At the sound of his approach she turned round, smiled, rose, and walked away through the swinging doors.

He sat down, abruptly, staring, puzzled. A man at a nearby table turned about and looked after her also. Another fit of yawning seized Malcom. Had seen her before, somewhere, surely. . . .

XIII

The next thing of which he was conscious was a waiter shaking him and Metaxa, urgent and unsteady, at the door, amid a crowd from the supper-party—Metaxa embracing and being embraced by the two girls who had climbed the stairs with him. They kissed Malcom also. One of them was crying. So was Metaxa.

'Goodbye, my dears, and thank you.'

'Goodbye, goodbye!' they called as the two went down the steps into a darkened and unfriendly London. The Greek caught Malcom's arm.

'Son,' he said, 'I'm bloody drunk. In a minute I'll be drunker. Down street, turn left, across street is garage. Unless it's moved. Moved.' He turned to wave a belated farewell to the empty doorway. 'Goodbye, goodbye.'

The fresh air had sobered Malcom. 'How the devil are we to get to Bulford?' he asked at the garage entrance as he wheeled out the combination and his battalion Sergeant Major stood leaning happily, if a trifle hazily, against a wall. 'You can't drive like that.'

Metaxa lurched to the sidecar, got into it carefully, and sat down. 'No. You drive. Sober, Presbyterian. Natural ascetic.'

Malcom knew little or nothing of the mechanism of a motorcycle. Metaxa appeared to have fallen asleep. He shook him.

'Here, how do you change gears?'

'Mm. Pull down for top, pull right for second. Wheel to the right, son Roger, he said, and the Lord God give you joy of it. Morris. Great poet.' He snored.

Malcom never knew how he did it, but he crept through London and reached the western roads about three o'clock in the morning. At Staines, as he stopped to peer at a signpost, Metaxa awoke and made a solemn declaration.

'I am a natural sceptic,' he said, and fell asleep.

At a quarter to six Malcom stopped again and awakened his passenger in front of their office in Bulford. As the Sergeant-Major stirred and yawned there flashed on Malcom, irrelevantly, answer to that question with which he had vexed his brain all the star-lighted miles from London.

'By God!' he shouted, 'That girl in the restaurant—it was Rita. . . .'

XIV

Forty-eight hours later they disembarked in France, and went south and east for days, by changing trains and camps. In a month's time they were marching up under the drumming roar of the great bombardment of July 16th, and going into action at Trones Wood.

CHAPTER SIX

THE DEFILE OF THE BEAST

I

He spent over two years in France; he was not once wounded or gassed or fever-stricken; he became a corporal and then a sergeant; he was twice pressed to accept a commission, declined like Metaxa, and was victimized in consequence; he grew to regard unclean equipment and unpolished buttons with passionate disfavour; he robbed a German prisoner of three hundred American dollars and then shot that prisoner as the man turned on him threateningly; he sat three days in a shell-hole at Bois Louange, he and two others, marooned in a maelstrom of retreat and advance; he found a rat-eaten woman's corpse in the depths of a staff dug-out in the Hindenburg Line; he commandeered an abandoned Leyland lorry in the Spring retreat of 1918 and drove a score of men for thirty miles, and fell asleep, and awoke still driving them; he lived a life so fantastic that his memory was to refuse to treat it seriously, or, in self-defence, became deliberately treacherous.

He never spent a 'first day in the trenches.' They massed in emplacements and sunken roads in front of the gun-clamour of that July 16th and then went forward into a draggled, corpse-strewn waste, a-vomit in sudden volcanic eruptions, drifting long clouds of gas. They jumped the last bank of the sunken road and yelled and went forward at a stumbling run. The air was filled with a whispering rush of bullets—Malcom was to remember that whispering sound first heard, like the sound of exhausted hail. The forward sky flickered and winked with gun-flashes; behind, the sound of the British barrage leapt forward and

123

forward on their backs, like the leaping of pursuing dinosaurs. The upper air was populous and filled with an insane racket, while from copses to left and right arose a whoop-whoop presently merging into the whoo-oo-oor of gunbelts. . . . Malcom found himself plunging forward, an interested automaton, above the rhythmic play of his Army boots. His company commander raced three paces in front of him, sobbing a foolish chant: 'Oh, you bloody bloody bloody—oh, you bloody bloody SWINE!'

Suddenly his hat vanished and with it the roof of his skull. He swayed and fell. Malcom tripped over him, stumbled, recovered, with vision below his eyes of a thing like an archaic cranium filled with a seething mess of dun-coloured jelly.

He was in 'A' company, 'B' was at its heels. Sergeant-Major Metaxa, grinning, a knobkerrie in his hand, raced past. By then the smoke-mist so patched ground that they lost direction and found themselves enfiladed from the right. The battalion's attack was north of the Bois de Trones and south of Longueval. From the trees to the right, lines of echeloned machine-guns raved at them. Men beyond Malcom doubled and crumpled and sprawled—he saw one man impale himself on his own bayonet—and suddenly a shell burst brightly against the infernal wood and the gun-flashes. Unharmed, Malcom ran forward through a raining spray of metal, saw Metaxa and a few others, joined them, and was presently fighting and falling and scrambling into the pits of the machine-gunners.

Then something happened which he was never to see recorded. The machine-gunners, as Metaxa's company leapt amongst them, cheered and laughed, as though it was some game. Malcom stabbed one of those laughing gunners through the stomach, and fell on top of him in an attempt to retrieve his bayonet and was trampled underfoot by the others. When he struggled up again his hands and tunic were soaked with blood and his mouth and throat sick with the smell of excrement.

Nine officers and four hundred and eighty other ranks of the battalion failed to answer that night, and were provisionally posted 'missing' until when and if their exact fate could be ascertained. The most of them had died like bogged flies in the spider's web of trenches and cellars which guarded the riven lands of Waterlot Farm.

Malcom spent most of the night in a captured trench, an acting-corporal, and, overcome by his queasy stomach, again and again very sick indeed because of the smell of his own body.

II

Delville Wood, Trones Wood, Longueval, Ginchy—they marched and counter-marched, took and re-took, stormed and fell back amid those immense names for three weeks. Then they were relieved and marched out and gave place to battalions of felt-hatted Australians who were to die in the mud and rains and futility of the Ancre. Thirty miles behind the lines, in rest-camp, the depleted Norsex were joined by drafts from England and set again to marching and training under an idiot colonel who believed in the imminence of open warfare. Malcom changed his tunic and acquired one that was unstained and had stripes sewn on it. He became smart and attentive in the presence of officers and blasphemous and capable in the presence of those who lacked both stripes and commissions. Metaxa organized vigorous football matches and Corporal Maudslay, battalion heavy-weight, became a centre-forward of considerable proficiency.

Indeed, the battalion Soccer team acquired a reputation. It would go miles in lorries to play rival division teams. In one away match Malcom tripped over and sat on a sturdy half-back who was blunt and blasphemous and Scotch.

It was his brother Robert.

He had joined the Seaforth Highlanders, but was then in training as a gunner for the Tanks. Amazed strangers, they sat either side of a packing case in the barn of Robert's company, and looked at each other uncertainly and unconvincedly. Robert tried to break through the veils of unreality.

'Christ—Malcom, little Malcom. A corporal—an . . . d'ye mind when I smacked ye for stealin oat-cakes? . . . Never sent me that six pounds, never wrote. Ginchy? Christ, I was at Longueval. Why'd you never write hame? Auntie Ellen's dead. We heard you'd left Glasgow; Auld Ian was there an looked in to see ye, and you'd gane. What'd you join an English regiment for?'

'What do you think of it all, Robert?'

'It's jist fair hell.' He sighed. 'Though I dinna say onything. Hae ye ever seen a German?'

Malcom nodded. Robert smoothed his short, brindled hair. 'Never seen ane o them. The daft B's. Why the hell did they start it? Mebbe they didna. We're as daft as they are.' He sighed again. 'God, I'd like richt weel a plate o new bannocks and warm milk, and then go ower the brae by Tocherty and see the Leekan lichts below. Mind them, Malcom?' He suddenly grew shy. 'I was married afore I cam oot. Ane o the Murray lassies.' He had a flash of the old, whimsical arrogance. 'Jean, the bonniest ane.'

'Jean was the bonniest,' Malcom said, gently. Robert kindled, his kind eyes shining.

'You mind her? I wantit you there for my best man. She's kept a piece o the cake for you. I'll write an tell her to send it. . . . She's lonely there, up in the cotter hoose at Pittaulds. A weet summer, she says, but the corn comin fine. The clover'll stand thick and bonny below the Stane Muir at Chapel—mind the lang field?' He glanced out below the barn eaves and muttered to himself. 'They'll be bringin hame the kye the noo.'

And suddenly all that was peasant in Malcom wept for his brother, this strayed, lost peasant. He sat and gripped his hands in his pockets and held himself from speaking, and went out to the darkness and the homeward journey with his heart wrung in a passion of pity and rage.

Ten days later, in the attack on Thiepval, he saw his brother, thrusting his gasping face from the port-hole of a Tank, go by into the hell of bright fires and smashed entanglements where the

Wurtembergers had died. He caught sight of Malcom, shouted something, and passed, a man in a dream.

Malcom never saw him again.

III

In late 1917 he lay in a field of wheat, among wheat-stalks and poppies, all one afternoon. It was a very quiet afternoon. Between the lines in the Picard country there was only an occasional rattat of snipers' fire. The Norsex had come in a week before, to take over from French troops who had previously fallen back a distance of some three miles. The wheat field now lying midway the long, fresh scarrings of earthwork was still a recognizable field. It was a freak field and a brigade curiosity. Several times both sides had tried to burn the wheat, but it fired ill in that late, damp autumn. One shell-hole, like a geyser-burst, lay almost midway the lines; and this shell-hole became a coveted point of occupation throughout the day. From dawn one watched for the Saxon sniper who was wriggling towards it; found, one shot him. Or the German look-outs watched for the Norsex sniper, and shot *him*. It was a sport without military significance. Occasionally those two snipers stalked each other among the poppy-stalks and wheat.

Malcom had been out since dawn, and had forgotten his water-bottle. Metaxa discovered this and crawled out with it, and then perforce held Malcom company, for the German trenches had been heightened during the night and at least half a dozen rifles had attempted to pick him off, following the undulations of the wheat. He lay a little to the right of Malcom, deeper in the shell-hole than the latter was. The place was pleasant enough but for the stench from a sprawling figure in dank grey-green. He lay half out of sight, that figure, his clumsy field-boots cocked at a comical angle. There was nothing dignified or impressive about him. He was merely an unpleasant object which stank.

'Poor devil,' said Metaxa. 'I like those Saxons.'

'It's a pity he's mislaid his face,' Malcom said, indifferently.

A movement on the new brown embanking of the Saxon parapet had caught his attention. Something greyish just verged the trench-edge for a moment, and in that moment, his finger gentle upon the second pressure, Malcom fired. Came the far clatter of a body falling. Malcom ejected the spent round, clicked home the bolt again, and slithered deeper into the shell-hole.

'Got him?'

'Yes. One of his eyes, I should think.'

They lay and listened to the shower of bullets pinging over-head. Their own trench took up the challenge and for a little a Saxon machine-gun bayed.

'You'd think there was a bloody war on,' murmured Metaxa.

Malcom glanced at him anxiously; he had always an absurd anxiety when Metaxa was with him under fire. The Greek knew it and caught his glance and smiled whimsically.

'I know.' He chewed a wheat-stalk and meditated.

'Though I've given up feeling that way about you. You'll be all right.' Then: 'But I think myself I'm fey.'

'Eh?'

He pulled a poppy and pressed his face against it, and for a little seemed to forget what he had been going to say.

'. . . flowers of Proserpine. A lordly Greek death for a Cairene bastard to die—among poppies and wheat. Not the kind that I'll come to, I think. Look here, Malcom, I know I'll go West in this show sometime. I know it just as certainly as I know that tomorrow's sun'll come up. It's like walking through a fog to the edge of a cliff. Somewhere I know I'll fall off. I'm not depressed or sick. I just know.'

Malcom had met several men with just such premonitions. Not one of them who stayed within his ken but had been killed. Perhaps some sixth sense awoke in one there, or evolved and shaped and came to being. He was to remember that he at-tempted then neither consolation nor contradiction. He just lay and stared at his rifle.

But Metaxa had turned on his back among the crushed corn-stalks and brown earth and lay considering the sky and inviting

128

a stomach-wound. 'And it's not unpleasant, this death-sentence. Once I thought a man would go mad with such knowledge as mine. But I feel as sane as ever. Only, of what remains—Christ, how I want to live it!' He was silent for a moment and then whispered to himself, remotely, almost in the thought images of the wistful Robert, dead and lost at Thiepval: 'God, the miracle of wheat. . . .'

He lay quiet for a little while, then turned his head towards Malcom, restlessly. 'Wonder what's beyond the cliff, after all? Thank God I'm an atheist! . . . Did you hear that R.C. padre last week asseverating that anyone who goes West in the front line goes straight to heaven—mixed symbolism and all?'

Malcom grunted. He considered the proper study of R.C. mentality a subject for the pathologist.

'Yes—right to a de-loused immortality beyond the reach of whizz-bangs. . . . What a life! What a death!' The Greek chuckled and stirred to exposition. 'Think of the collisions among the various denominations scooting skyward, all over the world at the moment, to their various vexatious heavens. . . . Lord, what post-mortem retreats there have been: Paradise, Avilion, Valhalla, Nirvana, Hades, Mictlan. . . . Wonder if those rival blisses ever go to war? Sure to. Must be fun to be an Aztec ghost under Huitzilopochtli and lead out a Mexican Expeditionary Force against Jehovah, captaining the defunct Israelites. Or serve under Gabriel when Jesus and Siva meet in dispute on some celestial frontier. Can't you imagine the trumpeting and tub-thumping and the posters pasted up all along the Christian heaven: "Why haven't you military wings up, young shade?" "Jehovah expects every saint post-dating the Reformation to do his duty." "Yahveh wants you." "*Armageddon Courier!* Brightest News and Pictures! Virgin inspects detachment under Henry VIII. Mohammed betrayed by a Houri: Reported in Flight from Paradise." '

This was the kind of blasphemy they both found exceedingly funny. Their laughter echoed up over No Man's Land. Malcom kept his eyes on the slumberous Saxon lines the while Metaxa lay and searched the sky.

129

'Mictlan. . . . Those Central Americans were the only logical theologians who ever lived. The Toltecs and Aztecs, I mean. Not after centuries of progress did they depart from the stern, unbending creed of their fathers. *They* never transmogrified the old agricultural cannibal sacrifice into a Communion with snippets of bread and sips of wine. All the necessary blood and none of the unnecessary squeamishness. Your Wee Frees were prinking Progressives compared with them. They sat down to table after each sacrifice, nicely dressed in scented clothes, and gossiped intellectually of art and the weather and palace-building and the latest Nezahualcoyotl ode the while they ate well-cooked cutlets sliced from the slaves dragged screaming to the altar-stone an hour before. Christ—logicians who weren't afraid of the price of civilization! Different stock altogether from the Mayans.'

Malcom was mildly fogged, but interested. He knew nothing then of Mexican archeology, except what little he had gathered in boyhood from the flowery pages of the genteel Prescott. 'Much the same as the Aztecs, weren't they?'

'The Maya? Good Lord, no. They weren't Nahuas at all. Doubt even if they were Red Indians. Never read of them? Never heard of your namesake, the Mayan Maudslay? The only interesting people of prehistory—oh, not because my father was an American and I've drunk cocktails in Greenwich Village.'

'Tell us about them.'

An aeroplane, black-crossed, droned overhead. A Fokker fighter. In the north, beyond a clump of hills, an artillery duel was creeping up to intensity against the greyness of the afternoon, like a thread of mercury creeping up a thermometer.

'. . . came south into Central America two thousand two hundred years ago, bringing with them a culture which was ancient even then. They were alien to the natives of the time: the Toltecs and Aztecs hadn't yet separated from the other Red Indian nations in the north. And for seventeen hundred years, like men in a nightmare, those Maya wandered Central America, building cities and rearing stupendous monuments—I've seen

130

photographs in the Peabody Museum and the architecture's extraordinarily good—and then abruptly deserting cities and monuments and fleeing in a night. They were old and decadent in Yucatan before the Danes came to England. They were cannibals at the time of the Norman Conquest. They left behind them, on temple lintels and stelae and a few manuscripts, a script which is still undeciphered. That's about all. They nearly made me an archeologist myself—I intended having a shot at Central America when the Meyrin-Beard do was over in the Mesaleekh. Think of them—cannibals with a script—a script more ancient and involved than the Chinese! If a man could read the Mayan glyphs, what story mightn't they tell?'

'Raids and rapings, wars and widowings, hates and horrors. The usual stuff.'

'Who knows? They may have been the last fugitives of drowned Atlantis. They may have evolved philosophy before Plato, discovered gravitation before Newton. They may have attempted and failed a civilization to escape the horrors of civilization—half history's a record of such attempts. They may have built the City of the Sun in some American bush—its ruins may lie there still. Compared with theirs our calendar is the work of a dithering infant. They may once have had keys to all the secrets of life and death and time.' He rolled over. 'Perhaps the undeciphered glyphs contain the key to even—*that*.'

He nodded to where the Saxon lines were already dark in the false twilight. Malcom lay beside him, his imagination kindling, caught as ever by the wonder of such fairy tale in the history of men.

'By God,' he said, unconscious how far in the years to come he was to pursue that resolution, 'I'm going to learn more about your Maya.'

131

IV

Early in 1918 they managed to get leave together—their first leave since their arrival in France—and went to Paris. There they spent a curiously oppressed eight days, putting up at a little hotel, "on the wrong side of the Seine," which catered almost exclusively for warrant officers and N.C.O.'s of the British, Colonial, and American armies. In Paris Malcom saw his first American; Paris was flooded with Americans.

'Negroes among them, too,' he observed, unnecessarily.

Metaxa, eyebrows a-tilt, remonstrated. 'Coloured men, Malcom, coloured men. No nigger alive admits he's black; he is quite passionately coloured. Spectrum-worship. Fancy a white man speaking of himself as a member of the bleached race! Still, we wouldn't like to be called blancers. . . . Another bottle?'

They were sitting in the open air, looking at Paris. Malcom shook his head.

'No thanks. Sour stuff.'

Metaxa ordered another bottle.

'I'll drink your half. Then I'm going out to get a woman. Coming?'

Slightly drunk, he leant his arms on the table and grinned at Malcom's unreproducible libel on Frenchwomen. After a solitary experiment Malcom had practised a fastidious continence in France. All his life there was something virginal in his nature which balked at such ogling, leering, pawing—and yet matter-of-factness—as characterized the practice of French lust. Unreasonably, he never ceased to detest the Latins for this matter-of-factness which he himself championed in theory. Metaxa finished the bottle.

'Of course it's foolishness and a waste of time—not to mention that other waste you've so delicately deplored. But what the hell does it matter to me? Humanity might as well play itself out that way as any other. I've no children or any intention of fathering any. I've no faith in the future of those that are fathered. Me, I'm for the ants.'

'Eh?'

'The ants. When man wipes himself off the earth as a disciple of Onan or in the next outburst of international sadism, some other life-form will rise to take control. Everything points to the ants. We blasted mammals have had our show: we're probably as doomed as the dinosaurs. Way for the Insectidæ! I pin my faith to the ants. Christ, do you remember how I bleated about the Defile of history that afternoon at Stonehenge? How the crook-boned apes might yet reach beyond the sewers and cesspools of civilization to the Light above the Pass? What a bloody bleary anthropoid I must have been!'

He had grown strangely bitter in the past six months. Malcom watched him blankly.

'The Light—God, never! A lump of seasonable carrion in my belly and a warm hide against mine—the best I can ever hope for. . . . Almost drunk again. I'm going. Go mad if I sit here and stare at the traffic and think of the Line back there.'

He rose up, staggered a little, then put on his Sam Browne and buckled it. 'How are you going to kill the rest of the day?'

'Going to hunt up a book about the Mayans. Those glyphs of theirs interest me.'

'The freak Azilian worrying over his grandmother's thigh-bone. I prefer such members flesh-clad.' He laughed, a little too loudly. 'Meet early tomorrow, shall we? Come to the Café Despruit at eleven?'

'Where is it?'

'Boul' Mich'.'

Next day Malcom sat in the Café Despruit from half past ten till half-past twelve, very little interested in war-time Paris, but deep in the book he had purchased that morning after a notable struggle to pronounce the word 'Maya' French fashion. It was the Abbé Brasseur's translation of Landa's *Relacion de las cosas de Yucatan* which he had finally secured, and sitting reading it he forgot for a little that aching unease awaiting him and Metaxa in the east. It haunted him probably as much as it did the Greek, though with an intense foreboding oddly impersonal.

133

There came a rattling of chairs. Metaxa sat down opposite him, ordered an absinthe, and drank the sickly liquid with twitching lips. But he was not drunk and showed no particular effects of dissipation but for an odd look in his eyes, as though they had been sprinkled with fine sand.

'Had a good time?'

'Bong, tray bong, as they say in the French classes in Aberdeenshire. Oh, damned funny.'

'What?'

'Nine years ago my wife sat here with me in this café. Her bag lay where you have that book. I remember the nick in the arm of that chair.'

'Your wife? I never knew you were married——'

Their eyes met and Malcom's shivered away from the meeting. The Greek's voice droned in a thin, flat sing-song.

'Nine years ago. We'd been honeymooning in England. Three months. Then we came through Paris and later went on to Rome and so to Cairo. My architect fees in Koubbah carried us through. We sat here one afternoon and watched the Boul' Mich' go by. She was tired, I remember, and laid her head against the back of that chair, and we were so friendly we had no need to speak. Nine years ago. What's the book?'

'Eh? Landa's *Relacion*. About the Mayans. Read it?'

'I went to a Blue Lamp last night, Malcom, and bargained for a second-class "amie," because my money was nearly done. The patronne had just one disengaged at the moment, and sent me up to her. I went into the room and—oh, Christ, Malcom—*it was my wife!*'

V

He looked up and saw a patch of starlit sky, powdered blue paling to a pearly effulgence. He stared at it uncomprehendingly for a moment. And then he understood. It was moonrise.

He bit his lips and lay still, listening. The ravine was filled with the mutilated undead. The stupefying shock of wound and blow had passed, and agony with distorted mouth whimpered amid the sprawling heaps. A man somewhere to the right and below him cried for water, pitifully, reasonably. 'Water—only a mouthful. Only a mouthful, orderly. Oh, Christ, only a mouthful. . . .' Further up the slope someone screamed and screamed, with a horrible rhythm in his screams.

Someone on the wire.

Presently, looking out and up, he saw against the moonlight the sprawling brakes of wire, with broken standards and torn stanchions, and beyond them, right on the crest, a zigzag against the sky, the German trenches. He himself, tripping and twisting his ankle in the evening attack of the Norsex, lay half-way up the slope, but it was plain that not a man in 'A' or 'B' companies had gained the crest. Dark bundles of bloody rags hung here and there amidst the strands. Above him, to the right, half-hid by a little dip from the German trench, but clear to his eyes in the ghastly light, one figure hung upon the wire with drooping head and arms outflung, grotesquely crucified. Then the Maxim bayed again and he ducked back into cover behind the body of Sergeant Morgan, burrowing his chin in the mud and feeling the dead body drum and quiver against his steel helmet.

The Maxim choked and spluttered to silence. Somewhere, behind, across the valley, a chloric light rose and poised and burned with a green incandescence. He turned his head and watched it and then fell to listening again. Should he attempt to crawl down the slope—or up to that party which had gained the shelter of a shell-hole just under the German wire to the left? Had they been wiped out? The bombing of the spot from the crest had ceased. . . .

A great cloud blinded the moon. The machine-gun opened again, raking the ground, apparently to guard against the crawling approach of night-raiders. A bee pinged and buzzed from the steel heel of his boot. His rifle-sling, jerking free in the darkness, lashed him across the face. The screamer on the wire ceased to scream. The cries for water fell away into a drooling under-moan.

Were there any Germans left at all on the crest apart from those gunners? Retreating everywhere, Metaxa had said.

Metaxa?

It must have been near midnight before the crucified figure on the wire awoke again to the torture of its torn body and broke into screams and pleadings in a crescendoing hysteria. The moonlight sprayed and dimmed through the flapping of the ragged cloud-curtain, and Malcom lay and heard the voice in the dance and sweep of the frozen shadows. He lay and twisted and covered his ears and whimpered.

It was John Metaxa.

VI

For hour upon hour—though they may have been only so many minutes—he seemed to lie and listen to the voiced anguish of the mutilated, mindless thing that had once lived and moved and questioned the world and loved him. And then an extraordinary calmness came on him, that slobbering agony in his ears. He rose and took his rifle and limped up the moonlit ravine, treading and slipping amidst the spewn lumber of the dead. He walked without concealment and without heed. Once the machine-gun rattled down the slope again. Not a bullet touched him.

With every upward step he took the screaming tore more fiercely at his ear-drums.

When he stumbled into the leftwards crater under the German wire he found some half-dozen men and a corporal still alive. He stumbled amongst them, and avoided a bayonet thrust, and was recognized.

'Christ, Sergeant, you! Thought you'd gone West with "A." Where've you been?'

Malcom laughed foolishly and sat down and heard his own whisper from very far away. *'The Defile of the Beast! The Defile of the Beast!'*

'Sorry I nearly jabbed you, but I'm jumpy as hell. There's a poor bastard on the wire there been screaming his guts out. Quiet now.'

'I killed him,' said Malcom.

BOOK II

BIRTH-PANGS

Some work of noble note may yet be done,
Not unbecoming men that strove with Gods.

Ulysses.

CHAPTER ONE

AN EXPLORER FROM MARS

I

Four years later he used to lie awake in his bed in the Buxworths' house in Chelsea and watch such crudely tinted, retina-projected chromos of the War years pass and re-pass in the darkness fading into London dawns, the while the window-curtains grew grey and then faintly stained with scarlet radiance reflected from the River. He had developed the habit of awakening at that hour, and in all he was ever to write there was dawn symbolism and dawn analogies *ad nauseam*. Some mental trick or twist such as awakens the fishermen with the tides brought him out of sleeping with the coming of light, into sharp and uncomforted wakefulness, to watch the slow beginnings of day upon his window-sill. In such hours every vivid incident of every year he had lived would unroll on the film of his memory against the fading twilight, torn pictures with ragged edges and faceless puppets sprinkled with a leprous dust.

But the Buxworths' house: it was old, narrow, semi-detached, with an enormous basement damp as a cellar, and sprouting grey-green fungi in unexpected corners. George Buxworth, sweating through this basement with a scuttleful of coal, would come unexpectedly upon those fungi and invoke Christ, dispassionately. Jane Buxworth waged unending war with them. The baby, Steven, escaping her eye a moment, would wriggle towards a new-silvered, lichenous growth ecstatically, prod it stickily, taste it, and be sick.

Like Malcom, the baby had a habit of awakening at dawn. He was thirteen months old, and very active, and neither George nor Jane got much peace after his ceremonial wailings and preliminary crowings had announced another day. He slept on a peculiar cot arrangement against their bed, but on a higher level, and would, every morning, crawl the plank on to the parental couch and land plumply and weightily on some portion of Jane's warm and placid body. Malcom would hear that thump in the room below him. The ceiling was so thin that George had resigned himself to the fact that his lodger was unremote from much of his private life. He said the position gave him the notion of a comfortably Jehovahistic universe. . . .

After the preliminary shock would come tentative scufflings. This was the baby exploring, seeking his guiding light—George's flame of red hair. The hair was never pulled. Jane said Steven just sat and stared at it in an unbelieving sort of way, or pried inquisitively into George's ears and eyes, or placed his hands on the sleeper's chest and peered into the cavity of his mouth. At that George would groan and wake, sweep the baby aside into the arms of the somnolent Jane, get out of bed, stamp illtemperedly and yawn, with a kind of hollow moaning proceeding from his wind-passages. At exactly that moment the alarumclock would go off. It was placed on the mantelshelf, at the other side of the bed from George—so placed by George himself, because he had found keeping it comfortably near at hand was useless; in such latter circumstance he had merely reached out in semi-consciousness, switched it off, and gone to sleep again. So it was relegated afar off, on the theory that he'd have to get out of bed and extinguish it, and thus be thoroughly wakened. But when the baby overslept himself to clocktime, the theory collapsed. Malcom would hear a pillow hit the buzzing machine, a faint crash as it and the pillow hit the floor, then a muffled buzzing trailing into silence. When, as was customary, Steven had evicted his father before the set time, George, struggling midway in his shirt, would be taken unawares by the buzzer and stumble blasphemously amidst chairs and other impedimenta in an effort to silence the product of his native land. . . .

And, like Jehovah, Malcom would lie above, listening to those

142

things and watching the mornings of 1923-24. Sometimes they were late in coming, for a dense foam of fog would blossom up from the River and drape the outside of the window with changing curtains of silk-shot yellow. Then George, after silencing the clock with a pillow, would reawaken late, start off late, doorbanging thunderously, and they would hear the clat-clat of his feet as he ran to catch a L.U.T. tram. Half an hour later Malcom would hear Jane coming up the stair with his delayed cup of tea. She would knock at the door and come in, yawningly and trailingly, George's old red dressing-jacket negligently looped across her breast, her pyjama-trousers belted so high that they always left bare six inches or so of leg and ankle. The lodger would sit up and take the cup, and they would yawn at each other, friendlily.

She generally sat on the edge of the bed and smoked a cigarette the while he drank the tea. She would sit on one imperfectly trousered leg and swing the other, her shoulders hunched, her short-cut brown hair falling over her eyes as she regarded her rhythmic slipper. She had the calmest of brown eyes and the calmest, Malcom thought, of brown souls.

'Where are you going today, M. M.?'

'No idea. Wet?'

' 'S a fish. Hear George last night?'

'No.'

' 'D nightmare. Fell out of bed.'

'Christ.'

'He said more than that. Fell on a nail, I think.'

They would smoke and meditate on the nocturnal gambollings of George. He would fall out of bed on the very least provocation. He dreamt very active dreams and insisted on living them.

'Eaoughh! . . . Have to feed Steven. Coming down to break-fast?'

She had been a Civil Servant in the days before George, on leave from the Rhine, had married her. She made horrible breakfasts, blackened and burnt. Malcom would shake his head.

'No. Not hungry.'

'Liar. All right. Oh, George said he thought there was a clerk's job going in the counting-house of the *Crocodile*.'

'It can go to blazes.'

'That's what I told him you'd say. . . . There's baby.'

Or George himself, early awakened, would appear with the same cup and stand beside the window going through complicated physical jerks while Malcom, with faint memories of Rita, advised and instructed him with parade-ground-like obscenity. George got little exercise as 'literary' editor of the *Crocodile*.

'Dry up, M. M. You'll corrupt our dear soldiers. See my yesterday's review of Blankety-Dash's new war book?'

It was the year of romantic war books, when soldiers still cheered as they went over the top, and loved the colonel, and spoke of the enemy, indignantly, and with a suitable aitchlessness, as Uns.

'No.'

'Sloshed the bloody rat good and hard. Knew him at Festubert. On the British staff; never saw the front line in his life. An empimpled little swine with a washy eye and a dirty vindictiveness. Eh? Oh, the usual stuff. "Such comradeship as men never knew before". . . . "If ever the mother country should send her clarion call ringing across the world again——"'

'What'd *you* do, George?'

'Me? Have the old lady smacked and put to bed with a mustard-plaster. Shoulder me gun like a simple Nero. By God, I would. And I don't think.'

He still found a simple pleasure in English slang and colloquialisms, occasionally disastrously wrecked by the insertion of an inappropriate 'gotten.' The son of a Chicagoan publisher, he had enlisted in the Canadians in 1915, had become an infantry captain, had transferred to the British Royal Engineers, had been three times wounded and twice gassed. Reversing the order of fiction and history, and following a very usual course among American younger sons, he had settled in England as the land of opportunities, his Army service standing him good for naturalization. Malcom had met him in the Rhine Occupation (they had both extended their service beyond normal War engagements), and they had fraternized with each other and the enemy to the prejudice of good order and military discipline. George had been demobilized in 1922, Malcom a year later.

'That bounty of yours must be slipping a bit low. Why don't you get a job? I can edge the *Crocodile* into providing you with something easy and lead-swinging, if you still want a rest.'

'Damn the *Crocodile*. Scavenging's not in my line, George. I don't want anything to do with Fleet Street.'

'We ain't in Fleet Street, sir, she said, but in the Lane of Shoe. What's your lay today?'

'Hawking. Door to door, as usual. Chocolates and Christmas cards.'

'But hell, it's Spring.'

'All the cheaper, both of them. Nice line in robins and homosexual saints, mum.'

'You're potty. Honest to God, M. M., what the devil are you wasting your life for?'

He would be honestly vexed over this matter at least seven times a week. He had a bright grey eye and healthy cheeks, and a broken, inquisitive nose. He got little satisfaction from the ex-sergeant.

'For fun, George. I'm still—an explorer from Mars. Don't worry. I'll pitch on something. There's Jane calling.'

So it would be. She would sing out 'breakfast' in a high, clear tenor. They would avoid looking at each other, elaborately, with visions of charred porridge and blackened bacon. George would reclaim his lodger's cup and prepare to go.

' "Oh, dust and ashes, once found sweet to smell——" See you tonight.'

He had discovered London. "I don't mean the place exploited in guide-books and literary weeklies by those odd little freaks of twitterment who imagine that London is Fleet Street and the City, and find every stone and corner hallowed by memory of that adipose conceit who trailed across the late eighteenth century like a disgusting slug. But the real London——"

Johnson's London came hardly at all into that Autumn-Winter of 1923 and Spring of 1924 when he knocked from door to door as agent for Christmas cards and gramophones and deaf-aids and vacuum cleaners and floor-polishes and photograph-enlargements and contraceptive devices. His range ran from the Buxworths' house in Chelsea north through Kensington and Hammersmith and Shepherd's Bush, Notting Hill, Paddington, Kilburn, Hampstead, north-east through Highgate, Hornsey, Crouch End, Walthamstow, south-west through Holloway, Stoke Newington and Kentish Town, out of regions where festered the ancient lowly, the cheated of the sunlight, with little money for sheer necessities, far less the luxuries he hawked, into areas of grubby respectability and 'No Hawkers'-defended semi-detachment. He became acquainted with innumerable coffee-stall people and such-like folk and an authority on the whereabouts of unexpected little parks and seats, haunted by mothers with babies in the daytime and by prostitutes with clients in the evening. He disentangled bus-routes and speediness from tram-routes and cheapness. He accumulated stores of wisdom regarding the inhabitants of strange roads and lanes and lost little culs-de-sac piled behind Euston and the White City and St. John's Hospital. Backed by the fact that his Army bounty was still unexhausted, and that failure to gain profits was therefore no synonym for immediate failure to exist, he did excellent trade in the most unexpected merchandise to the most unexpected clients.

There were scores of others in the same trade—many of them ex-Service people, like himself. Some wore their medals. Some, like Malcom, had their decorations lying at the bottom of the English Channel. Some favoured applying a sudden foot in a rapidly closing door, when the hour was between noon and four o'clock and no menfolk about, and using a toothy snarl to force the pace and trade. Others were experts in exhaustion and wan smiles. He met one girl, May Laymore, with whom he struck up a temporary partnership in a stationery-and-stamping machine business: the machine, after a few simple pressures and adjustments, stamped any address required. May carried the stationery. Malcom stamped.

They were ostensibly a married couple, and actually so one particularly wintry night which overtook them far up in the wilds of Whetstone, with much territory awaiting their exploitation next morning—exploitation to be carried out in haste, for their lay was being copied and others were on their track with reductions and scrolled lettering. So they stayed the night in a frowsy little hotel, sharing a room for cheapness and warmth and to keep in accord with their reputation. The dimly-illumined wallpaper represented strange things like ineffective green caterpillars crawling among decayed vegetation. The rain and sleet slivered up and down the window-panes and under the thin blankets the two hawkers hugged each other desperately, more out of cold than affection.

Yet even that incident, like every other of his hours and days, merely deepened his detachment. An explorer from Mars, unexcited, uninterested, he had watched the new years rise and fade and rise again, bloodily manured, from the fields of Flanders. In those London dawns in the room above the River he would lie unstirred and watch other Malcoms, dead, dispossessed, strange and remote, incomprehensibly enthusiastic, incomprehensibly alien: Malcom of the Dundon College, Malcom of Glasgow, Malcom of Salisbury Plain, Malcom in France. He would close his eyes and turn to the wall again, with the sounds of day-stirred London growing in volume below him, and the whistlings of some laden barge piercing up from the mist-hazed River.

III

George and Jane Buxworth charged their lodger ten shillings a week for his room and would beguile him into consuming carefully-plotted 'chance' meals whenever he was absent-minded enough or hungry enough to be unable to resist their charity. They would lay the most elaborate traps to feed him forcibly. The baby Steven was a notable auxiliary in their campaign. When Malcom first arrived from Germany to stay at the Chelsea house Steven was still being fed by Jane: she was the only woman Malcom had ever seen feeding a baby, and she did it in a fashion not only natural, but beautiful—"two very different things." She did it in his presence. She was the most calmly assured person he had ever met. "I watched her and almost felt proud to be a mammal."

The truth was that she found as deep—but no more deep— a pleasure in the feeding of Steven as she did in most things physical. She could eat her own charred bacon with sacramental enjoyment, she breathed into healthy lungs as though each breath of air was Alpine oxygen. She had a physical enjoyment in living that faintly interested and astounded Malcom, his own days in the Ring and at strenuous fatigues long past. He was told that while Steven was being born she had sat up in bed and demanded to see her baby before he was well in the world.

Fed, the baby would gurgle, sated, and then, if Malcom was present, would turn his head and crow, desirously, for his black hair. Malcom always obliged. Steven's tentative, sticky hands in his hair aroused in him the queerest feelings. The baby seemed somehow to share them. His starings of wonderment over Malcom's dark poll would cease suddenly and his solemn explorings result in abrupt and quite unwarranted gurglings of mirth. He would cling to Malcom's hair and rock over a secret jest, his toes curling ecstatically. When George was present he would grin over those displays and utter Rabelaisian warnings. Jane would survey lodger and progeny placidly.

'You ought to get married and have a baby yourself, M. M.'

'My God!' George would appeal, shocked. 'Women! What'll they want us to do next?'

Jane would be unperturbed. 'Oh, of course, I mean his wife. . . .'

One night, when they supposed him asleep, Malcom overheard a drowsy arguing between George and Jane.

'What's really wrong with M. M., George? Was he shell-shocked?'

'Eh? I dunno. Why?'

'Don't be silly. You know he's not, well—normal. I think he's married already and half lost his memory, or something. Did you notice his face when I said he ought to get married?'

'Hmph.' Sound of an impatient floundering.

'Don't wallow. . . . Well, did you?'

'You've been reading the serial in *Peg's Paper*—*The Mill-Girl's Triplets*, or something. Go to sleep, my good woman.'

Another grunt. Silence. Soliloquy.

'Some girl, I think. Perhaps in France. I think she must have been going to have a baby. He's crazy about Steven. Secretly crazy. Doesn't realize it himself. And do you notice he never talks about France? Only listens to you and then switches on to something else.'

'Kept a *vivandière* in a shell-hole, no doubt, and visited her twice nightly. Christ, you women! What do you think we did in France? Hung round red lamps all the time?'

'Blue for officers, weren't they, dear?'

Another silence. Then: 'Sorry, George. That was mean. But M. M. worries me.'

'Why?'

'What's he going to do with himself? He can't sell bootlaces and Christmas cards forever. He has twice as much brains as you have.'

'Thanks.'

'I've heard you say it yourself. And why does he hate newspapers so much?'

Malcom leant out of bed, picked up a shoe, and dropped it on the floor with a thud.

149

'Crikey! That you, M. M.?'

'No other.'

Silence. Jane:

'Sorry to gossip about you, M. M., but you *are* a mystery-bag, aren't you?'

'Shut up, Jane. And you go to sleep, M. M. She's gotten out of hand, but I'll silence her though I've to use a gag.

'Don't bother. . . . There's no mystery, Jane. I hate newspapers because I was fired from one for stealing money to finance a socialist group. I never mention France because I murdered my best friend there. He was caught on the wire and I went out and bayoneted him. The baby business is about as simple. I was the father of one that was never born. Its mother was killed in an accident before we could get married.'

He heard George say 'Hell,' inadequately. Then Jane's voice, clear and casual:

'Feel sleepy, M. M.?'

'Not a bit.'

'Neither do I. George'll get up and make us some cocoa.'

Malcom was already out of bed. 'He needn't. I'll bring you some.'

He sat on the edge of their bed and they all drank, in a dim radiance of starshine from the window. No light was turned on, lest the baby awake and demand a share, with his usual sociability. They felt they were stealing a march on him.

It was the end of Spring. Looking through the window, Malcom could see the far blur of whiskey advertisements over the Thames. The River had brought a ghostly warmth and sweetness out of its uplands into London, and suddenly, for the first time since he had left it, Malcom felt a pang of homesickness for Leekan. Jane, dim and cup-poising against the pillows, was displaying what George characterized, *sotto voce*, as the cloven hoof beneath the cocoa.

'You really can't go on as you're doing, M. M. Why don't you join the socialists again—or the communists? Or write something? You're—oh, you're very annoying to be fond of.'

'You're a dear, Jane. If we lived in Thibet I'd ask George to share you with me. . . . Oh, I know I'm a fool. But I can't help it—don't want to very much, perhaps. Anthropophobia. . . . You two people—and Steven—are the only people who don't make me sick to be intimate with. I'm poisoned, somehow. . . . And I can't read, far less write. I've tried. It's like—like going to the bottom of the sea without a diving-suit: I just go blind and fuzzy. Do you think I sell bootlaces from choice? It's the only job where I needn't know anyone for more than five minutes on end.' He thought of May Laymore. 'Or not much longer.'

Jane didn't seem to be listening. She was leaning across the bed to look out of the window. 'I think it'll be a good day tomorrow. Sunday. We'll all go and picnic in Epping Forest. You can carry the baby, Malcom.' She was again facing him. 'You know, all that you've said is—oh! silly.' Resolutely: 'I'll think of things tomorrow and show you it is.'

IV

Next morning George cooked an early breakfast while Jane flapped a negligent duster and Malcom squatted on the floor and built brick houses for Steven. As soon as one erection was complete Steven would gurgle at it, assume a cunning solemnity, reach out a sudden fist and demolish it shatteringly. . . .

Sunshine filled the smokeless London Sunday as they set out. It was nine o'clock and the River gleaming unfogged. Jane wore a pink frock and a cloche hat, George a horrible new suit with purplish effects, Steven the exiguous white and Malcom the shabby garments provided him on demobilization—all he possessed. At a kiosk on the edge of the Forest George bought the *Observer*, to sit on in case the grass should be damp and to spread over his face in case he should want to sleep in the sun.

They had lunch by the edge of a thicket and a pond. Steven, left unguarded, crawled off and attempted suicide by drowning, and was rescued by Malcom in the nick of time. It was very warm. The green of the trees sometimes quivered to purple. The birds all over the Forest were indulging in a quick, hot chirping, or standing and genuflecting as they drank with beady eyes round and unwinking. George, having read Mr. Garvin, greaned, sat on a portion of him, covered his face with the rest, and relapsed into sleep. A stray terrier came and sniffed at him, brightly and suspiciously, till the baby routed it with determined efforts to deprive it of its tail. Jane sat and clasped her knees and pondered her lodger.

She did most of the talking. Malcom sat and listened and watched Steven and occasionally looked at the talker's very white neck. He records a characteristic thought: his wonder then that two civilized beings, inculcated with the straying and shameful lusts of millenia, could sit and like each other without having anything in common in the way of food or desire. It was a stirring of his old, restless curiosity and he sat astounded at it. Jane seemed to know his thoughts.

'It's funny you and I are so friendly, M. M., and not a bit in love.'

He said something about George having been too quick for him, and suggested drowning the journalist while he slept. Jane observed her husband, placidly.

'He's too wicked to drown. And I'm not the kind of girl you want at all. I'm too English. You want someone more like yourself—a dark and excitable person.'

'I'm not excitable, surely?'

'Of course you are. *And* sentimental. This girl of yours who died, and your friend you killed so splendidly: they still live so much for you that they're killing your life.'

'Is that sentiment?'

'Yes. Pitiful, too, M. M. I know you've never really thought of that friend, either. He's just been an awful ache, a live abscess in your mind. . . . I think you've almost completely forgotten the girl. What was the colour of her hair?'

He pondered. A dim fairy smiled at him, colourless, across the years. 'I don't remember. . . . Well?'

152

'You've no right to forget—anything of her or of him. They're your life now. You're killing, while you keep them only abscess-alive, all the fine things they gave you to carry on. They can see and feel things only through you now: sun, moon, stars, and oh, all the rest of it: that pond there, and the Embankment under rain at night, and the fun of sleeping with a girl and seeing a baby twiddle its toes.'

She stopped, shading her eyes from the sun, and thinking. She was of all people he knew the least poetical and so could occasionally beat out poetry from sheer plainness of words. '*For these they gave their immortality*,' said a forgotten quotation.

'I'll certainly fall in love with you in a minute, Jane.'

'Oh no, you won't. Only with living again.'

'I don't think I was ever in love with living. It was something else.' He sought back through dusty memories. 'Religion, I think.'

'Religion?'

'Oh, not gods and prayers and altar-whinings. The light that never was. Something—some fairytale I lived. It had to do with the horizon and the Milky Way, I remember—Heaven knows why!'

She shook her head. George and the baby slept on the *Observer*, Goths deaf to its urgencies. They seemed very remote from the world of Chelsea.

'I'm not religious even that way. The good things and the plain things are what I want.'

'Sleeping with George and having his babies and—and eating kippers and toasting your toes in front of a fire?'

She took up the litany. 'And going through grass barefoot—we do every year on our holiday in Norfolk—and having a tide come splashing against your skin, and feeling sleepy, and sleeping, and. . . .'

'"And love it was the best of them and sleep worth all the rest of them." I agree. So what are you trying to make me believe?'

'Why, that love and sleep aren't the best of them—for you. You're meant for something different. You know you are. You'd

153

never really believe that thing you've just quoted—not though you lived it for years. . . . And that's why I like you, I think. That's why your friend did—oh, perhaps he was tired and sick as well in that wartime, but it was the real you he loved. Must have been. And the horizon and the Galaxy—they're still there, aren't they? There's still that Something you once believed in.'

He stared at her, half-startled. 'Once . . . Metaxa said that.'

'Your friend?'

He nodded.

'And he knew—he must have known. You yourself couldn't have borne to go on living if somewhere, deep down, you hadn't known it as well. . . . Sit and think of it, like a dear, and mind the baby. He's wakened again. I'm going to sleep down by that bush.'

The baby stopped crawling on the smooth, cropped grass. With determination in his eyes, his small posterior bulging, his legs strained and pillar-like for the great adventure, he was attempting to stand upright. He caught Malcom's eye, gurgled a little self-consciously, and promptly collapsed.

Malcom spent the afternoon teaching him to walk.

V

Next morning the Chelsea household overslept and George had to go without breakfast. The postman had brought a single letter. It was for the lodger and bore the Leekan postmark:

'DEAR MALCOM,

I have been long writing you but here I am now. We are all keeping well and getting on fine. I had a letter from Jessie in Canada and she was asking about you. Peter is foreman at Mains of Tulha. Tom and me manage the Chapel fine. It is three years come yesterday since father died. Tom has a lass now. Her name is Sarah Mondynes. She fell into a hole in the moor and nearly broke her legs last week. The hole was dug by Mr. Stevenson, looking for bones. He was asking about

you. We hope you are getting on fine in London. Tom saw the
Dominie in Leekan on Friday and he was asking about you.
Miss Domina is coming home for her holidays. She comes
every year. She comes by boat. Robert's wife married Jock
Edwards three weeks ago. They have gone to live in Dundee.
He is a butcher. That is all the news now so I will stop with
love from Lilian and Tom.'

Malcom took this letter out on the day's rounds and read it
at intervals and thought of Leekan. June. The hay would be
coming fine as—God, how many years before!—Robert, in the
filth of France, had seen it coming, that evening they sat together.
Robert, forgotten with all the rest of them, the 'bonniest ane'
whom he had adored in his shy fashion, who had lain in his arms
at the 'cotter hoose at Pittaulds'—she was now the property of
the broad-buttocked Jock Edwards whom he had kicked in the
broom-thickets of Leekan School. . . .

He sat and thought of that incident. He sat by the pond in
Ravenscourt Park, watching the ducks diving for worms, remembering Leekan, Robert, Jock Edwards. Jean—Jean something-or-
other, and Domina Riddoch, . . . The peewits crying and crying
down the sun-hazed Valley. The corn'll be coming fine.

He sat up. What was that but Robert, unforgotten, living in
him. Jane—who would have suspected her a poet!

A tramp came and sat down beside him and asked for money.
Malcom gave him a shilling and then disregarded him, and fell
to thinking again. His father, his mother, dark and still, his
boyish 'Azilian'—that boy who had practised gentlemanly ges-
tures on Stane Muir—Rita— Metaxa—Robert: if they were of
him, living and undead, all of them? For what? What had they
laboured to shape and bring to birth through him? Something,
surely, after all. . . . For what equipping of what dream-adven-
ture, all unknowing, had they lived and died?

And then, before his eyes, a vision in the sunlight weather, a
boy of five came up out of the years, stumbling and plodding,
a stone clasped in each small fist, his gaze upon the horizon. . . .

He ate his dinner in a fuggy little chop-house near Hammersmith Broadway. As he was going out the proprietor, a small, anxious man, called him back.

'Your pack, mate. Leaving it behind.'

'So I was.'

He carried it out and went down to Hammersmith Bridge and flung it overboard amidst a great circling of excited gulls. It fell, fountain-splashing, scaring a stray boatman. Malcom walked home to Chelsea, along the embankment, startling Jane at the washing-tub.

'Hello. No trade? Oh, if you've anything you want washing, bring it down to me. I've lots of hot water going waste. . . . Where's your pack?'

'It must be near Tilbury by now.'

'What?'

'You egged me on to do it. I dropped it over Hammersmith Bridge.'

Her eyes lighted up, placidly. 'You're mad. You didn't.'

'I did. I'm going home to Scotland for a while. Oh, I'm coming back. I must get away from London and think things out. You're to blame.'

'Have you any money?'

'I'm all right. I've about fifty pounds. Hello!'

He had felt something poke against his knee. It was the baby, Steven, pulling himself upright with a solemn determination.

CHAPTER TWO

THE WOMAN OF MAGLEMOSE

I

Two days later he was in Leekan, and the morning after his arrival was jerked out of sleep by the sound of a clear, cool voice below his window.

'Tom! Hello, are you in, Tom Maudslay?'

Tom? Still drowsy, Malcom sat up in bed and listened.

A low-voiced colloquy was taking place beside the garden wall. He could not hear a word of it. Once an ejaculation of surprise rose clear. Then a burst of laughter. Finally there was the sound of quickly retreating footsteps, as of those of a lightly-shod runner.

Malcom got out of the muckle bed wherein he and three brothers had once slept and put his head through the window. Directly beneath him his brother Tom, the short and ruddy farmer of Chapel o' Seddel, was standing, a canny grin on his face, staring down the road that led to the Valley. Malcom craned to look, but the steadings hid his view.

'What's the joke?'

Tom started and looked up.

'Hello, Malcom man. Sleep fine?'

'Fine.'

'That's fine. We've jist had a visitor to see you.' His grin deepened. His gaze strayed to the object he was watching cross the Valley.

'See *me*?'

'Aye, an she's comin back. You'll have to hurry up an come doon. Breakfast's nearly ready.' He shouldered the stable fork he had been leaning on, turned away, stopped, and grinned again, fascinatedly. 'God, I wish she bided in Leekan. She'd waken it up!'

'Who?'

But the exasperating Tom had disappeared into the byre. Malcom gave it up, indifferently, and, standing in his pyjamas, filled an early pipe. In the stable the three farm-horses clumped and tail-swished, each munching a swede. Lilian was clanking her milk-pails in the dairy. Malcom, pausing with lit match, was aware of some scent of the morning and the Valley momentarily puzzling him. He leant out of the window again.

Clover?

The Valley seemed drugged with the smell of it. He turned his head. Above Chapel o' Seddel, beyond its firwood, Stane Muir was being lit by the sun into polychrome sheets of fire—grey, wavering sheets of peatburn fading into the redshot yellow of wood-flame, into the golden purple of sacked palaces. . . . Heather?

Who the devil had the visitor been?

The sounds in the dairy ceased. Hurried footsteps below.

'Mal-com! Breakfast!'

He opened the bedroom door and leant over the stair-rails, demanding information.

'Lilian!'

His sister emerged from the kitchen, stumpy and red-cheeked as Tom, red-haired to boot, upturning a cooking-flushed, freckled face.

'Who was Tom's visitor?'

'Her? Och, that was only Miss Domina.' The Lowland Scots of Chapel o' Seddel, like that of the rest of Leekan, had been anglicized almost out of recognition in the ten years since 1914. 'She's hame at the Schoolhouse on holiday.'

'Domina? Domina Riddoch?'

'That's her. She came down the hill the noo nearly naked and I ran in, I was sic ashamed, and left Tom to go oot and speak to her. *He* didna mind!'

'Naked?'

'Gey nearly. Footba shorts and a vest. She'd been havin a run ower the moor before breakfast—to waken herself up, she told Tom. Found some rabbits in Tom's snares and killed them and brought them doon. . . . Gracious, that's yer bacon burnin!'

She fled. Malcom dressed, once or twice pausing to listen to the day-awakened Valley. Backgrounding the cry of the peewits, ceaseless as ever, was a sound as unending, but plangent, rhythmic—the plashing of the North Sea on the beaches of Pitgowrie. Chairs scraped in the kitchen. He went down and found Tom, Lilian, and the hired man—a colourless, ineffective youth, a nephew of Mayven of Cairndhu—each seated in front of an immense plate of porridge. Tom had a motorbike and sidecar and Lilian went to a picture-house once a week, but the porridge survived all changes. A smaller plate was set for Malcom. His bacon still frizzled in the frying-pan. No one else ate it at Chapel o' Seddel. He was being treated like the foreigner he had felt the night before.

'We're off to start hay-cuttin in the lang field, Malcom. But we winna expect the help you promised last night. The visitor'll be up for you at nine o'clock sharp, she said.'

'Impudence,' commented Lilian, fussing over Malcom's plate.

'Och, I dinna ken.' Tom swilled the creamy milk round his bowl, mixed it satisfactorily, took a long drink, and recommenced operations with his spoon. 'She's fine.' He grinned at his brother. 'Only dinna fa in love with her, Malcom. Ower much competition, they say, though you'll hae a clear day the day. "Tell him he can act as my beater," she said, when I'd given her leave to shoot rabbits up in the moor, and she'd found out you were here. "He'll do that fine," I said. " He's been a sodger and can dodge your gun a right." She laughed and then off she ran, licht as a deer, wi hardly a stitch or a steek on her. . . . God, she's bonny!'

The hired youth produced a faint smirk.

'Bonnier than Sarah Mondynes?'

'Och, Sarah's fine. Though she wears ower mony clothes a

the time.'

'Tom!'

This was Lilian. Malcom ate his porridge. His curiosity was mounting.

'This—it's the Domina Riddoch I used to go to school with, isn't it?' (Tom nodded.) 'I'd almost forgotten her. What does she want to see me about?'

Lilian ate bread and butter and marmalade. 'Hm,' she commented, expressively, but obscurely. Tom grinned again, without malice. He had turned out a cheerful character.

'Oh, nothing, I s'pose. Wants to see you. You baith live in London. She's a chemist there, ye ken. Comes hame for a holiday every year, an God, she aye manages to shock Leekan.' He turned to his sister. 'Mind that time in the kirk the year before last?'

The hired man guffawed, then choked on a final mouthful. Tom thumped the choker's back, helpfully, choking himself. Lilian compressed her lips. 'I mind it.'

'What happened?' asked Malcom.

'Och, it was only an accident. . . . It was, Lil. I dinna suppose she ever goes into a London church. D'you, Malcom? I wouldna myself if the picturehoose was open here on Sundays. . . . It was last year. She turned up at the kirk wi her uncle—the Dominie, ye ken. It was awfu hot weather, and the Reverend Stevenson's sermon was gey long an drawn oot. Aboot half the congregation was jist noddin in sleep when Miss Domina shook herself, pulled oot a case, cracked a match, an lit a cigarette. Auld Ian nearly fell oot o his pulpit. You could have heard a pin drop. And then she gave herself another shake, looked round aboot her, said "hell!"—we a heard it—dropped the cigarette, put her foot on it, an leaned back as though nothing had happened. . . . God, ye could hae lit another cigarette at her uncle the Dominie's face, it was so red!'

'Showin-off,' said Lilian.

'Och, she jist forgot. Anyhow, she'll soon be here, Malcom, an she wants you to bring some oatcakes on the jaunt. The

160

Schoolhouse'll supply the rest o the picnic, she said.'

Lilian got up. 'I'll pack you some in a parcel noo. You're gettin a fine day. . . . One thing, *you* haven't a wife who can cite her as a co-respondent.'

'A what?'

Tom gave a grunt and rose to his feet. 'You're in for it a. See you enjoy yoursel. Come on, Willie.'

Malcom turned to Lilian as they clumped out. 'Co-respond-ent?'

'Aye, she was, right enough. Twice. It was in a the papers.'

'*Twice?*'

'Aye. With only two years between the cases. The Dominie could hardly look a body in the face when the scandals happened in London. Puir man. And she wasna defended at the courts, and there's no speak o her marryin either o the divorced men. . . . Mrs. Greig o Redleafe was the only body in Leekan that spoke to her about them when she came north—and she got what she deserved, for she's a gossipin auld wife.'

'What did she get?'

'It happened in the post-office, and the news o it was a ower Leekan in an hour or two. Miss Domina just smiled at her, friendly-like, and said, "Quite true, Mrs. Greig, though I don't see how it's any of your b——" '

Malcom was refilling his pipe. ' "Bloody," ' he suggested.

'Aye.—"business, unless you're afraid I ask Greig to sleep with me. Give him my love and tell him I'll come and twist his nose if he calls to me across a field again." And out she went.'

A chicken strayed in through the open kitchen door, paused, chirawked urgently. Lilian glanced at the kitchen clock.

'Michty, she'll be here in a quarter of an hour! Run oot and feed the chickens, Malcom, while I get your parcel ready.'

A heat-haze already overhung all the Valley as Malcom crossed the courtyard. From the lang field arose the clang of Tom's mower and the hysteric barking of Tom's collie bitch in pursuit of a mower-roused hare. The chickens clucked and scrambled round Malcom's boots till he'd scattered them the last of the grain in the basket, abandoned the basket to a scuffle of inquisitive pecking, and himself climbed the steep grass bank that overlooked the road into Leekan.

Right across the Valley, unchanged, rose the Schoolhouse buildings. He stood and followed with his eyes the track leading down from there across the shelving ledges upraised of old by the Neolithic terrace-agriculturists. Deserted. Near Leekan River, however, just past the cotter-house where he and two others had sheltered one storming night in 1913, was a moving and nearing speck. . . .

He sat down and waited. Absurdly, he found his hands trembling.

II

He scrambled to his feet.

'Hello, Domina.'

'Hello, Malcom. Hell, isn't it hot?'

It might have been a tall boy—jacket, shirt, shorts, puttees, boots—who promptly sank down in the grass, almost into the place from which he'd risen. She shed her gun to one side, her game-bag to the other, tossed back her hair and looked up at him.

'You haven't changed much.'

'You have.'

They looked at each other in a queer silence, Malcom with sight of Domina's face grave in scrutiny, conscious that his own was as grave. He felt for his pipe. A little smile came on her lips.

'Well——?'

"She was twenty-five years of age, five feet six and a half inches in height, weighed one hundred and twenty pounds in the nude, possessed a mole on her right inquincal fossa and a scar across her left breast where six stitches had been sewn in after a motorcycle accident a few months before. A small head, brachycephalic, with exceedingly fine, blue-black hair growing higher on her forehead than she liked; accordingly, cut short except for a heavy fringe, like that of a medieval page. Lobeless ears. Eyebrows thick, but short-haired, meeting and matting in a level line across her nose. Straight, short nose. Eyes a little sunken, but set far apart, thereby, in combination with those brows which met across her nose, denying strict beauty and symmetry to her face. One eye a liquid bronze, but the other, startlingly, much darker: sometimes almost blue. Small mouth, full lips, the upper slightly overhanging the lower, and that in spite of the fact that her teeth bit as did those of the Cro-Magnon men: her upper and lower teeth met edge to edge, not in the scissors-like fashion of most moderns. Three or perhaps four teeth stopped; one, on the upper jaw, with a dark lead filling, to attract attention to her mouth in the same fashion as did the teeth-blackening of primitive prostitutes. Skin like a gypsy's skin: bronzed a deep olive from tip to toe through much exercise under-clad and much sun-bathing not clad at all. . . .

"Such daub for Domina, the sunlight wheeling on her beetle-wing hair that time we stared at each other above the courtyard of Chapel o' Seddel! A composite daub, over-smeared with later-learnt pigments, yet ineffective still. I'd ply the colours deeper yet if I thought she could ever live through any tri-dimensional art— procure the measurement of her ankles, an analysis of her tibia, an appraisal of her pituitary——"

'Well?' she asked again. It had been a silence of perhaps another minute. 'Do I pass?'

'Honours easy.'

Her hand swung out and touched the mere tips of his fingers as she jumped to her feet. She picked up her gun. She was almost as tall as he was. She smiled slowly, close to him.

'We used to head the bursary lists together, didn't we?'

'But he was right! Goodness, ever so right! A forerunner, your Metaxa.'

'How?'

'Why, this belief of his—about civilization. Everyone shares it now—or they soon will. Even the little professional thinkers share it. Read Rivers and Perry and Elliot Smith. The Darwin-Keith-Wells outlook is dead as the dodo. . . . Of course civilization's beastliness. There was never the raving primitive of the history-books. There was never the cave man with a club. (The damn lady novelists snooped round the Huxley laboratories and invented him as a copulative substitute, poor things!) There were the heroes of the Old Stone Age and then—the discovery of agriculture in one or two places—Atlantis and ancient Egypt. Seven or eight thousand years ago. And civilization burst on the world like a fever and an itch. . . . Goodness, the temperatures and the scratchings it's raised! Gods and kings and wars, priests and prayings and sacrifices. Man was man before these came with civilization. And for eight thousand years he's been an aberrant lunatic, with just now and then a glimpse of sanity. . . . Crikey, there's a deer!'

It was three o'clock in the afternoon. They were far in the broom-thickets on the western fringe of Stane Muir, and high above the Valley—so high that they overlooked both it and the sea. Even across this remoter distance the sea-smell was half-drowned by the smell of the hayfields. The Grampians strode up the northern horizon in purple robes. Remote beyond the miniature buildings of Chapel o' Seddel, cattle, like toy-automata, stood drowsing and tail-switching. Below them, leftwards, the sea-coast wound and rewound in splashes of grey, that were granite cliffs, in splashes of golden yellow, that were sand-dunes.

They had climbed and adventured, chased rabbits, shot them, missed them, talked and argued, lunched and drowsed in the sun, stirred themselves afoot again, crawled through brakes and thickets, waited by warrens innumerable since that meeting at nine o'clock. Domina's jacket had been abandoned on a menhir of the Devil Stanes; her khaki shirt, thorn-ripped, open-necked, was as mud-splashed as her shorts and puttees through a moment of excitement and misadventure in crossing a bog in response to the beater-hallooings of Malcom. Malcom, hatless, his single shabby suit stained green with mould, had suddenly found himself living and thinking again with an intensity that was startling.

They had begun talking to each other, intimately, unshieldedly, at once, the while they climbed from Chapel o' Seddel up to Stane Muir, without preludes of politeness or hesitation. What's this, and how's that? And where did you go from Glasgow, and how many girls have you had, and are you still a socialist and do you believe in God? . . . To be broken into abruptly by the bang of her shot-gun, her long-legged racing across the heather after a wounded rabbit, her shouted directions for him to drive the swarming game towards a point of vantage: Stane Muir swarmed with vermin which descended on Leekan in nightly hordes and devoured the crops. . . .

'Mal-com!' She'd appear out of clumps of whins, dangling a couple of rabbits, and throw them on the ground, and sink down herself, easily, gracefully, like a trim bird. 'Hear the banging? They came in a drove and I browned them. Missed most. Foul shooting.' She'd stretch out full length on the grass, hands clasped behind her head. 'Yes? Where were you? Bulford? . . . Go on.'

And he'd go on, sitting a yard or so away from her, looking down over Leekan, with an auditor who seemed startlingly not one person, but three—Metaxa in a fresh incarnation, Rita returned from the fields of asphodel, and the two of them welded in a strange amalgam, dominated, transformed, jeered at and bullied by the personality of Domina herself. . . .

Hidden together under a gorse-bush, watching a great open space pitted with the mouths of rabbit-runs, the sun in the mid-afternoon sky, he'd finished.

'And I've come up here to—think things out. I haven't thought at all since that night when I heard the screaming of Metaxa, impaled on the wire in the Beast Defile. . . . God, what thinking can answer that, what God or faith justify that horror?'

He'd sat for a moment with the brightness of the Stane Muir sunshine darkened by the awful memory that haunted his days. Not looking at him, she put out her hand and just touched the tips of his fingers.

Physically the most fastidious of beings, she had a horror of casual pawings and comfortings, and he was to learn that that light touch of hers was the utmost she ever admitted in casual caress. For a moment she'd been silent, biting a long stalk of grass with her even, Cro-Magnon-like teeth, and then turned to him.

'But he was right! Goodness, ever so right!'

IV

They lay and looked at the sunlight dappling the skin of the stray deer—a stag which had wandered down from the Grampians. For a moment the great beast, emerging into the open space of the rabbit-warren, stood and sniffed the air. Then it caught the dull glint of light on Domina's gun-barrel, wheeled, and cleared a near broom-thicket in one magnificent leap. They heard receding crashings. Domina whistled and jumped to her feet.

'That's the end of the bunny-business here. They'll all lie up with brain-concussion. Goodness, isn't it hot!' She glanced down at herself with disfavour. 'That's another disadvantage of not having lived eight thousand years ago—or five hundred hence.'

'What is?'

'Clothes, of course. Ugh, the beastliness of them! The fun to live in a time when a naked body or a naked thought didn't raise the sniggering of the padded civilized! Poets had sense when they saw Adam and Eve nude in Eden. One of those glimpses of sanity that haunted the world. . . .' Short, blue-black hair flung back from her forehead, she stood and looked down on Leekan; she

166

stood with a straightness that at a second glance robbed her figure of any boy-like illusion. Suddenly. 'And all this tremendous saga of yours, Malcom—all the things you've done and seen—Rita as well as your Metaxa—it stops being meaningless. There *is* a meaning.'

'I'd like to believe it.'

She made an impatient gesture. 'You *must* believe it. There's no other way to sanity. There *was* a Golden Age. We know it now. The legends didn't lie. Once upon a time there were neither metals nor wars, scandals nor clothes nor kings. Proofs everywhere: we'd have seen them everywhere if the last eighty years of science hadn't been infected throughout by Darwinism—oh, the blindest bats, the Darwinians! Eighty years of gouty formulas and fuzzy incompetence. The conclusions of biology clapped like a mustard-plaster on the skin of every living, healthy enquiry. Skinned alive we've been! . . . Cro-Magnon men, the people who painted the caves of Altamira, the matriarchal societies that lined the Seine when the Kelts came West—they were the last freemen in Europe for thousands of years. Let's make some tea, shall we? . . . Waken up, Malcom!'

'Eh? But—all this sounds sense to me. Sense at last. But—how does it help? We're a long way from the Old Stone Age. We're right in the middle of civilization——'

'Not us.' She had dropped her gun and was squatting gathering twigs for a fire. She looked round at him. 'You and I are proof to the contrary at this very minute.'

He thought and spoke slowly, looking down at her 'Because we're up here together—alone? . . . Isn't that proof how civilized we are?'

'Of course it's not. Goodness, proof that the horrible thing's almost past! If we were civilized—in Stage One of the disease— you'd be sitting austerely apart and waiting for me to cook your food and then share your bed; in Stage Two I'd be helpless and twitter and you'd be lighting this fire for me and oozing a ghastly patronage called chivalry and wondering how far you'd be able to go later before I'd scream! Instead of which. . . .'

Malcom heard his own laughter join with her clear, cool peal. He picked up the battered billy-can which had evidently done service in many a Schoolhouse picnic, 'I'm really not so helpless as I look. I'll bring water.'

They made tea, ate the last of the Chapel oatcakes, and counted the day's bag. Caches of corpses led progressively down towards the Devil Stanes. The sun was low above the Grampians. Domina lit him a cigarette and lighted one herself and sought her usual posture—the same one beloved of Metaxa.

'Lots of time. Let's argue some more. Where were we?'

'This Golden Age business. I suppose I'm stupid, but I can't see how it explains my—"saga." '

'But it does. You've been passing through the last stages of the illness. Like all the rest of us. Only with worse delirium. Brain-fever: that's all that civilization is. It fell on men and they fought and slaved and enslaved and imagined the filthy gods and built up the filthy social systems. World-madness and nightmare, a horrible film over the face of the earth—till the War came and split it from head to foot and men began to crawl out, shaking at the knees, sore-headed and dazed, but recovering from the disease at last——'

'Recovering?'

'Recovering. Haven't you seen? Climbing out of the pit of religion and morals and faith and fantasy and fear, escaping belief in authority and tradition, good and evil, gods and devils, heavens and hells, right and wrong. . . . Oh, the stuff clings to us still. Fevers *are* sticky. But it's falling to pieces around us daily. Like caked mud falling off us. And we're coming into our own again. That's what the years of your saga did, Malcom. Finished civilization. And it'll never come back.'

She laughed and sat erect. 'You should hear uncle on the subject. We're agreed on the collapse, but not on its desirability.'

'I can't even agree to the first. I see no signs whatever of the collapse of civilization. There are still towns and ships and aeroplanes and—shotguns.'

'These aren't civilization. They're things made by man in his madness! He tore up rocks and bridged the seas and counted the stars in his madness. And now he's wakened up to find all these implements and all this knowledge to hand, and he's going to use and improve them sanely. Splendidly. Resume again that Adventure the Old Stone Age men were out on when they lost and forgot it in the herding of cattle and the sowing of seeds and— and the castrating of eunuchs. . . . Atlantean man, Magdalenian man, Maglemosean man—coming into his own again. You're one yourself, Malcom, though you don't know it. Neither afraid of the world nor finding comfort in it. Only a challenge.'

'How the devil did all this come to you?'

She considered. 'Curiosity, I suppose. I'm an analyst, you know. And hating second-hand opinions. Found it out, read it, tried it out. Some thousands of people in every country now must know the thing—muzzily—from one angle or another. Some know it from all points.—Oh, I don't!'

'Supposing it's as you say—civilization's not the machine, and the machine can be carried on without it. What's going to do the carrying on?'

'Primitive communal anarchy. It's the natural association of all herd animals.'

'I've no fancy for the herd.'

'Can't help your fancies. It's inevitable. And even the ancient communes had chiefs—the men of wisdom. And the herd'll be a world herd of *men*—not the bestialized brutes that civilization has made of men.'

He lay and meditated this fantastic heresy that had yet such ring of sanity. Sunset was nearing Stane Muir. He looked over at Domina and found her looking past him, towards the sunset. An obvious question rose to his lips.

'And women—the business of the sexes?'

'What? Oh, we're almost beyond the divorce courts already!' Still not looking at him, something like a flash of amusement crossed her eyes. 'Primitive promiscuity, of course—with the aid of contraception, another weapon left from civilization's night-mare. In a few generations there'll hardly be a man alive who'll know his father, or, except in exceptional cases, care a tuppenny damn who his father was.'

Queerly, he thought of his own father. Any great loss, such severance of relationship? Was not indeed fatherhood the most artificial of claims? And the expounder of these outrageous opinions—what of herself?

'And how far do you accept that personally? Promiscuity? You're one of the women who've escaped or are escaping the codes and traditions. Supposing any chance acquaintance— myself—were to attempt to rape you up on this hill, what would you do?'

She abandoned the sunset. She looked at him from under raised, insolent eyebrows.

'Is this a proposal?'

'A hypothesis.'

'Oh.' The secret flash passed again across her eyes. 'It would depend. If I wanted you to, I'd go shares. If I didn't——'

'Yes?'

'I'd punch your head.'

V

'Droves of stars tonight.'

'Eh?'

It was an hour later. Rabbit-laden, they'd groped their way down through the Summer darkness to the circle of Devil Stanes. Around them now the ancient menhirs of the astronomer priests rose like ghostly sentinels of lost millennia.

'Stars, Malcom. Another herd just come out over there. Goodness, look at the Milky Way. I've never seen it so clear.'

Aldebaran. Betelgeuse. Venus low down in the west above the Grampians. And—unterrifying, the long-lost friend of Leekan boyhood—the arched galactic splendour of the central skies.

'Clear enough. Flat, like a biscuit, and we're somewhere near the centre.'

170

'I know. Centre of a finite universe. Einstein goes round it every morning before breakfast.' They stood and grinned together in the dim starshine. Domina again: 'Beyond the last shores of darkness—fun to know what was there!'

'We'll never know.'

'Why not? What are we alive for but to find out that?' She had left his side, searching for the jacket abandoned inside the circle earlier in the day. Out of the dimness: 'That's the Adventure that makes it worth while, now we've finished with gods and goblins. . . . Though we're hardly on the verge of it yet.'

'What?'

'Why, what all the Old Stone Age explorers were out on— what those Azilian ancestors of yours were on the track of when they set out for Argyllshire—the Expedition of Consciousness against the dead universe—and the Thing behind it.'

He was startled. 'Expedition——'

'Never thought of it?' A shadowy head appeared close to his own. All the Leekan night was very still, though growing colder. Here and there, in the Valley below them, the paraffin lights were kindling.

'Eh? Something like that—it was *my* private romance for years. Jules Vernesque stuff. . . . What kind of Expedition? Symbolic? Telescopes and spiritualists?'

'Goodness, no. Real. Actual. The plain Adventure we'll be out on again, now that the fever's over. Clearer every day. . . . Earth to the planets, to the fixed stars, to the Milky Way——'

'Yes?'

She was silent for a moment. Then: 'My game? Fun to play it! Why, then, somewhere beyond the rim of the Galaxy and the rims of time, ten million years and a day away, men'll reach the palace of God and storm it, and capture the engine-room and power-house, and then—and then——'

It was clearer. She was a starlit silhouette, struggling with a silhouette jacket. He helped her. She shivered and turned up her collar. But she made no attempt to move. He saw the faint sheen

171

on her stilled, upturned face.

'True—never anything half so true as that. . . . Though I've only this minute invented it. . . . Goodness, I'm to have children sometime—just that those Titans on the Rim of the Galaxy may have a little bit of me in them!'

Something flashed and quivered a whirling beam of light from the darkness of the coast. They waited. It flashed again. Todhead Lighthouse. There was the sound of a sudden yawn.

'The Adventure's challenge to the stars. See it, Malcom? Hell, I'm so sleepy!'

VI

"Domina of that day on the hills! Now that I pause and re-read what I've written, I seem, in my effort to explain how after a five years' mind-trance I began to think again, to have missed from the telling hours of that day that would clarify the evolution of Domina herself from an impish schoolgirl into an amoral anarchist. Of the story told as frankly as my own I've made no mention. For, after all—though I can see her, be-sworded, a reckless freelance amidst its future pages—this is *my* autobiography, not Domina's.

"She was a B.Sc. of London, a metallurgist specializing in phosphor bronze, employed in a semi-Government experimental 'shop' in Woolwich. Her salary was eight hundred a year.

" She had a flat in Chelsea, not half a mile along the Embankment from the house where I had been living with the Buxworths.

"She had allowed herself, at the age of seventeen, to be seduced by an acquaintance, a boy-officer in the Gordon Highlanders, who was killed in France a few months later, and since that first occasion—a very happy occasion—had apparently regarded the physical *dénouement* of sex-relations as a normal and healthy exercise, entirely unrelated to religion or morals. . . . But indeed, she looked at the latter things, in their conventional incarnations, much from the standpoint of a visitor at the Zoo inspecting spotted hyenas through the bars of a cage and vaguely surprised at their smell. . . .

"These, like journalistic headlines, becrossed the drowsy memory of her story as I undressed that night, and tumbled into the muckle bed of Chapel o' Seddel, and left to my subconscious the task of unravelling the day's impressions. But neither conscious nor subconscious grasped the fact that I had glimpsed but a single facet of a personality as vivid and varied and bewildering as the colours of a Stane Muir dawn."

VII

He was soon to "glimpse another facet"—dazzling, infuriating. Late in the afternoon of the day following the battle in Stane Muir a note came from the Schoolhouse inviting him to tea. It was a note in the clipped and angular hand apparently sacrosanct to the chemic mysteries of metallurgy, and was brought by one of the Dominie's scholars, who gaped when he delivered it, recovered, and fell into a garrulous account of an auld stane grave being dug into at that very moment by the Dominie and the minister. Up on Pittendreich's hill. And a the Dominie's class sent hame an oor earlier that they should hae been.

'A stone grave?'

'Aye. Ane o Pittendreich's men was ditchin round a bit hillock when the Dominie's niece—the leddy frae London, the fine ane that's aye laughin an can play footba so bonny—was speakin to him. His spade birred on a stane and the leddy kent it was an auld stane grave. So she sent him for Auld Ian an the Dominie an then came doon to the Schoolhouse hersel an bade me bring you the notie.'

By five o'clock Malcom had crossed the Valley and knocked at the Schoolhouse door. A new housekeeper was unnecessarily embarrassed over her befloured appearance. She had been making scones. 'You'll be Mr. Maudslay? Na, they havena come back yet. They're a up at the auld grave—carryin on daft-like.

173

Mebbe ye'll walk up an bring them doon?'

It was a field high up towards the rim of the Valley. In the centre of a shelving brae a grass-covered mound had lain unmolested for millennia, till Pittendreich's ditcher and Domina Riddoch had come upon it. Climbing to it, Malcom passed through gullies of gorse, and, turning once, beheld all the Valley adrift with a summer heat almost liquid. Then he came on the archaeologists.

The head of the mound had been shorn away. At the bottom of the pit lay a dismembered skeleton, doubled up on its right side, and singularly perfect. A little heap of stone implements was piled on the edge of the grave.

Domina and an old man were in the grave, kneeling, and measuring with a tape-line. Another old man, with a camera in his hand, stood and watched them, barking sharp comments. They did not hear Malcom approach, and it was a moment before he realized that the old man in the pit with Domina was the Reverend Ian Stevenson and the other the Dominie.

'The oldest Neolithic grave in Scotland,' the Reverend Ian was panting. 'Four or five thousand B.C.'

'But that lump of a thing—that axe. How could a Stone Age man have made it if he hadn't imitated a metal implement?' This was the Dominie.

His niece raised a flushed face, caught sight of Malcom, and laughed. 'Well, here's someone who ought to know. Azilian man.'

The old men turned and stared. Then the Reverend Ian wheezed bulkily in his broadcloth and wiped his hands and climbed out of the pit.

'Malcom!' He peered at the newcomer short-sightedly. 'Man, you haven't changed.'

'Nor you, sir. Hello, Mr. Riddoch.'

'Well, Malcom.'

They shook hands and stared at him, and looked from him to Domina, and seemed slightly uncomfortable. Domina in the grave wiped Stone Age dust from her hands.

174

'Let's go and have tea.' She put one hand on the edge of the pit and vaulted out of it, landing on her feet, like a cat. The Reverend Ian regarded the performance in delighted surprise. 'Could they do that in Neolithic times, Mr. Stevenson?'

He was gallant. 'There was nothing so bonny as you in those days.'

She was in a kilted skirt and sweater, dusty brogue shoes and stained silk stockings, but her dark hair and flushed face and limber figure made beauty enough against that colourful hillside. All three of them stood looking at her in pleasure. She glanced from one to the other of them, the secret flash of mirth for a moment lighting her unholily pigmented eyes.

'I know. But it'll all wash off.'

'I hope not.' The Reverend Ian again.

She took his arm. 'Come down to the Schoolhouse and we'll see. Tea?—Uncle?— Malcom? Oh——' She turned to the latter. 'We've found a job for you.'

VIII

'This job——' The Reverend Ian spoke the word apologetically. He put down his cup and looked across the Schoolhouse verandah at Domina and Malcom. 'It's not very well paid, I'm afraid, and I don't know if you would care for it. But Domina says you don't care very much for your present work as a—what is it?'

'Commission agent.' Domina supplied the euphemism softly. Malcom hastily raised an empty but grin-obscuring cup.

'Ah, yes, commission agent. One of those new freelance professions, I suppose? Well, the Hanno Society——'

The Hanno Society, a London organization of archaeologists, explorers, and such-like folk, had the Leekan minister on its council, and was at the moment seeking a paid assistant to act under the direction of its present unpaid but honourable secretary. An extremely difficult business. There were so few young men with either the necessary equipment or enthusiasm. He had mentioned the matter while they were excavating the mound on Pittendreich's hill, and Domina had declared it was exactly the kind of work Malcom was seeking——

'Well, Malcom?'

'But—have I the necessary equipment?'

Domina stirred in her chair. She had vanished after their descent from Pittendreich's hill and reappeared ten minutes later miraculously transformed, so that for a moment Malcom, rising with the others, had been aware of an acute sense of loss. There was no trace of the hunter of Stane Muir. In bland rose-red, a wisp of frock that was almost a tunic, shoes and stockings to match, she seemed to have casually sloughed a garmenture he had taken for a personality. This sleek girl out of the *Tatler's* pages—Domina! Her uncle had grunted. He had aged and grown peevish, quite plainly suspicious of his niece's intentions towards Malcom.

'Exercises to correct. I'll take a cup with me. Come up later, Ian.' And he had gone.

Now they sat finishing tea on the verandah and listening to Domina's flippant flouting of Malcom's hesitations.

'Of course he's equipment enough, Mr. Stevenson. He's soaked in all the old archaeological theories—all the dud ones that the Hanno people believe in. He won't come out of them properly for some time yet, and by then he can either desert the Hanno or start converting it. . . . Converting it, I imagine. . . . Do say you'll take it on, Malcom, if Mr. Stevenson can get you it. Great fun. In the enemies' camp, you know. They still believe we've progressed since the Old Stone Age.'

The Reverend Ian was genial and tolerant. 'Well, perhaps we haven't, Domina, and you're an original Maglemosean woman, uncorrupted, come back to tell us how much better they ordered things then. . . . No, I don't think we'll go into it again. I'm not so supple as I used to be and I just barely escaped with my life last time. . . . But what do you say, Malcom? Shall I write London and recommend you?'

'Splendid of you, sir.'

'Then I'll send off a letter tonight.' He rose. 'And now I'm going up to see the Dominie about those photographs. Come and see me in a week's time. There should be an answer by then and we'll be able to talk without this young woman of Maglemose'—he patted Domina's sleek head—'putting me out.'

The door into the Schoolhouse drawing-room closed behind him. Domina stretched and yawned in her chair.

'Decent old stick. Foul that he should be a parson. You haven't thanked me, Malcom.'

'I want to——'

'Oh Gawd!' She was on her feet, twinkling down at him amusedly. 'Let's go and smoke in the honeysuckle alley instead.'

'I can't be put off as easily as that. Only I suppose thanking you would be nonsensical. Those two days——'

He found himself in the Leekan evening, following a sleeveless figure in bland rose-red through the Schoolhouse garden, under the rustle of a gigantic yew, and on to the smooth grass carpeting of the honeysuckle alley. It was no true alley, but a secret garden, hid from the Schoolhouse by the waving plumage of the yew, sentinelled about by the honeysuckle bushes, and with no outlet at the further end, though a dip in the entanglements of honeysuckle lianas focussed a view of the evening Valley and remote Stane Muir.

Midway the 'alley' was a lichened block of red sandstone mounted with a cross-piece and gnomon much more ancient than the Schoolhouse. Domina strolled past it but Malcom halted and bent over the sun-dial. At no remote date an oblong section of the sandstone had been scraped and graved, amateurishly, but not unskilfully, and he read aloud the words round which besieging battalions of lichens were already preparing an assault.

> *'Th' uncertain day is mine in shadow-wars*
> *With splendour of the sun:*
> *But ah! the standing steadfastness of stars*
> *When all my hours are run!'*

177

'The old inscription was foul.' Domina had turned about and come to his side. 'Something about grasping the sunny hours with humble joy. Used to give me tummy-ache even as a child. So I spent a couple of days last year testing myself as a stone-mason—not to mention as a doggrelist.'

'I like a "standing steadfastness of stars." ' He straightened up. 'Those two days, Domina. . . . That stuff you talked about—the Adventure. What are we going to do about it? What's our job to help its beginning again in this collapse of civilization?'

She had bent over a clump of honeysuckle, a dismayingly altered and troubling figure. She turned round with a bloom in her hand. A drowsy bee fell out of it and boomed away into the evening.

'Do? Nothing that I know of, except heave a brick now and then at the bleary bards still squatting in the carrion-caves of civilization.' She looked at him over the bloom amusedly, impatiently. 'Oh, we can't always be serious. Life's so short, we've such a little while in the Adventure's march—and it'll march anyway, whether or not we try to help and organize it. . . . And it's a bit of a bore.'

He felt as though she had struck him in the face. 'Bore? What's the use of realizing the thing at all if you do nothing to help it?'

She yawned. 'No use.' She flicked the honeysuckle bloom over the hedge. Apparently it bored her also. 'What are *you* going to do about it, anyhow?'

He stared at the sundial. 'I don't know—yet. But something.'

'We have lit in Malcom this day such a flame——Me, I'm going to live. Who was that little poet man with the profile—I can never remember his name—the man who was going to live to kiss a thousand girls and write a thousand poems?'

'Brooke?'

'Was it? Well, I'm going to dance a million dances, read a million books, run a million metallurgical combinations, have a million lovers! I've thought——'

'Yes?'

'All those mothers of mine—I'm going to live the lives they

178

were cheated, collect and spend the wages that you defrauded them!'

'Eh?'

'Why, my own mother's, her mother's, *her* mother's, and so on back to the early Neolithic—all those poor damn women who went through hell to give the dirty peasants and priests and patriots and poets of civilization easy times and well-cooked food and all the crazy satisfactions of lust and torture and sadism which were yours. I'm going to live every unenjoyed life of those starved mothers of mine who were killed and eaten in cannibal rituals, starved to death, beaten to death, crippled in crinolines and ghastly codes, robbed of fun and sunshine and the glory of being fools and disreputable for over six thousand years. . . . And I'm going to get every woman alive to do the same!'

She stopped and laughed at herself and wandered to the hedge and plucked another idle blossom. But he had seen her face the face of a crusader.

'And where's all this emancipated female cavorting and caterwauling going to lead?'

'How should I know? Or care? . . . That's not our business. Goodness, no! Our children's, maybe, if we have any. Journeys end in mothers' meetings. . . . You men have made the world the dirty mess it is. So you've unchained us and expect us to clean out the Augean stable—still without wages. You don't mind us wearing grooms' breeches if only we'll be nice and respectful stable-lads. But we're not having any, none at all.' She swung round on him, abruptly, mockingly.

'Oh, Malcom, how long do you want me to sermonize? You *are* dull.'

'Am I?' He considered her. 'I suppose so.'

He took her in his arms then, and raised her face in the evening light, and kissed it. She kissed him in return with a cool, sweet deliberation. Cattle lowed in the Leekan pastures beyond the secret garden. She discovered an amused practicality.

'Let's go over there.'

They went over and Domina was tender and a little amused

and then kindled, waywardly, to a moment of passion that drowned them both. When he came out of that long kiss her head lay back on the grass and her throat was a white column in the dusk. She sighed and smiled up at him, whimsically.

'That was lovely. Adventure enough?'

He did not answer, being still a little dizzy. The love of Rita had been that of a passionate fairy, his chance lustings in the intervening years affairs small in range or experience. It was his first revelation of the fact that love of a woman's body might indeed ensnare a man his whole life long, even when that body had withered beyond desire and left only the memory of its magic to encolour and enslave all hope and courage and dignity. . . . They sat and smoked cigarettes, Domina leaning her shapely back against the sundial, Malcom asprawl at her feet. Suddenly he jumped up, startling her.

'By God, I never knew that before. You can see Todhead's light from here.'

She looked towards where he pointed, to that greyness in the mountain-block that marked the cleft to the sea. They waited. Whirling, a great beam smote the evening sky.

'By God!' said Malcom. Then: 'Eh?'

She had dropped her cigarette. She was clasping her knees and staring seawards as well. She laughed at him, but with an odd catch in her voice.

'Oh Malcom, my dear—if that—if that *were* the answer!'

IX

She went away next day, on a sub-visit to another uncle. Returning to Leekan a week later she learnt that Malcom, in response to a telegram answering the Reverend Ian's letter, had departed for London as assistant secretary of the Hanno Society.

180

CHAPTER THREE

THE RIDDLE OF THE GLYPHS

I

He was assistant secretary of the Hanno Society for over five years. He assembled and dispersed councils, engaged translators and corresponded with members, edited the quarterly journal of the society and carried out innumerable other offices. He became an expert in matters as far apart as the morals of Marco Polo and the fauna of Kerguelen. He talked with big-game hunters, explorers, archeologists, anthropologists, geographers, artists, flat-earth freaks, hollow-earth faddists, people who believed the earth went round the planet Jupiter. He travelled across England several times and across Europe once (to Prague) in pursuit of rare documents bearing on early exploration and discovery. And for four out of those five years an exasperated impatience drove his interests now this way, now that.

The secretary—the honorary secretary—of the Society, the Hon. Reginald ffrench, an ethnologist of the British Museum, was a small, polite, and agreeable man engaged in an unending History of Exploration. This was to begin with the voyage of Hanno and to end with Scott at the South Pole. His new assistant flippantly suggested beginning with Adam discovering the Persian Gulf and ending with the first explorers reaching the moon, thereby rousing interest in the first chapter with a well-known character and closing on a dramatic episode in the last. ffrench had been so long lost among manuscripts and crania and ethnic calculations that he took Malcom's flippancy for advice—at least with regard to the lunar explorers—and entered into correspondence with every 'expert' who had a 'rocket' in mind or being and sufficient mental glibness to believe he could send a projectile to the moon.

Those experts could be met at any hour of the day pushing through the swinging doors of the British Museum, under the cynical stare of the Maya priest one side the entrance and the Easter Islander the other. They would search out ffrench and stagger his politeness and credulity with large-scale diagrams and small-scale models. Inevitably they would wind up with requests for subscriptions. Sometimes they cornered him so desperately that he would ring up Malcom at the Hanno office in Bloomsbury Square, five minutes' walk away, and beg help towards a decision. This was a euphemistic phrase for scaring out his lunatic visitors. At Malcom's questioning they would wilt, pridefully, jocularly, or resentfully, and bang the Hon. Reginald's door with great force.

One, however, a retired major of artillery, proved to be of different quality. He kept ffrench and Malcom a long afternoon poring over his calculations and checking them as far as their knowledge of mathematics and ballistics went.

'With money and a Government grant and a proper lab.——' He sighed and smiled wryly. He had won Malcom's support, for he was neither showy nor cocksure.

'If your gun was for killing——'

The experimenter shrugged. 'Quite. I'd be mobbed with State offers of assistance if I intended to blow up New York from London. But the moon—oh, that's impracticable, and there mayn't be anyone shootable there.' He rolled up his plans. 'There's no such thing as science, you see. Quack-medicining and muddlement. There are hundreds of people who with leisure and proper equipment could really build a science of science and abolish unemployment and every other social question *en route*. Where? Everywhere—starving in doss-houses or working eight hours a day in coal-mines or nineteen hours a day as general practitioners, or what not. . . . Can't be helped. They're outside the scientist trade unions, and the B.A. yawns politely when it hears one or two of them annually.'

182

'But it ought to be helped. Parliament——'

The artillery major stroked a silver-grey moustache and stared at the Hanno's assistant secretary in amiable amusement. 'Parliament? What political party would bring forward a bill for the Handsome Endowment of Genuine Research? Might lead to the abolition of politics entirely. Damnable, what? And the moon's too useful as a repository of political promises to be tampered with. . . . Besides, it would need a pretty intricate test to separate the freak and sham from the genuine worker.' He smiled again. 'It has taken you two an afternoon.'

He was killed a month later at his bungalow in Sussex— 'blown up,' said the newspapers, and what became of his calculations or what led to the accident neither ffrench nor Malcom ever learnt. Besides, by then ffrench had secured a holiday and gone to Germany to interview fresh rocket men.

Malcom found himself astounded by a feeling of pain as over a personal loss. Why on earth should he be? Reaching the moon?

He went out of doors that night and stared across a quarter of a million miles of space at the giant reflector in the sky, that world of blazing deserts, ink-shadowed ring-mountains and tenuous breaths of atmosphere that mist the crater-bottoms under the telescopes of a Pickering or a Warren de la Rue. Remote and strange and not so very far! . . .

And then for a moment he seemed to understand that sense of loss he had felt at news of the experimenter's death. Domina Riddoch's fantastic visioning of human destiny, his own boy-dreams of the penetration of the horizon, the storming of the World's Wall—the symbol of the Adventure itself hung there across the wilds of space, challenged, if unconquered, by a fellow-adventurer.

The Adventure of men—How to read the riddle of the million roads that awaited it?

II

The Hanno specialized in publishing not only modern works dealing with genuine exploration so few in number out of the piles of MSS. which arrived daily from half-baked male globe-trotters and lady explorers who had not been even mildly grilled—but also reprints of the accounts of early travellers, like its contemporary, the Hakluyt. Most of the editing and translating was done free of charge by members of the Society, and for several years Malcom immersed his leisure moments in the writings of Ibn Batuta, Gonsalez de Clavijo, Jon Olafsson and others of even more remarkable adventurings and nomenclature: they fed his wonder-lust as once Flaubert's Matho and Spendius had done.

He had returned to the Buxworths' house in Chelsea, to the boisterous welcome of George and Jane and the sticky congratulations of Steven. Jane took a proprietary interest in his work, reading odd volumes of the Hanno publications and voicing her gladness that she had (in spite of this new view of civilization propounded by her lodger) been born in the twentieth century and not in one more primitive and undrained. The *Crocodile* had begun to flourish, and its 'literary' editor with it. Malcom had not been back in London three months before the Chelsea house was overhauled from roof to basement, the lichens evicted, the tiling renewed. The ceilings were strengthened as well, so that he could no longer carry on a conversation with Jane or George lying in bed below.

Jane's announcement that she was determined to have another baby Malcom suspected was a direct result of the new privacy. She and George wrangled over the matter in the manner of people arguing the purchase of a new piece of furniture.

'But what's the poor little rat to live on?' George would demand with some heat.

'Oh, he can become a literary critic, like his father. There are always funny little things writing books.'

'Or found a school of journalism,' George would snort. 'Nearly

184

everyone can blight. . . . Christ, Malcom, did you ever hear the like? Another kid when the two staple industries of England are book-reviewing and the "littery" vomitings of the unsmacked. "Littery" is just right. . . . Little swine. Ever seen them at their little troughs with their noses all pointed?'

'Who?'

'The aspirants to five thousand a year and the shoes of Shaw— "in your spare time, too." Look here, you've nothing on tonight. Meet me and I'll show you a selection.'

It never seems to have struck Malcom that the 'selection' of young writers which he scrutinized that night may have been far from representative, and that George Buxworth may have been— quite certainly was—a prejudiced guide.

"We pushed our way, as unostentatiously as possible, to the back of the room. It was crowded—mostly by young women with cigarette-holders, fountain pens, and negligently unbuttoned jackets. The evening's lecturer, a bloated little man like a toad which had hidden too long among lichens, I had never seen or heard of before. George had, however, and kept whispering biographical details omitted, I suspect, from *Who's Who.* . . .

"My brief career as journalist had never brought me in contact with fiction-writers. I learnt it was a good thing to steal magazine plots indiscriminately, because, of course, it wasn't stealing. They had all been used before. Another good point, when one took to writing novels, was to get acquainted with likely reviewers. . . . He thought bedroom scenes were being overdone, and foresaw the swing of the pendulum towards the more virile and open in fiction, though one must remember that Cannes, Lido, and night-club studies, with strong plots, were ever-popular. Detective stories——"

The young women sat around, scribbling busily, the only disturbing factor being, one gathers from Malcom, George Buxworth's frequent grunts and violent nose-blowings. At the end of the lecture came questions. What was the best length for a novel now? Did the libraries really insist on about 100,000 words, because their subscribers preferred thick books? Would 'moral experiment' novels go down? The lecturer's point about becoming acquainted with reviewers—wasn't it also a good plan to cultivate publishers' readers—invite them to lunch, and soon? . . .

'Bitches,' said George, succinctly, when they had groped their way out. 'Wish one would invite me to a lunch "in a private room." I'd give her enough copy for her next six novels—if she ever came out of hospital. Ever read their stuff?'

'Don't think so. What's it like?'

'They've got formulae—and technique, oh, the technique's generally damned good: they work things out in advance as an engineer blue-prints a bridge—for every occasion. . . . Stale unmarital beddings and kippers fired on oil-stoves: that's Bohemianism. Baedeker, Lane Poole, and a heterosexual native: that's Romance. A collier with complexes and an over-developed pituitary: that's Realism. . . . Christ, the young school of novelists!'

'And what's the remedy?'

'God knows. Drown the lot—especially the detective storyists—sadistic little swine!' They had reached Piccadilly Circus. They stood and watched the flickering of a film advertisement high up on the cliff-wall of a building. George knocked out his pipe, refilled it, and meditated. 'Though, of course, there are exceptions. Sometimes you'll open a young novel and find it naked as a knife and as clean as rain, without any of the dirty old swathings and stammerings. The kind of book impossible to any of the Victorians, or even to the Edwardians. Makes you believe in the first chapter or so that there's something new coming. But the promise never lasts. The damned thing either turns out a re-hash of Huxley-Lawrence phallus-worship, or a re-boost of the R.C.'s, or a wallow in psychanalytic cess-pools. . . . As though the author had stared out of a new window for a minute and seen nothing and pulled down the blind—with a shiver. . . . Eh?'

He found Malcom's cold-blooded blasphemy amazing. 'Nothing? But, Lord God! *Can't they see*?'

Apparently Jane won, for the new baby was presently forthcoming, and was christened Malcom George.

Before this event, the *Crocodile's* prosperity had run to a maid and a telephone and Malcom had suggested that it was perhaps time that he took up his quarters elsewhere. The Hanno paid him £300 a year—about the same as the Glasgow *Tribune* (now long defunct) had done. But the Buxworths would not let him go and reproached him for the effect his desertion would have on the health of Jane. So he stayed on, refurnishing the room himself and having a soundless typewriter installed—a machine into which one inserted a page of paper prayerfully, for the page was likely as not to be discovered inside the spring or the oiling-works as emerging on the roller.

He came into the habit of doing much of the Society's work in that room overlooking the River. Here also it was that he tapped out those strange sonnets and lyrics which were privately published by Harding under the title of *The Darkness Behind the Stars*. It was also in those early days that he began to meditate the beginnings of his immense *Autobiography*.

When he did not wish to be disturbed he posted a card outside his door. Sometimes he would hear Jane's feet on the landing below as she stopped to apprise herself whether or not he was at liberty to gossip. Steven had to climb further. He would pant up each step, sit down on the topmost one, and regard the card dolefully. Malcom would hear him and his shuffle of disappointment as he prepared to turn about and descend, and would generally relent and open the door.

''Splolin',' Steven would explain (he heard much of explorers), and grin ingenuously, and sidle past towards the bright and glittering machine on Malcom's table. The lodger told him innumerable stories, mostly paraphrases of narratives from the Hanno publications, and Steven, even thus early, had determined to become a traveller. He would pant up from the hall with messages, somewhat delayed owing to the necessity of ''splolin'' *en route*. Then thump agreeably on Malcom's door: ''Phone for Ma'com! 'Phone for Ma'com!'

'All right, Steve.'

'All ri', Steve. Phone for Ma'com'—urgently.

Late one afternoon, three days after the telephone was installed, he panted up to Malcom's room with the usual formula. Malcom, busied in writing a polite letter of congratulation and encouragement to a member of the Hanno—one Newman, who was about to investigate the geological formation of western Central America, and appeared to expect the outside world to regard his intentions with awe—abandoned his typewriter, went downstairs, and picked up the receiver.

'Yes?'

'Hello. Is that Malcom?'

'Yes.'

'This is Domina. . . . Say *Yes!*'

'Oh. . . . Where are you?'

'In bed.'

'Good Lord, what for?'

'Had an argument with a jar of acid in Woolwich. No, no-one threw it at me. Tests with some nitrates—and the nitrates won. . . . Oh, only a scalded arm and shoulder. But that's not what I want to talk about. Why haven't you looked me up in London?'

'Forgot your address.'

'Liar.'

He abandoned that point. 'How did you find out mine?'

'Girl who does illustrations for the *Crocodile*—Dorota Maxwell—knows Buxworth—knows me. Buxworth talks of you morning, noon, and night, it seems, and I recognized the prophet. . . . Are you listening?'

'Yes.'

'Then you'll know what to do now. I'm having tea in half an hour.'

He was admitted, by a maid of exceeding prettiness, into the barest flat he had ever seen. There did not seem to be a super-fluous article anywhere, except in Domina's bedroom where chairs and side-table were heaped with magazines, cigarette-packets, and unopened cartons of chocolate. A disingenuous camibocker garment which the invalid had been engaged in embroidering with one hand had been hurled into a corner of the room in boredom.

Domina was lying on her left side, facing the fire. Her right arm and shoulder were swathed in bandages.

She twisted round to see him, hurt herself a little, and swore. Her face was pallid, the heavy blue-black fringe disarrayed on her forehead, and her eyes too bright.

'Hello, Malcom. Look prosperous. Tea, Iris.'

A bare arm came from under the eiderdown to meet his hand. She nodded, expectantly. He bent and kissed her, covering his mixed feelings with: 'Why on earth do you use scent?'

'It's the harlot in me,' she explained, and put her head down on the pillow again, and twinkled at him. Abruptly, moving, she winced. Thereat he put his arm under her, raised her up, punched the pillow and rearranged the sheets.

'Thanks. You're my only man visitor who has any sense. They mostly dither and call for Iris.'

He learnt that the accident four days before had been serious enough. The whole of her shoulder still burned like fire. She had fainted, but had recovered in good time to refuse the sanctuary of a hospital. She had a horror of hospitals and being pawed over by callow and aseptic hobbledehoys in search of experience.

The maid brought in tea while he was telling her of ffrench's lunar explorers. In the midst of laughter over a Rügen rocket which had fallen off its pedestal in a field and killed a straying and enquiring cow, she suddenly reverted to his failure to call on her.

'Why?'

He had foreseen that question, but had no answer ready. He sat and looked in the fire, searching for the answer. It proved incredibly difficult. He put down his cup and got up and walked

189

to the window and looked out at the Thames. He turned and found her eyes on him.

'Because—Good Lord, you don't think I didn't want to come? Especially after that incident in the honeysuckle alley—oh, even though there was no chance of a repetition! . . . I've wanted to at times, quite damnably. But you spoiled me for these things that day on Stane Muir. You painted a clear picture of something that has haunted me—dimly—all my life: the Adventure. And I'm going to follow it—like hell. You preached a view of human history and civilization that was like a revelation to me: I'm going to pass it on to others, if I can. . . . To you they're just melodrama and mud-slinging. To me they're worth more than you or any other human being.' He paused. 'I must sound the damnablest of prigs. I kept away from you because—I thought you immoral, I suppose.'

She nodded to that, understanding. It had nothing to do with her lovers. She had turned to the pillow and he saw her face in profile, the black silk eiderdown leaving sharp and clear her pallor of neck and cheek up to the darkness again of her hair, her insolent upper lip a little relaxed, the long, thick eyelashes drooping beneath her brows—like a swift line painted from side to side her face, those brows.

'Perhaps I am—immoral. Sometimes I'm sure of it myself. I want—oh, all the things I said—and did!— in the honeysuckle alley. But the others as well; I want the lot, Malcom! Melodrama and mudslinging? Goodness, do you think I haven't seen the real thing as well—that it hasn't made me drunk and frightened? But how real is it, and how many realities are there? And what the devil can one do though it's the only one?'

She moved impatiently. She whispered to the dancing firelight. '. . . God and Mammon. . . . But I'm God's man, Malcom, if you can find him for me.'

IV

Presently she had recovered and returned to work with her mysterious metals in Woolwich. George, entering Malcom's room one evening and finding his lodger struggling into evening dress—a shoddy, ready made suit he had bought that day—shouted with laughter and, unkindly, summoned his family. Malcom stood in front of the mirror doing futile things with his tie the while the Buxworths, George, Jane, and Steven, sat on his bed and regarded him with mirth. George declared his preference, any day, for a proletarian hawker to a boorjoy archaeologist. . . . He wanted to know who the skirt was.

It was two o'clock in the morning before they left the ball and walked home along the Embankment, Domina cloaked and in silver shoes and bare-headed as usual. They stopped at one point and looked down at the gurgle of the Thames. And Malcom made a sudden discovery.

'The worst of Mammon, you know, is that he's such a bloody bore.'

'Who?'

'Mammon. The castrated Mammon. Dressing up and dancing and playing and galumphing to music, eating unnecessary food, drinking unnecessary drinks, swinging unnecessarily squawking squaws round a room by their unnecessarily shaved armpits. What a bore, even though there was nothing else! . . . Lord, how I'd like to help clean a sewer now or spread manure on a turnip field or—anything that's real!'

'But exercise and amusement. . . . Malcom, that's just the old Presbyterian in you.'

'Is it? He's real, anyhow. Exercise and amusement—when there's *that*!' He pointed to a frieze of stars above the Surrey bank.

Domina kicked a silver shoe against the parapet. 'You're obsessed. Those stars—what can you do about them? How are they to take the place of dancing and singing and fun?'

'If I knew!'

191

She lighted a cigarette, found it distasteful, and flung it into the River. They watched it sail down through the darkness till the water extinguished it. For a second its sharp aroma was left in their nostrils. Domina yawned. 'I'm thirsty.'

They had coffee at a small stall, deserted but for themselves, a rickety, frowsy contraption whose proprietor recognized Malcom from his hawker days. He glanced doubtfully at Domina after he had served them, and then, winking at Malcom, became hoarsely confidential.

'I don't know,' said Malcom, and then was aware that his own hushed tones were ridiculous. 'Wait.' He turned to Domina and explained.

'And you can't tell him? I should think it's the first thing to make sure of in the organized Adventure. Men!' She laughed. She was angry. 'Five children already and his wife too shy to find out? Tell him to come over here.'

She entered into a startlingly direct conversation. She wrote down several addresses, and the coffee-stall keeper's sweating confusion passed into gratitude and relief. When they left she was silent for a little and then laughed inconsequently.

'Remember pointing to the stars? Where's Venus?'

Malcom laughed and touched her hand, admiringly. '*You* are real enough, anyhow.'

The morning was growing white above the Thames by Westminster. Domina yawned and peeped at him darkly, from under her long lashes.

'Don't feel a bit sleepy, but we must get warm. Let's toss to see who's going to do the entertaining.'

So he tossed a penny, Domina called heads, and the penny fell outside the radiance of the lamp under which they were standing. They searched for it with a match and a policeman came along the deserted pavement and stood and considered them suspiciously. It was heads.

He took her up to his room, turned on the gas fire, went down to the Buxworths' kitchen and made cocoa. When he came back he found her asleep in his armchair. She heard him coming and woke and smiled and he kissed her and they forgot the cocoa.

Next morning Jane did not enter, but woke them with a discreet knock and a tray with two cups left on the mat. They had both overslept and Malcom went out to find a taxi to take Domina to her flat and then to Woolwich with all speed. When he came back he found her sitting in the kitchen discussing domesticities with Jane and running her hand through Steven's hair. Jane and she had established complete understanding.

'But don't you want a baby?' said Jane.

'Often. But I don't want a husband. . . . Goodbye, Steven. Kiss Auntie Dom. Goodbye, Mrs. Buxworth.'

'Goodbye,' said Jane. 'Come often.'

Domina's secret smile peeped out at them.

'Not *too* often.'

V

Almost daily, passing into the British Museum, he found his eyes travel from the enigmatic stare of the Ancient Maya priest to Laurence Binyon's lines engraved in smoky indistinctness on the Museum façade. There seemed some subtle connection between them.

> *They shall grow not old, as we that are left grow old,*
> *Age shall not weary them, nor the years condemn:*
> *At the going down of the sun and in the morning*
> *We will remember them.*

Nor had he ever forgotten Metaxa's Mayans or that long-lost book of the Abbé Brasseur's he had bought in Paris. They had merely receded into the mist-land of memories along with Metaxa himself. In the years from 1918 onwards they had seemed to fade to meaninglessness with other foetal dreams and enthusiasms.

But now he began to find remote images and phrases stir to the challenge of the stela-cast. He would see again the Picard shell-hole, hear again the fantastic theorizing of the one man he had ever loved. '. . . the key to all the secrets of life and death and time. Perhaps the undeciphered glyphs contain the key to even—*that*.'

And he would see the Greek's handsome head nod towards the twilight and the Saxon lines, and then the picture would roll up like a scroll and vanish, and, a little heavily, he would trudge through the corridors to ffrench's department or enter the Reading Room for an hour's immersement in reports from the battle that was already beginning to split the ranks of historians and archaeologists.

For the leaders of the heresy championed by Domina on Stane Muir were assailing the comfortable certitudes of half a century, and the startled evolutionists were retorting with a barrage of invective and insult. A fight affecting the very foundations of human society, it went unnoticed in the Press. Not so in the Hanno Society. Malcom discovered members who would have delighted in burning the heretic diffusionists as an auto-da-fe in the middle of Bloomsbury Square. He had difficulty in preventing each issue of the Society quarterly from developing into a concentrated assault and battery on Professor Elliot Smith and his lieutenants. He himself, his sympathies instinctively with the root-beliefs of the heretics, maintained a disappointed neutrality.

For this new-old view of history—that man, like the other anthropoids, had been originally a decent and kindly animal, no blood-drinking ghoul of the fevered Darwinian imagination; that civilization—wars, cruelties, gods, agriculture, temple-building—had been no more an instinctive and inevitable development in the wide-scattered communities of the early world than it is instinctive and inevitable for an orang-utan of the forests to develop the tea-drinking habits of his kinsmen in the Zoo; that with the passing of civilization's codes and tabus the aberrant horrors of ten thousand years might pass away as well: with all these opinions Malcom agreed. But the diffusionists enormously weakened their case by maintaining that civilization first arose in but one locality, and that locality Ancient Egypt. To Malcom it seemed plain that the germs of the world-disease had fecundated in at least two or three localities, and spread about the world and met and overlapped and stewed to a greasy ferment. . . . He devotes a large portion of his *Autobiography* to proving that Ancient Atlantis, the home of Cro-Magnon men, was the continent from which the early American civilizations originated. He goes on, rather naively, to upbraid the diffusionists for not following out their conclusions to the logical extreme and attacking contemporary religion, morals, ethics, politics. "Domina is the only logical diffusionist I have ever met."

But, looking out at the world from the windows of his Bloomsbury office or his room above the Thames, it needed something of the faith that moveth mountains to believe in Domina's assertion that the War had liberated men from the civilized code and habit and outlook. Religion, reinforced by the dreary mummeries of a shamanistic spiritualism, held its own; it did more. It invaded the ranks of the physicists, stormed their laboratories, and retired triumphant with the rather shaky and illegible signatures of Einstein and Eddington appended to a Declaration of Faith that there was Really an Anthropomorphic Something. The jerry-built commercialism misnamed capitalism had been propped and pilastered anew on the bones of the dead. *It* showed no sign of collapse. Demos, unaltered, unchanged, sporting, obedient, fatuous alike in his grovelments and growlings, grubbed an unchancy livelihood in commercialism's packed cellars or starved and whined on unemployment doles. Below them all the faces of the ancient lowly still haunted the imaginations of men like Malcom.

> *'Oh, slain and spent and sacrificed*
> *People, the grey-grown, speechless Christ!'*

'Well, what are we going to do about it?' Domina would demand. 'Join the Labour Party and get presented at Court?'
'Co-respondents aren't eligible for either honour,' he would

tell her, severely.

'Oh, I forgot,' she would say, contritely. 'These little habits——'

'But seriously, what the devil *are* the intelligent people who think like us to do?'

'Nothing. Leave it alone. There's nothing to be done with it. For an archaeologist you lack perspective, Malcom. The world'll cure itself. It *is* curing. Civilization's rotten right through, and all this religious revival and war-mind and so on—they're just temporary back-ripples on the tide——'

She failed to follow her own advice with the coming of the General Strike of 1926. She deserted the Woolwich 'shop' and, undaunted by Malcom's declaration of neutrality, hired a motor-cycle and sidecar, packed an admirer—possibly one of the co-respondents—into the sidecar, and toured the home counties distributing *British Workers* and egging on the strikers generally. George Buxworth, with a grin, enrolled as a defender of law and order, wore a special constable's brassard, and appeared to spend most of his time collecting exhausted revolutionists and shepherding them inside Jane's kitchen and outside cups of cocoa. Malcom, retiring to his room for nine days' neutrality, abandoned his *Autobiography* and devoted himself to the writing of the propaganda novel of 'primitivism' which George Buxworth had urged him to attempt.

He had finished a third of it when the strike ended. Domina, unrepentant and apparently indispensable, went back to the Woolwich 'shop'; and George climbed the stairs to see how his lodger was getting on.

He sat with the MS. in one of Malcom's arm-chairs and grinned and chuckled and wiped streaming eyes as he went through the pages. 'Hell, M. M., you'll be the death of me yet! Life with a vengeance—without fig-leaves or cherry-blossom.' He finished it regretfully. 'It's the kind of thing James Joyce used to dream of before he mislaid his English dictionary and took to writing in a mixture of shorthand and Irish.'

'Well, what are its chances?'

'You might get it published in Milan—or in the millennium.'

And still the enigmatic Maya stela looked down on his diurnal journeyings into the Museum.

What if Metaxa's jest had been no jest? What if the strange tribes of Atlantean refugees which descended on Central America in 200 B.C. had indeed in their isolation developed some primitive approximation to twentieth-century civilization, and fought the thing, and failed to conquer it, and left enshrined in their unread writings account of both fight and failure?

Unread?

Half-amused at his own romancing he began to read books on the Maya problem; in a fortnight's time he was attacking the subject with the sharp-edged singleness of purpose of an athlete who had at length found a contest worth his training. He revived his early Spanish with the aid of a private tutor at the Berlitz School, and at the same time, in the Museum Reading Room, plunged into study of every document which dealt, even remotely, with the pre-Columbian Central Americans.

He was no more an ideal archaeologist, I think, than he was an ideal writer. Both trades were auxiliary to his purpose and dream. But within a year he had as good a knowledge of the Maya and Mayan quarter-history as may be obtained from the written materials—mostly speculative or commentary—at the disposal of the modern world. Then, with the confidence of ignorance, he set about learning the modern Maya language.

He unearthed two grammars in the Reading Room and struggled with them for a month, discovering an insane language with innumerable rules, no examples, and marshalled hosts of exceptions so numerous that "a Maya conversation must have been fought with nothing but irregular troops." The reality was, of course, that the Maya tongue, evolved and used far from Europe, made no submission to Western grammatical rules, least of all to those of out-of-date Latinists. Thinking that there might be more modern works, he consulted a Spanish publishing house. It had never heard of them. And then a chance meeting put fresh materials into his hands.

It was at the Luxembourg frontier, returning from his single journey across Europe. A fellow-traveller, a tall, burly man with hair as black as Malcom's own, had his luggage strewn in front of him and was hard beset by officials. His knowledge of French appeared to be as limited as his knowledge of German. He appealed, in desperation, to the waiting and stamping queue.

'¿Hay alguien en este cuarto que hable español?'

Malcom sought among Castilian accentuations. 'Si, señor. ¿Que se lo ofrece?'

The burly man was a Yucatecan, a sisal-grower attending some exporters' conference in Berlin. He travelled to Paris with Malcom, heard of the latter's difficulties in the matter of Maya grammars, and promised to do what he could in the matter.

A month later Malcom received a small package from Merida in Yucatan. The package contained a tattered little volume, together with a letter of much courtesy and advice from Sr. Benito Torres, the distinguished Americanist. Maya—it was practically impossible to learn it from a textbook. Why not come to Merida and learn it orally? Sr. Torres proved himself a philologist, and covered several pages with remarks on the Maya language. The little grammar he enclosed was a copy of that compiled by Pio Perez, and much used by Le Plongeon.

Malcom abandoned the Museum for a time, and set about devoting his spare hours to study of the horrible tongue presumably used by the temple-builders of Xibalba.

George or Jane would occasionally climb to his room those Spring or Summer evenings of 1927, and attempt to drag him out to a theatre or picnic; they would sit on the bed and turn over photographs of Maya objects—probably the most depressing-looking objects in the world—and ask him irreverent questions about the ancient civilized cannibals. Did they prefer it stewed or grilled? . . . Steven would stare at the temple-photographs and say 'Pritty' in a bored tone. The new baby, Malcom George, was still at the stage of somnolent uninterest.

Domina was member of a Thames boating club. She insisted

on Malcom joining it, and he developed considerable skill and thumb-callosities as results of long, solitary rows from Chelsea to Mortlake and back again. But of Domina herself he saw less and less. She appeared to have abandoned many of her social gaieties, and, transforming a room of her flat into a laboratory (after shameful wheedling and bedazzlement of her landlord) from which would issue dreadful stenches and occasional flares of fluid metal, experimented in pursuit of some German research prize. Young men arriving to take her to one or another promised amusement would be blandly turned away by the pretty Iris, or else admitted and conscripted as unpaid and unhonoured assistants in odoriferous and frightsome operations.

She alternated those absorptions, however, with light-hearted "orgiastic weeks" in which Malcom had no part. But twice, returning homewards late at night and attracted by the light from his window, she dismissed disgruntled escorts and climbed up the Buxworths' stair to lounge in their lodger's armchair in glistening garments and enjoy herself by attacking Malcom and the Maya impartially. . . . They were merely an insanitary Neolithic people: Mongolian and Red Indian in stock: well-known facts from the shape of their heads. As for their unread glyphs, so far from being alphabetical, they were probably the crudest pictographs; and the Maya themselves, so far from being in any way mysterious, were trite and obvious both in their history and their religion. They meant nothing to modern life and modern needs. . . . As for Malcom, he was the unsubdued romantic, creating fanciful pictures in the forests of pre-Christian Guatemala, because he shirked twentieth-century Europe.

He told her about Metaxa and the poppy-field of Picardy.

'So this Maya study now—it's a kind of sacrifice to the manes of Metaxa?'

'Don't be an idiot, Dom.' He yawned and stood up, and hunched himself against the window, his hands on the sill and stretching himself in some weariness, looking at her with remote eyes. He had never forgotten Jane Buxworth's words that Sunday on Putney Heath. 'It's search, not sacrifice. And maybe all that

Metaxa wanted of himself to survive survives in me now. I am as much him as I am myself in lots of those things: more, I sometimes think.'

He yawned again, very weary, and bent his head in his hands, and Domina has told me of a swift and vivid and foolish thought she had at that moment, looking at him—that he was neither Metaxa nor Malcom, but Man himself. . . .

VII

Gradually, out of all those months of study and concentration, he began to upbuild in his mind, in speech and gesture, thought and belief and habit, the people who reared the great cities of Chiapas, Guatemala, Honduras and Yucatan, set the dated stelae in their plazas, and lined those stelae with pebble-shaped glyphs in the days when Christianity was dawning in Europe. And all this was but a preliminary to an intensive study of the undeciphered glyphs themselves.

In mid-April he resolved on a fortnight's holiday before beginning glyph-elucidation. He went down to a little town in Devonshire, taking with him, with a kind of shamed cunning in his attempt to cheat himself, a copy of Förstemann's book on the Dresden Codex—one of the three surviving Maya MSS.—and a large photograph of the most mysterious piece of sculpture in Maya art: the Sacrifice of the Temple of the Sun in Palenque, depicting two priests engaged in mystic devotions while to right and left stand column on column of calculiform characters, unread and unapprehended for over eighteen centuries.

His first day at the seaside town he passed in bored misery, wandering the sand-dunes or the inland muddy lanes where the Spring was so burgeoning. In the evening he walked the beach under a great globular moon and every pebble he kicked reminded him of the quest he had resolved to forego for a fortnight.

Next day he gave up the pretence, stayed indoors, and set to work on the glyphs of the right-hand panel of the Sun tablet:

those glyphs which stand behind the most perfect figure in Maya sculpture. He disregarded everything which seemed to bear any allusion to a date. Sun and day, moon, weather and numeral signs, all known since the discovery of Bishop Landa's manuscript or slowly spelled out by German and American investigators, too frequently misled the modern investigator. Also, it seemed to him that the probable solution lay, not—as usual—in concentrating on a single glyph all the student's erudition, but in attempting to read the glyphs in groups.

He had accustomed himself to steady hours of uninteresting work for the Hanno Society: He had soaked himself in Maya lore for over twelve months. But he had never endured such mental strain as on that first day, and at the end of it he was no further advanced than at the beginning.

Next morning he abandoned the first two glyph-columns—they are read in pairs—and took to the next two. And there, presently, it seemed to him that he had found a clue: a sign which he was certain represented the single Maya word 'long lands.' It was about noon when when he came on it, and his excitement in attempted checking and verifying was too much for his unreliable stomach. He hastily abandoned both his lunch and his original plan of studying the glyphs in groups. Instead, he commenced the detailed investigation of each character.

And then took place one of the most tragic and thrilling events of his life, and of all the explanations of it that were afterwards advanced to him—mental collapse, delusion, and what not—he never found one that was satisfying, not even Domina's triumphant assertion that he had somehow tapped back through the 'time-spirals' to the minds of the original sculptors of the Palenque panel, fascinating though that supposition was.

Without a scrap of evidence to support the statement he records his belief that he succeeded, glyph by glyph, with here and there unfilled gaps, in elucidating the entire inscription on the Tablet of the Sun.

Of that his memory remained quite definitely assured. But it was memory of watching another man seated at work and making discoveries at which the spectator peered ineffectually. Glyph by glyph he elucidated the inscription which has puzzled and enthralled all Americanists for the past hundred years and has stood unread in the Chiapas forests for over eighteen centuries. At the end of four days all that remained for him to do was to work out a coherent rendering of the inscription. Because of the peculiar twist of Maya thought and speech and script, he was in the position of one who had all the letters of a puzzle in his hand—a gigantic anagram—but with still the work of setting them in a frame so that they might coalesce to meaning in the eyes of the alien European.

It was a windy night of stars in his sitting-room when he arrived at that stage. He was to remember having the windows wide open and leaning out to look at the sea, and noting the rising of the gale. As he turned away from the window the curtains bellied wildly behind him, but he sank into a chair and clenched his temples over the beginning of a headache which threatened to split his skull.

Next morning, his room a wreck from the effects of the gale, he was discovered raving in some species of cerebral fever, and while his landlady, greatly upset, was fetching a doctor and sending a telegram to the Buxworth address in Chelsea, his transcript of the Maya inscription was (he was afterwards convinced) drifting far out on the winds of the English Channel.

"Poor Metaxa!"

VIII

George Buxworth came down from London, stayed four days, saw Malcom's delirium abate and pass, and had him taken to a nursing home. George assumed airs of shocked remonstrance. 'Cerebral fever? Good God, Malcom, it's a novelist's disease!'

Domina also came down, though she was not allowed to see the patient. But she and George, going back, took upon themselves to interview the Hon. Reginald in the British Museum and obtain from him three months' leave of absence for his assistant—granted very willingly and kindly by the Hanno, with Malcom's ordinary salary left uncurtailed.

It was his first real illness since childhood. He lay helpless and fretting in the nursing home while his late lodgings were turned upside down in search for his lost transcriptions, and the sunshine danced outside on the clean-smelling waters. He would wake and doze and wake again to that sunshine and sea-smell and fret his temperature up to improbable heights as he thought of his desperately wasted labour over the Palenque panels.

Domina came on the scene again, six weeks later, when he was convalescent and sitting on the veranda of the nursing home meditating his return to London. She held his hands, gravely.

'We're going for a walking-tour,' she said.

He seemed in robust health but for the nervous twitchings of his hands. 'I can't. I've got to go back to London.'

'Harvest's early down here this year. We'll meander up through Cornwall, sleep in ricks and steal milk from cows in the early morning. Take a hotel now and then, when the weather seems dangerous for you. But it's going to be a perfect fortnight. I know it is. We've got a whole fortnight to spend.'

He was moved almost to weeping with irritation at her density. 'You're talking nonsense. I've got to find out about my lost transcription and then go up to London and see the Hanno——'

She stamped her foot, though the peeping smile came from under her long eyelashes.

'Then it's me or the Hanno, Malcom.'

He fretted at her, his hands shaking. 'Don't be an idiot.'

'I'm very serious. You see, I've won my research prize. I'm going to Germany for a year. Sailing in three weeks' time.'

They went west into Cornwall for a week and then turned northwards. The weather up to the time of their setting out had been doubtful, but they followed on the skirts of halcyon days that took their thoughts back to the Leekan holiday two years before.

Domina, hatless, was clad in the simplicity of a tartan kilt-skirt—a tartan to which she had not the remotest claim—an open-necked sweater, and low-heeled brown shoes with those over-flapping, be-slashed tongues beloved of Gleneagles. Her only luxuries of apparel (Malcom compared her to a tramp steamer with a state room) were the silk stockings and under-clothes for which she had such a sensuous passion, on which she spent a tenth of her income. . . . Of all sounds of the Cornish roads Malcom was best to remember that dim and faery under-rustle of silken garments.

He himself was in ready-made flannels, hatless also, upheld by an immense walking-stick, and carrying their joint luggage in a tourist's pack: pyjamas, towels, a comb which presently aged to a grinning toothlessness, Malcom's razor, soap, a ground-sheet, two feather-weight mackintoshes, an elaborate saucepan-kettle-teapot, a pound of chocolates (constantly renewed), Carlyle's *Past and Present*, and a copy of *Comic Cuts*.

'If you fell down a hole and got killed with that lot,' said Domina, cheerfully, 'wouldn't the archaeologists of the future have a devil of a find!'

It weighed light as a feather on Malcom's shoulders as he swung along the roads, up long, meandering paths, down through sudden gullies to the sea, the sunlight browning his skin, his nerves reasserting control, and something like happiness in his heart.

Domina, sometimes beside him for long, quiet minutes, on other occasions would vanish into wood or thicket or up some shelving hill-side—for no particular reason except that the Summer was in her blood, every copse a mystery, every glimpsed footpath with a 'No Trespassers' notice an invitation. She would disappear, and in ten or twenty minutes he would see her remote in some field, deep in converse with a pipe-smoking farmer, or emerging from some farm-house, waving him to come up and share the glass of milk that was always offered her. Below her sophistication was an enviable, elemental simplicity which allowed her to make friends without effort. Those highway friends of hers—farmers, tramps, game-keepers—would stiffen a little into formality at Malcom's approach, and when they were tramping on together again he would vivisect his soul for reasons.

'I suppose it's that infernal defensiveness that the Army instilled into me in pre-natal days.'

'Ye-es. People don't like you readily, though there are some. Generally I think it's just your otherness that freezes them up.'

'Otherness?'

'Don't you know it? As though you were looking at something beyond the horizon.'

'It's probably hunger.' He would consult a map for the distance to their next meal. 'I never had such an appetite.'

They slept one night in a half-mown hayfield, on swathes of ammoniac hay, with a waning moon above them as they went to sleep and a fir-wood to their right. Far away in the west the sun had gone down in a drowsy, Leekan-like wailing of peewits. In the night-time a dog from a nearby farm came prowling and scented them out and, in outraged propriety, barked and barked despite their wheedlings and soothings. They endured it for a time and then emerged simultaneously from under the hay, loaded themselves with stones, and chased the dog for a quarter of a mile or so across stubble soft and yielding below their bare feet. They had started in anger, but soon it became a game, a play in the uncertain moonlight, and they ran and shouted, daftly, pelting a cur which raced round them and finally fled with frightened 'woof!' being unaccustomed to moon-dazed lunatics. They could smell the sea by then and were too wakeful to go to bed. Sketchily clad, they explored hand-in-hand through shadowy fields, scaring great horned cattle and once a horse, which galumphed away into the dimness with thunderous hooves. They found the sea at last, a smooth beach of shingle. They shed what little clothes they had on and ran down into the chill of water in the moonlight, splashing each other and breasting out into mysterious water still and silent, till a great comber would suddenly erupt from it over their heads and smite the quaking beach behind them. They came out and ran races to dry, having no towels, and Domina, declaring herself a Mayan priestess, danced a scandalous dance in the moonlight till the moon, apparently overcome, went out. . . . It was hours before they managed to reach the hayfield again and shelter and warmth under the swathes from which the dog had evicted them.

They inspected grave cathedrals, basked on hill-tops, lunched at public-houses—at one of them Domina drank too much cider—and spent only two disagreeable and stuffy nights in hotels: buildings raised to meet the needs of the after-War automobile tourists. Rain drove them to those hotels, and the first one refused them admittance because they asked for a double bedroom and Domina wore no wedding-ring. Also, they were probably disreputable-looking enough: Malcom's suit of flannels considerably the worse for wear and Domina decidedly crumpled and gypsy-like, her nose freckled by the sun, her vivid blue-black hair an electric banner, not the smooth, dead, unguented cropping of respectability. The hotel manager who declined their custom was fat and perspiring, his clerk a pale thing like a blindworm, and their glances and refusal infuriated Malcom. But Domina was merely amused.

'If it's a wedding-ring that's wanted, we can soon settle that.'

So they went to a branch of Woolworth's and spent an exciting ten minutes illegally investing Domina with the symbol proper to a double bedroom. She could not keep her eyes from the sixpenny ring as they left the store.

'I feel like a prize chicken,' she said. 'Or like Redleafe's bull in Leekan. Only *its* ring is through its nose, very sensibly.'

But the ring put a certain constraint on them, all the same, and that night—in another hotel from the first—he asked Domina to

206

marry him.

She was brushing her electric hair. It was a warm and cheerful room, deceptively homelike and comforting. She looked at him with puzzled eyes, hesitated a little, seemed about to laugh. Then she drew off the ring and dropped it into the fire, crossed the room and opened the window so that the curtain streamed. He turned round and exclaimed as the draught hit him, and suddenly found Domina's arms round his neck.

'Stuffy. We're both getting it, M. M. That damned ring! What is there to sell our freedom for that we can't have now?— Aphrodisiac bishops and eunuch editors?' She thought for a moment, her chin pressed against his cheek. 'Or—do you want children, Malcom?'

He had a desperate desire to lie, to tie her down if he might, to win a den and a warm room and her unstraying loyalty. And then, as in a blaze of light, he saw her the laughing dancer of the Cornish beach, his comrade of the dusty roads.

'No,' he said.

'Then there's no excuse for marrying.' She sighed whimsically. 'We'll just have to burn.'

X

But as their holiday neared its end, as London and everyday life and Domina's Germany drew nearer, a foreboding of loneliness as desperate as Metaxa's in 1915 would come upon him. They camped one night on the edge of a little fir-wood perched at the top of a Dartmoor tor. They had walked that day from Okehampton, and up in this evening calm, with the windy spaces of the moor about them, they made tea and boiled eggs and then lay down side by side, reading Carlyle, and deciding there was nothing in him. Presently the distant crying of sheep lured away their attention from the dull acres of Victorian bombast, and they lay and looked at the evening. They even neglected to follow up with the usual antidote—a passage from the stained and tattered copy of *Comic Cuts*, which also did duty as a tablecloth. (It had been Domina's idea to doctor the rolling Carlylean periods with excerpts from *Comic Cuts*, and Malcom confesses an inability, in the Buxworths' house later that year, to avoid picking up Steven's peculiar literature and following the adventures of his heroes.)

But that evening his old restlessness was back.

'What the devil am I to do when this is over? I can't carry on with the Maya—not for a long time, if ever. The Hanno keeps me going only a few hours a day and—Lord God!'

She ruffled his hair, and then, realizing the inadequacy of that, brooded on him and Dartmoor.

'You're the kind of desperate person who's always made the world uncomfortable for himself. . . . Oh, I'm different. I *can* amuse myself, I can at least pretend that God doesn't matter, can enjoy novels and cinemas and staring at pictures—all of which bore you to exasperation. Do? Why start to clear up the mess and preach the Adventure.'

'How?'

She lay and thought. 'Perhaps you were right, and I ever so wrong. Perhaps we'll never escape from civilization except by fighting it. Its foul marriage rings. . . . I thought once its end was inevitable, but now—Oh, I don't know. All the signs of the change seemed clear enough, but now they're as muddled a riddle as your glyphs. It may come back worse than ever—wars and gods and classes and cruelty—unless we fight it. Start the fight. Organize a society for all the shocking people like ourselves. . . . Something new in politics, with a platform of all those things that are never mentioned and are uncomfortable and real. . . . *You* could do it.'

He was silent. But Domina sat up in her enthusiasm. It seemed to her a plan that had been in her mind for years.

'Why, goodness, it's what the world's waiting for! All the young and intelligent of England and the world. . . . We've no choice in things, no voice in things. We can never do anything through the old, cobwebby religions, and the old and useless political parties—the Conservatives sighing for the eighteenth century, the Liberals dreaming of a chloroformed world in side-whiskers and crinolines, the Labour Party—like a Nonconformist dinosaur, with its nice little respectable brain in its spine, not its head! You can never fight the returning beastlinesses through them—they're part of the beastliness themselves. Let's fight them and it in the open!'

He stared at her. He put his hands on her shoulders and shook her. He jumped to his feet.

'By God, Dom, you're a genius!' He threw back his head in challenge to the dimming, unpenetrated horizon. 'I will! . . . I wish we were back in London!'

CHAPTER FOUR

THE NEW SATANISTS

I

'But what's the good?' George Buxworth wanted to know. 'There are scores of piddling, ineffective little societies like that. They yap at the heels of the Labour Party and spend their lives seceding from this and that, or hunting for heresy among their members. They're mostly manned by scrubby little writers who've mislaid their chins——'

'For God's sake leave your infernal novelists out of it,' pleaded Malcom. 'Listen to what I intend. I'm not proposing a spare-time political home for aesthetic progressives. What I want to see organized is all the good constructive immorality which is running to waste.'

'Sounds like a harlots' trade union,' said George. 'Still, go ahead.'

So Malcom went ahead, into interminable expositions and discussions, first with George for audience and opposition and Jane and Steven and Malcom George sitting by as a sort of Distinguished Strangers' congerie, then with George as ally and fellow-expositor and each of their new nominations as audience and opposition, then as secretary of the temporary committee, finally——

Finally, in February of 1929, eight months after Domina's departure for Germany, the committee agreed on the issue of an advertisement to the weekly papers.

The list of weeklies included every journal which seemed to cater for 'professional' people, and the advertisements (financed by the committee and quite ruinous to its pocket) were all of a kind, displayed in a neat little enclosure, so:

> SECULAR CONTROL GROUP: It is proposed to found a Politico-Social society with the above name and with an opportunist philosophy, policy, and outlook based on organized and documented knowledge. Inquiries by letter are invited to the honorary secretary, Malcom Maudslay, 33A Nunquam Street, Chelsea, S.W. 6

The wording had been fought over again and again before the advertisement was published. Malcom had never before realized the difficulty of conveying in a set space at once enough and not too much.

'It looks,' said George Buxworth, coarsely, 'like a cure for piles.'

'It's intended to be,' said Malcom.

II

The committee had met in the Buxworths' drawing-room every Saturday afternoon for six weeks before the issue of the advertisements. The smart maid would admit the members and George and Jane receive them and ply them with tea, while Malcom hovered, lightedly, from the door to the fire, 'like a small boy with his first birthday party,' said Jane. . . .

The Secular Control Group rolls afterwards specified the foundation members as George Buxworth, journalist; Stephen Harding, publisher; Malcom Maudslay, archaeologist; Ivor L. Moxon, garage proprietor; Bhupendranath Pratap, student; John Stanley, aircraft designer; Jane Buxworth, ex-Civil Servant; Stuart Isham, general practitioner; Dorota Fenton Maxwell, artist; Domina Riddoch, chemist.

But Domina's part in the preliminary discussions was played by letter only for she was in her laboratory in Chemnitz and not expected back until April of the year.

Malcom had talked to Buxworth and Moxon; the latter was a member of the Hanno Society and a man of singular energy and imagination. Those two had secured the interest of Harding and Stanley respectively, and Dorota Maxwell, an acquaintance of George on the *Crocodile*, had appeared on the scene in response to letter-urgings from Domina in Germany. She it was who brought in the Bengali—"the son of a Calcutta factory-slaver," says Malcom, whatever that may mean. Jane had produced her young doctor, Stuart Isham—a woman in spite of her name. They might easily have secured others to begin with, but Malcom vetoed this method of recruitment; they did not want a family party. So they cut themselves apart from propaganda efforts while they hammered out the question of a creed.

This proved difficult enough. It had to have definite meaning, and yet not be so close and rigid as to exclude those moderns with comparatively harmless fads attached to them like barnacles. Malcom made no insistence on his diffusionist view of civilization. Domina was not so accommodating. Stanley—thirty-three years of age, ex-pilot of the Air Force, part-designer of Schneider winners, and a believer in helicopters—proved to be enamoured of a kind of Wellsian-Shavian God, a harmless and agreeable enough deity, and wished to have the Group described as 'politico-religious.'

Moxon, lean, rakish, and middle-aged, with grey-streaked brown hair and grey-streaked blue eyes, a gold-framed pince-nez and a gold-mounted petrol lighter, would arrive from Berkshire in a large and impressive touring-car to combat any such idea.

' "Religion's" a mistake. You're bringing in Jehovah by the back door.'

'Robbed of his night-shirt': George.

'And with a copy of the *Outline of History* under his arm': Harding.

'The Lord *is* a shoving leopard.' This, *sotto voce*, from Stuart Isham, and her only contribution to the preliminary discussions.

But Stanley had as supporter Dorota Maxwell, in possession of very short skirts and hair, a piquant face and a Bengali adorer.

212

She would wave her long cigarette-holder against Moxon's poised petrol lighter.

'You're like Swinburne—whom your ancestor was frightened to go on publishing back in the sixties. It's not that you disbelieve in God. It's just that you've got a spite against him.'

' "Pioneers! O Pioneers!" ' George would remonstrate, soothingly. . . .

Moxon himself, however, was a Wellsian, believing the world could be saved by the 'scientist.' Domina's letters combated this idea with considerable pungency and authority. 'Politico-scientific' would be ridiculous. The average scientist was the most timorous and tradition-bound of beings outside his own particular sphere of research. 'Listen to the British Association in session, yapping its respectful admiration of the Throne and the bishops' bench, and you'll feel more inclined to hand over control of the world to the nearest union of dustmen.'

There was also considerable debate over a name for the proposed society. Malcom had begun with 'Union of Scientific Control,' but 'union' was vetoed as suggesting a trade union, Court dress, Empire Loyalty, and fatuous sentiments on the dignity of being grimy; 'scientific' was quashed by the journalist, the publisher, and the chemist. Domina herself, in a letter, was ribald enough to suggest 'The Neo-Satanists.' Buxworth, in a shocking raid on Mrs. Eddy, capped this with 'Science and Health.' Harding proposed 'Immorality Unlimited.' Stuart Isham, still *sotto voce* and irrepressible, advanced 'The League of the Leopard' as a Spooneristic concession to Stanley's religious convictions. The admittedly clumsy 'Secular Control Group' was a bad compromise for which Moxon could claim chief credit.

Desultory if good-natured wrangling on all issues was the rule. Not one of the committee had the same urge and seriousness in the matter as Malcom. Like him, like nine-tenths of the intelligent men and women in the after-War years, they had contributed to public life no more than a shrug of contemptuous indifference. It was a meaningless simian brawl. Changes of state and industry and social convention had gone on over or below them and their kind, at the mercy of professional politicians, propagandist journalists, priest-leagues, and what not—"the half-educated swarming to power from both the gargoyles and the gutters of the rotten cathedral of civilization."

Attracted though they were to the idea of a society which would crystallize into a code of action, however loosely, their own straying hopes and likings and passionate rejections, the committee members found it hard enough to slough years of cynicism and irreverent wit. The repartee was extraordinarily good, but Malcom would fret and shuffle his chair and George, the temporary chairman, would glance at him and the rest of the room with upraised brows.

'I think we'll get down to business. Otherwise our secretary may burst a blood-vessel. . . .'

They treated him, Malcom records, with a patronizing trust, and this is not difficult to believe. His thesis that the Group's 'philosophic' standing was "belief in modern ability to organize and direct the Adventure of Mankind" coupled with "complete scepticism of all traditional authority, codes, conventions, and dignities of civilization unamenable or hostile to constant re-testing and re-stating" was accepted almost unamended.

No such unanimity, however, gave birth to the political programme. Cutting it to an un-unwieldy minimum proved the difficulty. Stanley was prevailed on to abandon his demiurge, but endless other contentious matters arose. Dorota Maxwell wished them to declare in favour of 'free lust' ("The futile fool!" comments Malcom, bitterly and unjustly), and George Buxworth, probably in revulsion from his daily diet of authors, wished to have a vegetarian declaration of the Rights of Mammals. Thereat Harding, seizing the opportunity for a joke, protested on behalf of all plant life, quoting Sir Jagadis Bose on the terrors suffered by the common cabbage uprooted and devoured. Pratap had Dravidian ideas of dress reform, and his byronic shirt was kept out of the programme only through the agile manoeuvrings of Malcom. Shorn of individual fads and obsessions, they found themselves agreed on Eleven Immediate Propaganda Points:

SOCIAL AND POLITICAL

(i) *Abolition of the Legal Status of Marriage.*

(ii) *State Propaganda and Enforcement of Birth Control.*

(iii) *A General Tax to be levied for the Endowment of Each Woman's First Two Children.*

(iv) *Complete Secularization of Education.*

(v) *Disestablishment of Churches.*

(vi) *Repeal of the Blasphemy Laws and Censorships.*

INDUSTRIAL

(vii) *Nationalization of Banks.*

(viii) *State to Acquire Controlling Shares of Principal Industries.*

SCIENTIFIC

(ix) *Compulsory Periodical Dissolution and Reorganization of all Chartered Learned Societies.*

(x) *State to Acquire all Patents and establish a Department for the Endowment of* Bona Fide *Individual Research.*

ANTI-WAR

(xi) *International Organization of Associations pledged to both Passive Resistance and Sabotage.*

Each Point was elaborately documented and its implications made clear. The latter half of Point No. 11 Malcom pressed through with a majority of one.

'You'll have to be damn careful of the wording,' said Harding, who had been in opposition. 'Otherwise, when a war comes, the Secular Control Group'll be declared an illegal organization at once.'

'Of course it will.' Malcom lost his temper for once. 'What the hell else do we intend?'

215

Answers to the advertisements began to come in from all over the country in a thin stream of query. George and Malcom sorted them out into four groups: The Flippant, the Threatening, the Curious, and the Owlish. They decided to disregard the second and fourth classes—there were amazing specimens in both, ranging from a solemn warning by an English Mormon that Science would soon be overthrown by Revelation to a pathetic charge of plagiarism from a member of the Fabian Society—and concentrated their attention on the Flippant and Curious, knowing that modern flippancy generally covers a childlike longing for faith and belief in the ultimate sanity of things. The 'thesis' and the Eleven Points, set forth in a neat little booklet printed gratis by Harding, were posted to selected enquirers, with a note that the 'Points' had been merely tentatively agreed on.

They despatched six hundred and eighty packages and had between three and four hundred replies. For over a fortnight the two of them, working in the evenings and far into the nights, read and classified and filed those replies. They were assisted by Jane and much coffee, and worked amid an unending stream of mind-relieving ribaldry at the expense of their correspondents. Then a roll of names was drawn up and another letter despatched to each individual who had swallowed 'thesis' and 'points,' stating that it was intended to hire a London hall for the inauguration of the Group and enrolment of members, and inviting subscriptions of ten shillings per head for this purpose.

'That'll dowse them,' said Harding, calling in and producing his wallet. 'If there's one thing an intellectual can't bear it's parting with his money. I know. I'm one.'

Replies came in more slowly than before. They were sorted out into the Sincere, the Apologetic, and the Frankly Abusive. From the last group the perspiring organizers, attended by Jane, learned that they were confidence men, sex perverts, workshys, and certainly agents of the white slave traffic.

At the end of a fortnight, however, they discovered, rather

breathlessly, that they had received over £70. They set about hiring a hall.

IV

The first meeting was fixed for the 15th of March, 1929, at 6.30 p.m. in the Lamont Hall in the Strand. On the night of the 12th, while the Buxworths and Malcom sat in the drawing-room at 33A, busied over interminable Group questions, a violent peal was heard on the door-bell. Followed the sound of the maid's footsteps, a subdued colloquy in the hall, a remembered laugh, then the drawing-room door was flung open and Domina walked into their presence for the first time in nine months.

They all stood up, talking, Malcom the last to find his voice. Domina kissed each of them, impartially and unembarrassedly, and then sank into a chair.

'Well, how are the Satanists? Goodness, it's good to see you all!'

She was a little thinner, but still with that upright carriage and clear, fine-textured skin. Her brows were such a fine line of tracery from tip to tip across her forehead that Malcom realized they must be tweezered: some German frivolity. And then he saw her left hand. The little finger was missing, and the polished tips of the remaining fingers faintly but ineradicably stained a metallic blue.

'Good Lord, what have you been doing with your hand?'

'Oh, a little experiment. But it's all right.'

'You'll blow yourself up some time.'

She twinkled at him delightedly, leaning forward in her chair to the warmth of the fire. 'Like the frog in the fable. . . . Where's the baby? Oh, in bed. . . . I ran through the German course ahead of time. Going back to Woolwich on Monday. Now tell me about the "Group."'

Two hours later she and Malcom walked along the Embankment towards her flat under the frosty glitter of the March sky,

217

Rossetti's 'spacious vigil of the stars.' To their right the river swung in a long, black glittering curve down towards Hungerford Bridge.

He told her he was to give the opening speech at the Group meeting, and then abandoned that topic abruptly, his attention caught by the cold overhead splendour.

'Horribly remote. . . . Do you remember that night on Stane Muir, Dom, and your human archangels on the rim of the Galaxy millions of years away? That was the beginning of the Group.'

'I know,' she said, softly.

But he could not bring down his fascinated gaze. 'Do you think we ever will—our descendants, I mean? Lucky devils to be born a million years from now!'

'I know,' she said again. 'Remember Friedlander?—

"For us the heat by day, the cold by night,
The inch-slow progress and the heavy load,
And death at last to close the long, grim fight
With man and beast and stone: For them, the Road!——" '

'You've a lovely voice, Dom.' A remote memory stirred in him. 'Lord, Rita once said that about my own—ages ago in Glasgow! . . . "Man and beast and stone"—the likeness of ape and tiger that the wheel of civilization has imprinted in us all, down to our very bones. . . . Can we ever beat them, after all—ever do anything real? When I'm tired like this. . . .'

Her maimed hand touched his in the darkness. 'I didn't finish Friedlander—

"And yet, the Road is ours as never theirs!
Is not one joy on us alone bestowed?
For us the master joy, O pioneers—
We shall not travel, but we make the Road!——" '

'*We* make the Road! In spite of the ape and tiger. Even though

218

they pull us down, what does it matter? We've Man on our side, and he'll beat them yet. . . . And those stars—Goodness, America was once a million times more remote!'

'God!' he said, as at a sudden revelation, 'how I've missed you!'

V

The 15th of March, seven o'clock in the evening, and before the eyes of Malcom a sea of faces as he rose to speak. It was probably only a moment—though it felt like an hour—before the initial stage-paralysis of his tongue and senses ceased, and he became conscious of his own voice, a trifle high-pitched, and of standing detached, criticizing the content of his speech and the cut of George Buxworth's hair, seen out of the corner of his left eye.

There were nearly three hundred people in the hall—thirty more than had sent in subscriptions. But anyone was allowed to enter and the extra thirty was at least partly composed of pressmen, among whom Buxworth and Harding had been carrying out publicity work for some time. The members of the temporary committee were scattered throughout the body of the hall, excepting Dorota Maxwell, who acted as stenographer and wrote with such rapidity that she would pause in occasional unemployment and tap her teeth with her pencil—an idiotic and aggravating idiosyncrasy. He could see Domina midway the chairs, her hair gleaming, her shoulders hunched, sitting chin in hand and with her head a little down-bent. Jane Buxworth was at home with Steven and the baby. Harding showed up in the front row, a sardonic thorn set about with overblown young reporters looking about them disinterestedly. Moxon sat far down to the right and was rapidly and nervously kindling and rekindling his gold-mounted lighter. Stanley and Stuart Isham were somewhere in the vague blur of whispering back towards the rear; Bhupendranath Pratap glinted, Gandhi-like, near the door. Every now and then George, who had elected himself chairman and introduced Malcom, 'the founder of the Group,' to deliver the opening speech, would shuffle his feet unnecessarily. Malcom suspected he was bored.

"I became aware how thin and feeble my vocabulary was, with what clumsy brush I was painting that vision of sky-storming achievement Domina and I had glimpsed. Could it really be conveyed in words to alien minds?

. . . I remember floundering in a bog of surmise over that, arguing the analogy of music to the music-deaf, and finding, with a jolt of surprise, that while I had been debating the matter I had still been speaking. . . . What had I been saying?

"I closed with unnecessary speed, hardly touched on the infamous Eleven Points, and sat down with an abruptness which left George comatose and uncomprehending in his chair for a moment."

That moment supplied the first of the comic interludes. A woman in the middle of the hall stood up, pointed a finger at Malcom and shouted 'Blasphemer!'

George Buxworth stood up. 'Keep quiet, please. You can speak later.'

'I will *not* keep quiet!' She had black, frightened eyes and a pale face with a rabbit-like mouth. She waved a sheaf of papers. 'I will give witness as a servant of God. That young man who has spoken is a luster after women, a destroyer of religion, a forerunner of the Antichrist——'

'*Will* you sit down?' ('Christ, M. M., it's Kate from Hyde Park!')

'I will *not* sit down! I bear witness——'

The rest of her speech was lost by George snatching Dorota Maxwell's note-book from her hands and thumping the table vigorously. People had been turning amused faces towards the woman, but the chairman's action evoked surprising results in the rear of the hall. There came shouts of 'Leave her alone! Give her a chance!'

This was accompanied by cat-calls and cheering. Three young men stood up near each other and began addressing the audience at the tops of their voices, one declaring that birth control filled him with horror, as he himself wanted to mother a large family, the second appealing to all teetotallers to go home, the third, with hair as bright and red as George's own, demanding monotonously what Gladstone said in 1888. At this the two back benches burst into vociferous song, the main consensus of opinion apparently being that in 1888 Mr. Gladstone had prophesied that it wasn't going to rain any more. . . .

The interrupters were medical students, hobbledehoys of the London hospitals, and George's callings were entirely ineffective in stilling the tumult. Pratap had vanished—very sensibly, and to summon the police, as afterwards appeared—and Stanley was to be seen arguing and struggling vainly in the midst of the student phalanx. Malcom had had enough. His voice penetrated to the front seats at least.

'Any men here who'll help to clear the hall of those damned schoolboys? War-time chaps preferred.'

A dozen rose up, the platform was deserted, and the next few minutes were mixed and impressionist. The volunteers were arranging their ties and hair and Malcom, considerably soothed, was wrapping up the bloody knuckles of his right hand in Domina's handkerchief, when the Bengali returned with a policeman. Not a single student was in the vicinity.

George Buxworth was panting a little as he and Malcom regained the platform. He indulged in a hot whisper.

'By God, M. M., I believe you broke that young clodhopper's jaw. You damned idealists aren't safe. . . . Say, that speech of yours: we'll have a million copies printed!'

The members of the audience had kept their seats, all except Kate from Hyde Park, 'who had apparently balked at bearing witness in a police court.' The volunteers pushed back to their places. The reporters scribbled busily, and a hum of talk and laughter ran all over the hall. As it was to prove, the Group could not have had its first meeting better salted. George thumped the table.

'You people, you've heard Mr. Maudslay. All of you agree

221

with his general thesis, or you wouldn't be here. We've about two and a half hours to settle three matters: the Eleven Points, the temporary constitution, and the formal enrolment of members. I propose an hour and forty minutes to the discussion—ten minutes to each question, speakers three minutes each and one minute for a vote. If the Point is entirely rejected it'll come up at the next meeting. Any objection to this procedure?'

There was none. George nodded. Malcom smiled down at his bloodied knuckles. 'Point No. 1: *Abolition of the Legal Status of Marriage. . . .*' He surveyed half a dozen figures standing up. 'The lady in red.'

Malcom, with a sudden, naive memory of a sixpenny ring, leant forward to listen as Domina Riddoch, her eyes on the clock, began to address the audience. . . .

"At two o'clock next morning George Buxworth and I, re-elected honorary chairman and secretary respectively, were yawningly sorting out the last of the sheaves of memoranda handed us during the debates and looking up in 33A's *Who's Who* the particulars of Seymour Redland, described as a writer and schoolmaster, who had been voted honorary treasurer. We had enrolled two hundred and eighty-three members (including two of the reporters), collected subscriptions from over two hundred, and arranged a full-time discussion of the constitution of the Group at a meeting to be held a fortnight later."

VI

The newspapers gave them a mixed reception, some sneering at them as 'Utopians,' others entrusting to their readers stickfuls of account of how medical students had attempted to break up an 'atheists' meeting' at the Lamont Hall. But two distinguished socialist writers contributed articles of destructive criticism of the Group's programme to two Labour weeklies, and the day after those appeared a Sunday newspaper with a wide circulation took up the Group as a stunt, denouncing it in a leaderette as composed of advocates of free love, abortion, industrial sabotage, and Army mutiny. . . . Next week a shoal of enquiries came to 33A and Malcom succeeded in extracting four hundred and seventy-eight new members from the ranks of the enquirers.

It was but the beginning of a crowded seven months. To Malcom it seemed he had never worked before, that his struggle with the Maya problem had been child's play in comparison. Committees, organizing work, lectures, debates—he flung all his energies into them, yet in intervals of midnight silence in the Chelsea house found time to continue that immense *Autobiography* of his. Right up to October of 1929 he continued it and then abandoned its scattered pages to dominance of an unstirred desk in a deserted room.

" Worked—God, how we've worked! George Buxworth has deserted the *Crocodile* and taken to editing our weekly, *Control*. I've been offered a paid secretaryship and declined it. Our London membership has passed the six thousand mark; the Bristol, Manchester, and Glasgow Groups are flourishing. We have designed a constitution we believe unique, a series of rotating committees which include all members in active compulsory work throughout the year, and ensures no dead wood in the Groups. Bye-election candidates begin to be startled by queries from the Group office and our members are already working through nearly every professional and scientific organization in the country. We have been denounced by Conservative ecclesiastics and Labour atheists, by deans, dons, and dunderheads innumerable. Domina, chairman of the political committee, has been interviewed by the *Berliner Tageblatt*. France is sending us enquiries. George Buxworth, through Chicagoan connections, is already threatening the morals of his native land with shocking consignments of turpitude. Our Annual Conference meets in October to thrash out numerous questions, including the final wording of Point Eleven——"

The Annual Conference met, sat in session throughout two drizzling October days, and decided by an overwhelming majority to delete the word 'sabotage' from Point Eleven, leaving the

223

Group committed to passive resistance only in the event of War. Malcom sat and listened to the decision, George, Domina, Harding, and all the original members of the Group, with the exception of Stuart Isham, voting against him. He looked round the tables, then got to his feet and walked to the window of the Conference room overlooking Trafalgar Square. Below, a stranded party of Welsh miners had huddled all day on the benches round the fountains. Malcom pointed to them.

'We needn't worry about those people being murdered by peace-time commercialism now. In ten years' time, while you're passively resisting, they'll be dying like flies on the wire entanglements of the next war. I resign my secretaryship.'

And, in the midst of a dead silence, he turned and left them.

VII

His action astounded the Group. George Buxworth was empowered to ask him to reconsider his resignation.

'Hell, M. M., you can't leave us in the lurch like this.'

'You'll be all right, George. You're chairman of quite a respectable organization now. And if another war does come they'll merely give you a non-combatant job as a nice little Conchie.'

'That's damned unfair, Malcom.'

'I'm sorry, George, but I don't go back to the Group.'

Domina did not leave it at that. On the afternoon after the Conference they met, as they had previously arranged, and hired a boat and rowed away up by Castelnau and Barnes. It was biting weather. Both of them were in shorts and sweaters and the upstream row was in vigorous talklessness. They turned round at Mortlake and rested on their oars while the River carried them down into a London kindling here and there in the face of the dusk. Trees and bushes and cliffs of buildings hesitated and hovered to right and left, and an almost deserted flow of water swept eastward under bridges quivering against the bronze-black sky like dark rainbows.

'You're behaving like an unsmacked schoolboy, Malcolm.'

'Oh.'

She had twisted round to speak to him. Her face flushed darkly.

'Oh, the *damnedest* schoolboy. This resignation business. You know perfectly well the decision to cut out "sabotage" was inevitable. . . . Forced on the Group. The police were making things difficult already. We were as near being illegal as it was possible to be. If we'd kept the old constitution until the next General Election and the Conservatives wiped the floor with the Labourists—well!'

Malcolm said nothing. There was appeal in Domina's eyes.

'What's wrong with you, Malcolm? What is it? The anti-war point isn't the whole of the Group's programme. What about the other things you're deserting?'

'The survivors of the next war'll find them amusing to read about in the Group's minutes.'

'You're war-obsessed. Sabotage! Blowing up arsenals and munition-factories and derailing war-trains. . . . It's a dream.'

'So I've realized. Much better to lie snug in bed, passively resisting, and hear the guns across the Channel.'

'Do you think we will? Do you think, as a last resort, we mayn't come even to the melodramatic stuff you champion? But why put it in the constitution? . . . We've got to go on and fight the war-mind and prevent a possibility of war. We're going on. Don't think your desertion has killed the Group. Only—oh, foul of you to desert!'

He could not resist that. They drifted under the gilded pinnacles of Hammersmith Bridge. He tried to be reasonable.

'I'm deserting. I know. No excuse—except that as I sat and listened to the Conference's decision I saw I could never have any hand in planning the Adventure. Not for me. Realized I could never do anything in policy and tactics. And then I looked out of the window and saw those chaps in the Square and—God, the faces of every one of them seemed the face of Metaxa that last

225

time.' He laughed. 'I suppose I want a holiday.'

She scowled at him stormily from below her straight line of tweezered brows.

'You want shooting. Do you think Group work'll always be easy for the rest of us, that we won't have to submit to the discipline of it? Do you think I fancy the opinions of Harding and Redland and those other damned Wellsians and Darwinians? But we've a common objective, and I'll stick it, though you couldn't. . . . Just plain lack of discipline.'

'I know. I've no excuse.'

She swung away from him. Her hands were clasped round her bare knees, her mutilated left hand with its faintly stained fingers making deep indentations on her skin. A fine down covered that close-textured olive skin of hers, and he brooded absently upon the unreasonableness of physical beauty: this wonder of her skin and teeth and hair and eyes that made a corporate beauty, something delicate and fine that never came in his arms or was touched by his kissings——

The tide was coming up-River. They rowed for a little. Suddenly she stopped, turned round. Bright-eyed.

'But it's not. That wasn't true—and I knew it. It was irritability—oh, and a little spite. You're—Goodness, the lone beast, Malcom. People like you: I think they must always have loneliness. You can never march with the others, but always on the flanks or lost in front. You fret and toil organizing the Expedition, but advancing with it drives you frantic. . . . Don't come back to the Group, Malcom. Your resignation may have been the best thing ever—may keep alive in our memories that ghastly dream of yours if ever other means fail. . . . Get away from us all, somehow. Go out into the wilds and explore for the Hanno Society, and be lost and desperate and happy. . . .'

'But how?'

'Oh, I don't know. Go and convert the Eskimos to the Adventure. Get sent to the moon by one of ffrench's rocket experts.' She had sudden inspirations. 'Why, there's your Maya——'

VIII

And, as though he had been awaiting the moment, Simon Stukely Newman, in appearance and speech an impossible American out of Sinclair Lewis, in profession and hobby a desultory explorer, came into Malcom's life.

Malcom had known of him as a member and voluminous correspondent of the Hanno Society, had replied to his letters and queries briefly and compactly and never given him a second thought. Now, on the 19th of November, just emerged from several years of exploration in the Central American bush, he called on ffrench at the latter's office in the Museum, overwhelming that polite personage with data of research 'along the geological line of the Azoic from Mexico to Southern Guatemala.' A trifle mazed, but indefatigably courteous, the Hon. Reginald learnt, among other things, that his visitor intended returning to his stamping-ground at the earliest possible date, after the inevitable month in Paris. . . . It all seemed particularly harmless and uninteresting and American.

But a few minutes later, in a state of much excitement, he was ringing up the Hanno office for Malcom. The latter, abandoning the proofs of his translation of Cogolludo's *History of Yucatan*, went across to the Museum and was introduced to a short, sandy, fidgety person with large, horn-rimmed glasses and exceedingly yellow boots. He clasped Malcom's hand with Babbitt-like impressiveness ('Boise City?' said the experienced George, later, 'oh hell!') and sat down and wriggled a little and looked at ffrench. . . . Then the whole business came out.

During his latest penetration of the Pacific littoral above the Gulf of Tehuantepec the American had learnt from a trustworthy guide that a great ruined city lay in the eastwards bush, in a deserted tract of country. This guide himself had once seen it, though it was unknown to white men and only a rumour among the natives generally. Newman had had no time to attempt a visit to it, because of the rains; besides, he himself had not sufficient experience as an archaeologist to carry out a detailed investigation. But he intended to make the place during his expedition in the Spring of 1930, and wanted a competent Americanist to go with him, photograph and map the ruins—almost certainly Mayan—and look for inscriptions.

'You should find plenty willing to go,' said Malcom.

The Boise City man had allowed ffrench to explain so far. Now he came to the point himself

'It's this way. I read an article of yours in *Antiquity* about the old Mayans, and I said "That's sense." And the Honourable ffrench here says you're an authority, and a competent young man whom the Hanno Society might spare on research for a long vacation. My proposal, sir, is that you come with me into Chiapas and Guatemala on a year's exploration. I'll pay you anything in reason. What do you say?'

'I'll come,' said Malcom.

IX

They were to sail for Panama on Christmas week and from there proceed up the Pacific coast to Soconusco City. They lunched together several times at Newman's hotel, and Malcom records, in those last few pages of his *Autobiography*, his amusement at the patronizing deference paid to him. He took notes of the kit and equipment needed and was given *carte blanche* to order both in London. Details of khaki drill, leggings, and mosquito nets strewed his room at the Buxworths' house, plaster of Paris and paper squeezes for the making of possible casts had to be ordered, a medical chest laid in, two large and complicated cameras purchased and tested innumerable times in the studios of the Butcher company. In spare moments he refurbished his Mayan in Pio Perez' grammar and took to reading Spanish newspapers from a Chelsea kiosk. Newman had gone to Paris and it was a month before they would sail.

Domina was acquainted with young Lagniard, an archaeologist from a Liverpool museum who was in London at the time, and who had been on one of the official expeditions to Lubaantun and the surrounding country. She invited him and Malcom to dinner at her flat. Lagniard disclaimed personal knowledge of the Western Chiapas country, though he believed it had the worst of reputations for various climatic reasons. It was really outside the Maya territory proper—Old and New Empire—and he did not conceal his polite opinion that Newman was a credulous crank.

'If there's anything at all certain it's that the city-building Maya had little intercourse with the Pacific. They were cut off from it by the Cordilleras. The only peoples in those lands were barbarian Quiches. If there's a ruined city at all in that district it must be comparatively small and unimportant. Probably Late Mexican-Toltec.'

Malcom laughed. His eyes had that remote, lighted look that Domina knew so well. 'Perhaps it's the ruins of Tula, Tollan, the American City of the Sun from which all the great heroes set out.'

Lagniard also found that idea amusing, and played with it jocularly, but later, after he had left them, Domina wanted to know more about it, and Malcom told her of that strange city which haunted the memories and imaginations of the pre-Columbian Americans—the home of Kukulcan, whom modern research would identify with a sun-myth, but whom he himself considered an Occidental Buddha. The city—no doubt a dream city, a New World Cosmopolis—of some lost Atlantean poet.

She did not seem to be listening and he thought he was boring her till, crouching in her chair, chin clasped in her mutilated hand, she looked at him.

'You only half believe that, Malcom. . . . Perhaps there was once such a city and Newman's guide has seen its ruins!'

She turned away from his dreamy face and stared into the fire. He had never been more remote. The chill November air blew through the open window from the River. He thought aloud.

'I half think he's a crank myself—Newman. And his city—but Lord God, Dom, he was like an answer to prayer!'

Then she asked a strange question, not looking at him.

'Have you made your will yet?'

He stared. 'No, but I will before I go. Not that I've much to leave, but what little there is goes to you, of course—if you'll have it.'

Still she did not raise her head as she put her next question.

'Then don't you think you'd better complete the business and marry me as well?'

X

They were married a fortnight later in the Chelsea Registrar's Office, with George Buxworth and Dorota Maxwell for witnesses, very solemn both, and George with his hair cut. Domina, unhatted even for that occasion, went through the short ceremony casually, as though carrying out a light social duty. Malcom felt and probably looked like a man in a dream.

Mrs. Maudslay. . . . Lord God!

'But—you've never explained, always put off answering— what on earth have we got married for?' he asked, as their train crawled out of Paddington, leaving the waving George and Dorota behind. She did not answer his question, but leant dangerously out of the window, her cropped boy's hair blown in the wind, curve from shoulder to knee taut and strained, staring at the vanishing reek of London. Then turned and dropped down beside him.

'Good-bye, Domina Riddoch! . . . What for? Oh, just fun. Are you to have all the adventures? Besides, we can get divorced when you come back. . . . But don't let's bother about that. Oh, Malcom, we've ten days together, and then——'

'It might have been the moon. Central America's nothing to that. It was you who pushed me out on this. Don't you remember that evening on the Thames? It's just a chance I'm not on the way to Copernicus or the Lunar North Pole in some infernal rocket!'

She sighed and closed her eyes. And then a naive thought came to her. She uncovered those unevenly coloured eyes again.

'Malcom, do you love me? Do you know we've never said we love each other?'

He questioned the past. 'God,' he said, 'neither we have!'

XI

They went to Wiltshire (because Domina wished to see Salisbury Plain) and spent their ten nights at the Stonehenge Inn and their nine days, mostly sunny, frosty weather, in wanderings as far afield as Salisbury and Devizes and Upavon, near which latter place they sat one long afternoon watching little fighter aeroplanes wheeling and bucking in aerobatics over the country of the Sunstone Men. It was the region Metaxa and Malcom had toured on the stolen motorcycle thirteen years before, and one morning he prevailed on Domina to go with him on a bus-ride to Bulford. There were miles of empty huts there, derelict, though a part of the camp was occupied, and he obtained permission from the Royal Engineers' office to look round. And there still, at the bottom of the remembered hut where he had once smitten his tormentor Wilsom, was the little office in which he and Metaxa had sat remote into joyous nights and jeered at militarism and Guizot's *History*.

He peered through the window. An old table rested in front of it. It was the same table: he saw the black, burnt patch where Metaxa had been wont to leave his cigarettes till they smouldered to ash. . . . He stared at that undying past till Domina caught his look, and shivered, and drew him away, and outside those lines of rotting memories he found the sun again and forgetfulness and tiredness in a long tramp back to their room in Stonehenge Inn.

They played the lovers they had never declared themselves throughout five years of intimacy. He discovered in her depths of tenderness and mystic poetry she had never before uncovered to him. That haunting aura of aloofness disappeared. He discovered

231

that he had never known even real physical intimacy with one whose passion was as deep as those secret wells from which she refreshed her spirit. They would lie unsleeping far into nights and hear the sound of rain on the roof, the woof-woof-woof of nightwings, and go back to their childhood in Leekan for memories that seemed inexpressibly dear little things of touch and glance forgotten and resurrected to startle the darkness with low laughter. They talked in those hours of things deeper and more secret than may ever be found in a book of such century as this. In some strange, inexplicable way each seemed to the other matured, with all the uncouth sophistication of youth put by.

Every morning when they rose from bed they would see pillared Stonehenge rising from its hillside. It drew them often, those two who could never escape the fascination of the lands and times and the dim peoples who enghost the fringes of history, who rose out of millennial peace into red centuries, whose gods are not even names, nor their kings a memory.

'But all their blind, wasted lives and histories—oh, they'll find meaning yet!' she said one evening, when he had been talking of the Chalcolithic priestmen and slaves who had dragged the great menhirs into position. 'Sometime. When you and I are lost and forgotten dust in these our bodies as they are, my dear Azilian!'

'They'll probably dig up my bones and yours and swear we were low-grade Celts,' he laughed.

And then they would remember, and across them for a moment would fall a shadow like a bright, keen pain. Yet I think he had never the remotest suspicion of that adventure to which she had committed herself, for which indeed she had married him. Once he came on her sitting silent in their room, looking across the dusking fields at the great standing stones, and when he teased her she said an inconsequent thing.

'I was thinking—of your adventure and of mine.' It seemed that she was about to say more, and he waited. For a moment her face was resolute. Then she laughed unsteadily and turned to his arms while the hours wheeled by like homing birds. . . .

They were past. There came an early December morning and Waterloo Station in a drenching downpour of sleet. That, and a last picture: Jane waving farewell with an immense blue handkerchief snatched from George's pocket, George's red hair gleaming in the mirk like a damp beacon, and Domina herself, perilously poised on top of a pile of platform luggage, one hand on George's shoulder, standing mute and rigid until obscured from view behind the window-blocking goodbye gesticulations of Simon Stukely Newman.

CHAPTER FIVE

THE VERGE OF ADVENTURE

I

Even before they landed at Soconusco City and went up by rail through a pass of the Cordilleras to San Juan Pachuca, the entries in Malcom's diary are of a facetious quality that entirely fails to conceal his exasperation. Soconusco witnessed a witless delay of weeks, visits, applications, and the presentation of unnecessary credentials to scent-reeking and adipose Mexican officials. The hospitality of those officials and their polite and sniggering suggestions of diversions appropriate to travellers provided Malcom with sardonic reflections on "that festering immersement in virgins and voodoos which has been the principal activity of the Latin genius for the last eighteen hundred years." The only English books he saw on sale were works by Miss Victoria Cross and Mr. James Branch Cabell. . . .

At Pachuca there was a similar wasting of precious weeks and it was mid-March before they at length set out on the south-eastwards trail to the village where Newman was to pick up his guide. In front rode the American, short and stocky, with an immense sombrero like an inverted cuspidor, on his head, and a gigantic sporting rifle slung bandit-wise across his shoulders. His mount was an exceptionally long-eared and pessimistic mule with the bunched-up face of a cocker spaniel. In the middle of the procession five more mules, laden with baggage, provisions, and instruments, straggled along under the charge of three abject Indios and four unabject but scrofulous meztizos—one of them wore a British Army tunic with the crown of a major still adhering to the shoulder-band—whom Newman had hired to supplement the activities of his personal servant, a vacuously grinning Jamaican negro whom they had picked up in Panama. In the rear rode Malcom, straight, dark-faced, spruce enough in his new drill, one imagines, and making little attempt to conceal his angry amusement over the straggling inefficiency of the little expedition.

His mood of the time robbed him, I think, of much of the brightness of sunshine and appreciation of the quaintness of the people's speech and dress and appearance. In ordinary circumstances they would have kindled his ever-ready interest. He saw only a filthy, straggling land, hot and moist and mindless and unclean, the natives a sickly folk with lacklustre eyes and voices, every horizon the same unwinking bright painting of emerald overhung by dark mosquito clouds. Newman had engaged him as archaeologist, but appeared to imagine that this term was synonymous with photographer. At Malcom's pointblank refusal to waste half their plates posing the expedition's leader amidst groups of dusky and unwashed native belles, or chatting with unauthentic caciques, or taking pretty-pretty views of woodscapes, Newman commandeered one of the Butchers himself and trained his servant to carry out the constant snapshotting. He had as great a passion for being photographed as he had for arousing (as he sagely believed) the awe and wonder of the natives. He would smile puffily and fatuously as some languid group would gather round his geological fussings above an outcrop of rock or his minute and clumsy mountings of butterfly specimens or the like. He was convinced that he was looked on as a medicine man, a witch-doctor. . . .

"He is a type common enough to our modern world, though I have never encountered its American variant before. George and Metaxa have been my only Americans. . . . His large and unearned income, I gather, comes from an oil company, and he has spent his life alternately poking about in various more or less unexplored corners of his native continent, and then returning to New York or London and posing as the traveller-savant. He has, like most of those who have never known mental discipline, a cocksure certainty in all branches of modern knowledge—a certainty derived from the study of innumerable 'popularizations' apparently written by the half-educated for the benefit of the half-witted. He quotes those odd works of American and English 'erudition' as though they were complete and final authorities. His mind contains as odd a hotchpotch of theories as his rucksack contains geological specimens. He thinks Darwin was 'wrong,' and that the human stock had a non-anthropoid origin; on the other hand, he has the utmost faith in the truth and efficacy of some shamanistic formula called the 'Survival of the Fittest.' This, as far as I can gather, he takes to be a divine revelation of 'Science' giving authority for all parasites of oil companies to draw dividends without working for them, for Cook's-tourist explorers to browbeat and maltreat Indios at pleasure; in fact, for most of the dirty white scoundrelism in the world. . . . His intellectual guides are a trifle incongruous. He has, as a 'scientist' himself, a particular admiration for Professor Henry Fairfield Osborne, and, as a business man, for that champion of idealistic Big Business, Mr. H. G. Wells, whose distinguished initials he insists on pronouncing as 'Hay Jee.' "

That 'Hay Jee!' Malcom would sit and bite his lips and wait for it, watch for its approach the while Newman boomed like a bombastic bittern, and the oil-lamp hung from the roof of some native hut would collect the oddest coverings of winged insects. They would pile upon that lamp in strata, and as the lowest stratum calcined the next would take its place in ecstatic suttee. The beds—hide strung from four wooden corner-posts—would exude at night marauding battalions of giant ticks: one would pick off the sated and bloody monsters from one's skin next morning, generally under the vacuous grin of Newman's Jamaican servant. Newman in sleep moaned and snored fatly. In the dawn light he would show up greasily under his mosquito net, for he rubbed himself from head to foot every evening with a vile-smelling concoction which certainly seemed to be efficacious. Rather than attempt the penetration of his hide, so protected, all the tick battalions in the hut would enter on indefatigable route

236

march across the floor to Malcom's bed. . . .

He was sparing in washing, but when Malcom caught a slight fever a week out from Pachuca through bathing in a scummy lagoon, Newman ascribed his own immunity to his 'good Amurrican blood.' (He was of Jewish extraction, in spite of his meandering nose and sandy hair, but either he or his ancestors had ratted to the Nords.) He insisted on treating Malcom as a tenderfoot, posed himself as the seasoned explorer, and the fact that the expedition's archaeologist could out-run, out-shoot, out-march him made not the least difference. His Spanish was of the poorest and he knew not a scrap of any Maya dialect. He made solemn protests against Malcom using the latter tongue.

'Say, you're green to the country. You don't get the mentality of these nig-pigs. If they hear you speak their own lingo they take liberties. It's up to them to have had some Spanish knocked into them by this time.'

"I pointed out that there were no statistics proving that the inhabitants of New York had all learned Chinese on the off-chance of being accosted by a stray Celestial. This led him into a booming, unhumorous disquisition on white man's prestige and the Nordic destiny. . . . I gather that my black hair puts me outside the triumphal Nordic march."

II

Before they reached the guide's village Malcom was spending long hours in puzzling how Newman had ever managed to carry out previous explorations and penetrate into the bush as far as he had certainly done. The man was incapable either of detailed organization or a reasonable time-table. At the village the matter was soon solved. The solution was Ramon Pech.

The guide showed up on their arrival as a tall, pure-blooded Mayan, a Yucatecan from Campeche, as his name suggested, with a sloping forehead that might have been copied from the Palenque panels. He had a sardonic mouth, slit eyes, and a permanent puffiness on the left cheek, induced by snake-bite. On the first morning after joining Newman's party he and Malcom took the lead. It was impossible to ride and they had to plod along the dry bed of a stream, with the mountains rising green and pale saffron on their right, lacquered with sunshine. Presently Malcom began to practise his Mayan on a guide who stared his slit-eyed astonishment.

'You have been in this country before?'

'No. . . . Those expeditions are organized and captained by you, aren't they? Well, what became of the last two white assistants whom Sr. Newman brought up from Soconusco?'

He had heard rumours of those assistants in Pachuca. The guide avoided his eyes, as Malcom noted.

"He told me that one had died of fever and the other: of him he is not sure. It had been towards the season of the rains. The señor assistant had been left to collect botanical specimens and they had arranged to return for him. 'Then the rains had come. They had not returned. The Sr. Newman had declared that the assistant was making his own arrangements to proceed to the coast."

He was unwilling enough to part with this information and Malcom listened half incredulous and half furious. He could see each scene as though it had been rehearsed before his eyes: the young tenderfoot from America allowed to catch fever, lectured, improperly doctored, finally dying. And the second case—had it been pure treachery or just cowardice on Newman's part?—fear of himself being caught in the terrible rains?

As they slowly fussed along under the Cordillera shadows Malcom came to a curious conclusion. It was this: In his original straying up from Soconusco, years before, Newman had discovered the value of Pech as a guide, and under that guidance had on each subsequent expedition penetrated exactly the same distance as on the first. They were in a tract of terra incognita— or rather, on the fringes of one. On those fringes Newman had meandered and 'explored' spasmodically for the past two years, never penetrating any further through the bush to the south-east, always making sure of his retreat in advance of the rains. . . . The colossal vanity and cowardice of the little man! Malcom saw at last the reason for the assistants. Each time Newman had set out with the determination to have some discovery of note made—by an assistant. . . .

Ramon Pech's story of the ruined city was straightforward enough. He and a party of Mexican miners had once penetrated the country to the south—though they had done it from the east, not the Pacific Coast—in search of reputed silver lodes. They had found nothing but dysentery and malaria, and, after losing themselves for days, had abandoned the search and made their way out to the Usamacinta River.

But the day when they had turned back—this had been in the midst of flat and thickly forested country—they had seen a strange sight at sunset—or thought they saw it: a serration of hills rising above a thinning of the western forest, and on one of those hills, so Pech had thought, was a giant ruined 'church' and about the foot of it more buildings and great pillars upright and prone. The mining party had seen all this picture with some clearness in the fading light, though the hills were five miles or more distant and soon blotted out in the darkness. They had made no attempt to cleave a way through the jungle depths to it, superstition restraining them no more than the common knowledge that at the sites of such lost cities and buildings there is generally neither water nor fruit. They had turned back. But the size of the ruins in the sunset glow had stirred the wonder and kept green the memory of Ramon Pech.

'And you believe we can reach them from this side, that they're beyond the jungle there?' Malcom asked, and pointed to the dark eastwards bulking of the forest.

'So I believe, señor. But——' the guide glanced round at Newman, and then, confident of the American's ignorance of Mayan, shrugged his shoulders—'there will be no attempt to find them.'

The *Diary* fades out into laconic notes on halts and sunsets and temperatures till the entry opposite the 8th of July:

"10p.m. 109° my tent thermometer is registering even now. The hottest day we have had, but the darkness is worse. One can hardly breathe.

> *"Oh that the wild west wind might blow,*
> *That the small rain down might rain—*
> *Christ, that my love were in my arms*
> *And I in my bed again!——*

"Christ, I wish she was!"

The 18th of August breaks into voluminous record:

"9.30p.m. 105°. We are as far along the Cordillera fringe as Newman has ever penetrated—that is, further than any modern white, though Pech tells me that in a cenote thirty miles away to the east he once found a casque and sword and other rusty pieces of armour. Probably some straying Spanish conquistadores once perished there, either of hunger or at the hands of the natives—Quiche. But those natives have long vanished or—which is quite possible—live in villages hidden in the jungle-scrub.

"I have had neither the time nor inclination during the past three months to convey to paper my opinions of this imbecile pottering which Newman calls exploration. We have dawdled from camp to camp along the unending mountains, watched the sun rise over the miasmic forests each morning, gone to sleep with the croaking of the bullfrogs in our ears every evening, listened *ad nauseam* to our 'leader' berating or occasionally even beating his grinning Jamaican. Sometimes Newman has halted and commanded meaningless ascents of the Cordilleras foothills or unnecessary sorties into the eastwards jungle. Those sorties require hours of hacking with machetes before we penetrate a few miles and then Newman, who generally stays in the rear while the cutting is going forward, will give orders to stop, saying that he has acquired 'sufficient data' for the time being. . . . At last, this morning, I flatly refused to go botanizing in his company, telling him that I had come out from England as archaeologist and nothing else, and that if he has no intention of attempting the Maya city I intend turning back and taking half the bearers with me.

"We have parted for the evening with relations more than slightly strained."

Next evening the quarrel was resumed again. Newman blustered and swore at the mutineer and then confessed that there would be no time to reach Pech's ruins that season—unless Maudslay cared to go on alone?

'I'll see you damned first,' said Malcom, agreeably. 'Do you think I haven't heard of your other assistants?'

He looked at Newman closely. 'Suppose we leave the mules and bearers here with Ramon Pech and push on alone?'

. . . insane. Who was he to give orders? The rains would soon be on. . . . Anyhow, it was doubtful if the guide had not been mistaken or lied about the whole matter.

'We'll soon see about that,' said Malcom, and shouted 'Pech!'

The guide came and stood with his face in the light of the tent lamp. Questioned in Mayan, he answered in that language.

How long would it take to reach the eastward hills? Perhaps ten days, perhaps longer, and it would be very desperate and uncertain travelling. The rains——

But Malcom had made up his mind. 'Listen. Get a mule ready for the morning. We'll take some clothes, two rifles, and two machetes, the camera in my tent, and some food. You and I will start at six tomorrow.'

The guide was alarmed. Newman's interruptions in Spanish had not left him unacquainted with the situation. 'But the Sr. Newman is my employer. He will not let me go. He is afraid of those forests and of the carriers. I wish to come with you, Sr. Maudslay, in spite of the rains, but he would stop my wages, have me arrested by the alcalde of Pachuca——'

241

"I told him I would settle things with the Sr. Newman, and dismissed him. When he had gone I made the situation clear. I have seldom seen anyone in such a blue funk. He had no objections to me making the attempt on my own—indeed, it is probable that he brought me from England with that thought in mind—but to rob him of his irreplaceable guide! He threatened, unconvincingly, to shoot me, to have Pech arrested by the carriers, till I told him that if he prevented us leaving or refused to await our return for three weeks or so I would get back to Europe somehow and publish full details of his so-called 'explorations'; also, that I would have the fullest inquiries made as to the death of his last assistant, my predecessor, whom he had abandoned to die in the rains.

"He shivered at that, very evidently wavering between his immediate fear of the forest and Indios and the more remote but shocking disaster of being shown up in the scientific journals for which he has such reverence. Finally he gave in."

IV

The forests closed around them, greener than ever, stifling as death, with a vivid, damp heat that foretold the approach of the rains. Malcom, who had Newman sworn to await their return for a month, commandeered the bearers to hack a way through the three-miles band of jungle that arched the encampment. Beyond that were scrub and cactus bush waving high and yellow and bursting in a distempered foam on the sides of the Cordilleras. Then the bearers turned back and the two men with the mule, loaded with camera and equipment and paper squeezes and a little food and water, went on over the brow of the nearest foothill, and next day turned east and began to hack a way for themselves through that tundra that was half a cane-brake.

And for the first time in long months Malcom was light-hearted again. His notes, indeed, are characteristic. "What a bloody animal is the mule!" says the entry opposite the 22nd of

August, and nothing more. The 23rd blossoms out into a long account of their progress that day—the worst they had made so far, over treacherous ground riven here and there—"sun-cracked, like the moon." Pech behaved wonderfully, to the surprise of Malcom, who was incapable of understanding how he himself, who at bottom cared so little for human beings and so much for ideas, could arouse love in others. Machete-swinging, the Mayan stamped in advance. Behind, sweating, and swearing at the mule, you must picture the advance of Malcom, thin since leaving the coast, his narrow brown face sun-rawed and an incongrous beard beginning to cover his cheeks and throat. He tells of the agony that shaving was—"Like pulling out the hairs with a rope and pulley." Unexpectedly, he fills the rest of that page with the old joke about the best way to avoid the necessity of shaving— "Wait till the hairs appear and then knock 'em back with a hammer"—and wanders into a disquisition, with examples, of characteristic English humour: how fleas are best killed by being turned on their backs and tickled to death with feathers. . . . One gathers that Ramon Pech was plentifully stocked with the common flea.

Next day was the 24th. They progressed only three miles and, camping at night, saw that the forest was coming down upon them again: the real forest, gigantic in ceiba trees, festooned with creepers, choked with grasses and cane and alive with vermin. There was still no sign of Pech's 'little hills.' Out of the flare of sunset came a squall of rain. They shivered all night under a dripping ahuehuete tree, when, so Pech states, Malcom insisted on talking about the lost Maya civilization, trying to penetrate the 'time-spirals,' perhaps, through the guide's subconscious. In the morning they found the mule pawing and intractable. Great shallow, watery bloatings were appearing under its skin. Ramon Pech averred that it had been badly bitten and that they had best turn back.

Malcom swore at him. 'We'll go on until the tenth day though we've to crawl on our hands and knees. Or at least I will.' And then records in his diary: "Ramon swore also, in Mayan too erudite for me to follow. I think he felt inclined to punch me on the nose. Under similar circumstances I'd not only have felt inclined, I'd have done it. Fifteen miles today by my pedometer. Speaking of pedometers, I tried at lunchtime (baked beans and sour oranges) to translate Mark Twain's story about that night when he got up and wandered his bedroom, looking for some object or another, with his pedometer in his pocket. When finally he found a light, hours later, he discovered that he had walked fifteen miles since getting out of bed. . . . It was an instantaneous success. Ramon has been grinning over it ever since. I hope they had jokes like that in ancient Xibalba. And of course they had. The soft-headed 'reconstructions' of Old Empire life which represent the Ancient Mayans as perpetually immersed in building temples and carving panels and indulging in 'phallic orgies' (though if Domina's parody of a Mayan priestess that night on the Cornish beach was anything like the real thing, phallic orgies must have been good fun) are mostly written not by historians but little dried-up runts out of museum corridors.

"We are now on the borders of Xibalba, the edge of the ancient land where the Maya flourished so splendidly and in such isolation about the year 100 B.C. All those tracts to the east of us, now 'of life forsook,' once swarmed with the only civilization that has ever appeared in America."

He follows this up with a very vivid picturing, too long to quote here, of those pre-Christian years and of other aliens who may have wandered up from the far Soconusco beaches through forest and bush: stray Polynesians or Chinese, perhaps, arriving amazed at last on the borders of the Maya land, being captured and carried to Piedras Negras or Copan, spreading the seeds of Buddhism.

"And it all fluffed out like a rush-candle caught in a draught of wind, though how and why there is nothing more uncertain. Perhaps the glyphs of some lost inscription tell the reason. Perhaps they stand recorded in this very site we are seeking, and

I'll scrape round them unavailingly, and photograph and paper-squeeze."

He reverts on the 27th (the 26th is a blank page) to a fantastic possibility regarding those hypothetical Chinese sailors wrecked on American shores. "Perhaps a party was wrecked in the last years that saw the collapse of Xibalban civilization, and fled westwards from the Central land, with other refugees, to Ramon's ruined city. Perhaps one of them knew he was living history and wrote an account of it all in the Chinese script, and that account still survives sealed up in some tomb or treasure-house.

"I wonder if any of those Ancient Maya ever saw their civilization, detachedly, as the diseased thing it was, and something to be murdered before it murdered them? Perhaps Old Empire Copan had once its visionaries and its Secular Control Group: even its Domina.

"They seem no more incredibly remote in these forests than does European civilization, London, its kings, its priests, its gods, Salisbury Plain and the Secular Control Group. Tramping behind Ramon Pech this afternoon I fell into a reverie from which I could hardly shake myself free (and I hope I'm not in for another bout of fever): We seemed not merely Ramon Pech and Malcom Maudslay, but two eternal travellers from that Time itself which the Maya worshipped, stumbling over weed-grown civilizations innumerable, finding beyond the next horizon no lost Atlantean city but the ruins of London itself, forest-smothered and forgotten for twenty hundred years, with the wild beasts lairing in its palaces. . . .

"Ramon discovers himself as a vigorous proletarian. He tells me he always votes on the progressive ticket and that the present Governor of Yucatan is not only a pure-blooded Mayan but an equally pure-blooded socialist. When the shades of Karl Marx and Ahmekat Tutul Xiu join hands it is time to sing Nunc dimittis."

And then, for the 28th, the seventh day out from Newman's camp:

"Camped at sunset. Hills on the horizon."

V

Next morning they found a warm mist raining on them like a fine white spume. The sun came up a red flow of light, no orb, and for long the surrounding forest was invisible beyond a few yards on each side. Then they discovered the mule. It was dead and bloated and stank most vilely. Ramon surprised Malcom by weeping over its remains—a comic incident which so cheered him that he equally surprised the guide by insisting on writing a lugubrious epitaph for the mule and pinning it above the tree-bole where they left the unfortunate beast. Behind them was close on a hundred miles of forest and scrub land to be retraversed, and they had seen practically no game. Pech considered the provisions anxiously. Malcom attempted to hearten him by pointing out that such journey was nothing to that carried out by the Mayan's own ancestors who fled from the Old Empire into Yucatan fifteen hundred years before! . . . Meantime, there was no question of turning back, with the lure of those hills at last in the east.

But the hills were not so near as the sunset had seemed to bring them. As the mist cleared they showed as a faint tracery against the sunlight, at least fifteen miles distant. Through his Zeiss glasses Malcom saw their slopes mantled with the usual jungle-scrub. Ramon confirmed that, as far as he was able to determine by looking at them from a back view, those were the hills on the eastern slopes of which he had seen the lost Maya city.

'Then we'll start,' said Malcom.

He was in a fever of impatience to set out, as Ramon Pech records. They loaded themselves with a camera, the paper-squeezes (though how they were to transport to the coast any impressions, without a mule to carry them, Malcom does not seem to have considered), a machete each, and half of their food. The guide carried two waterskins, one empty, one full. They cached the other half of the provisions, their rifles, and various other impedimenta. Malcom carried on his back a pick-axe for use in clearing the Maya city-site, and they entered the forest.

The heat and the going were punishing, he tells. "It was by far the oldest forest-land we had passed through, and the detritus was knee-deep and sometimes thigh-deep, and swarmed with red ants. But the cane-brakes thinned out after a bit till one could see long vistas between the trunks, with the hills for background. We rested at eleven, having done four miles, and I had an inspiration. I asked Ramon if those hills had any name, and he said None, as far as he knew. The map does not mention them either. So, as Ramon renounced the right, I christened them the Domina Range before we reached them. Domina's name goes well with hills, unlike some of the sweethearts and wives with whom explorers have afflicted the atlases. We started again at two o'clock, after a siesta that was broken by a mamba crashing on broken sticks not three feet from my head."

They were holding in almost a straight line from their overnight camp, and this was bringing them to the southern edge of the Domina Hills. According to Pech's story the lost Maya city must lie on the extreme northern foothills, eastern aspect, but this could not be helped. It was impossible to strike a north-easterly tangent, for in that direction the forest abruptly wallowed away into a poisonous puzzle of slime and over-flowered ponds. They intended making the southernmost fringe of the Hills, passing round it, and then holding northwards till they reached their objective.

Towards five o'clock the forest began to thin out, but, unaccountably, the air grew heavier, greasier, and breathing became an agony under their heavy loads. To save their water, Malcom drank at one of the pools and something in the water was so poisonous that he vomited immediately afterwards, and felt odd spasms of dizziness as they held on again. In the south he saw the sky being painted by multitudes of shadowy fingers—now a fine line of purple, now amethyst, now garnet, each limning disappearing as another succeeded it. He stopped and pointed out the phenomena to the hastening guide.

The Mayan cursed. 'It is the coming of the rains,' he said.

They plunged on ahead again, through the bushes and shoulder-high coarse grass which had succeeded the forest. Almost immediately afterwards the accident occurred.

Malcom's dizziness, he himself states, was the cause. He missed a quite obvious crack and plunged into it the full length of his right leg. The crevice was scarcely eighteen inches wide but the edge caught and jarred his falling body "intimately. I screamed like a rat and then the pain was gone. I heard the crack of my fibula and then I think I fainted—incompletely. I recovered to find myself vomiting again in an unrestrained manner, and Ramon, having dragged me from the hole, doing excruciating things to my leg below the knee. He tried to mend me further up, but I was so sick he had to stop."

They were less than a mile from the Domina Range.

VI

There follows both from the *Diary* and from Pech's account a record of splint-making, bandaging, crude surgery, and desperation at the coming night and rain which may well be omitted. Briefly, the Mayan succeeded in staunching the flow of blood from Malcom's injured pelvis, and in setting his leg in rough splints. Not only that, but he picked him up and carried him across the remaining half-mile to the Hills. Shelter of some kind was necessary, and the breath of the forest at evening was poisonous.

But under the immediate brow of the southern hill there was no shelter at all. It was scraped bare, glistening volcanic slag, and the guide, after a rest during which Malcom again lost consciousness, set out round its slopes in search for some clump of bushes or projecting ledge to ward off the coming storms. In the west, behind them, setting the watching, silent forest alive with dark manes and straining heads, as of great feathered serpents, the sunset lingered. The guide had completely rounded the shoulder of the hill when he observed, a few feet up the twilight slope, something that looked like the mouth of a cave. He rested again,

248

and then pantingly bore Malcom up to that blackness against a lighter dusk.

It was no cave, he saw then, but a shallow scooping in the face of the rock, as though a quarry had been begun by the men of ancient times and then abandoned. It pierced eight or nine feet back into the hill, however, and faced to the north-east, with an overhang projecting beyond the entrance floor. Pech laid Malcom down after flashing his electric torch over the dry floor in search of snakes. Then he turned and ran down the hill and hastened back to the spot where the accident had occurred. By the time he returned, the wind was sweeping across the Domina Range, and with the wind came presently the first moaning downpour of the seasonal rains.

VII

"Ramon at first refused to go," Malcom records in his *Diary* for the 30th of August, after an account of the foregoing happenings. He writes in his usual floriferous hand, but in pencil. "But at last I made him see sense: that he could do no good and would be little better than a nuisance, that it was absolutely essential to get back to Newman's camp and bring Newman himself to doctor me and a mule to get me back to the coast. The rains aren't so far advanced but that that can't still be done. With the track more or less cleared he should be back inside ten days. He swore that it was desertion and invoked the saints—a thing, as I pointed out, that no good socialist would ever do in Yucatan—against any such plan. But at last he rebandaged my leg, which feels completely numb from the knee down, cut away the leg of my breeches and bound me up with a puttee and a handful of green leaves. The bleeding has stopped, but the moving was damnable. If it were only my leg. . . . Then he rigged up the cover of the Butcher to protect me in case the wind should veer and drive the rain into the mouth of this recess. He has filled the two water-skins, and if I go slowly the food should last. Then he put my machete beside me, saw that the blanket was all right, and fussed around till I had to point out that the rain had stopped and he had better start out. That was three hours ago. We shook hands and he kissed me. Amazing thing to be kissed by an Ancient Maya face from the Palenque stuccos! I shouted after him: I wanted to tell him to make Newman bring up the other camera and the plaster of Paris, now we've reached those hills. But I suppose he didn't hear, for he didn't come back."

He had never been so completely alone in his life, as he realized that night. The rains were descending again, a solid sheet of water washing over the Domina Range, and he lay for a long time in the darkness, wakeful, seeing the ghostly play of water outside the entrance of his shelter. He dozed and woke and dozed again till dawn, and then woke to find his pelvis burning. That burning pain did not wear off for several hours, and it was noon before he noted that the rain had ceased.

" It has not rained since then. All the afternoon has been quiet but for the dripping of the water and the sound of the rivulets streaming off the hills. But it is impossible to see more than a few yards from the entrance of my recess. The fog is as thick as wool and winds and changes continually. I lie crosswise to the entrance, and lizards slip in and out and halt and stare at me. Once I thought I heard some animal come padding up to the entrance, and stop and breathe and go away again. But I must have dreamt it. I was very bored all this afternoon and the light was fading before I noticed something that had escaped me before. Ramon was right. This is no natural hole in the face of the hill. It is the beginning of a quarry. More exciting still, the quarrying must have been done not with stone tools, but with copper or bronze. The vault has a green tinge that comes only from copper. . . . Our journey has not been for nothing. Ramon's city must be a fact—and a city built by a bronze-using people!"

The first of September says simply, "If only the fog would clear," the 2nd, 3rd, and 4th are blanks, but the 5th is lengthy, though the writing is curiously strained and unfamiliar:

" It rose today. The rain came on again just after ten o'clock, and two hours later a hurricane that seemed to rock the hills. The Butcher canvas was thrown down on top of me and I was half-smothered and almost fainting before I got it firmly wedged in position again. I did not dream about that beast after all. It is a puma. It came rushing in with the hurricane, and snarled, and slithered on its feet at sight of me. I threw a stone at it and it bounded out with a squawk. Only then I saw that the mist had gone. Almost the whole of the Range lay bare. It is not a straight sierra, but curves in an arc, so that the further tip is almost due opposite. But on all that further tip the shroud of fog lay unmoved.

"There, if anywhere, is the city.

"I could not get at my Zeiss. It is back in the rear of the recess with the camera. Even with its aid I doubt if I'd solve the mystery of that further tip, though it cannot be more than half an hour's walk away. Oh, my God, if only I hadn't been such a fool as fall in that crevice. . . ."

There is no entry for the 6th, the eighth day after the accident, and the entry of the 7th appears to have been attempted several times, abandoned, and resumed.

"An hour after sunrise the fog rose for a moment, then closed again as exasperatingly as before.

"Got very little sleep throughout the night."

Curiously, his thoughts strayed to Newman:

"Not a human being at all with whom I wrangled and bickered, but an ape, one of the horde of shiftless beasts our civilization has manufactured, their simian excrement befouling the passage of the Defile, their gibbered fears and meaningless treacheries dogging every step we take."

The 8th opens with something illegible, and then:

". . . here, lost in the wilds of Central America, in an old quarry of the Maya masons, perhaps within sight of a city lost for two thousand years: this is a romantic enough saga from the Azilian caves of Argyllshire and the muckle bed in Chapel kitchen! Ten months ago, yet it seems only yesterday that I rowed up the Thames with Domina, by Mortlake, and heard her urge me out on 'desperate adventures.' . . . All my life, it seems to me now, I've groped and struggled on the verge of some tremendous adventure. Is this a glimpse of it at last?"

"9th September: The stench is overpowering. I think gangrene has set in."

"10th September. That puma came again today and would not go away for a long time. . . ."

And then, somewhere in evening hours of alternate waking and unconsciousness, while Ramon Pech, after a fortnight's staggering Odyssey to his village in pursuit of Newman, was again nearing the Domina Range with a carrier and three mules, while in the cave above the slopes a beast squatted and licked its lips and crept nearer a silent figure and halted again, the mists lifted and swung aside from all the sierra, from the tips of the further hills. And Malcom lifted his head and cried out and searched desperately for his notebook and pencil the while the puma backed snarling away.

For it was no ruined city at all that crowned the Domina Range. Purple-blossoming, its terraces climbed the slopes. Golden-towered and minareted, the City of the Sun itself, it flashed in the evening light, a city immense, banner-hung and splendid, recorded by a straying pencil on an impossible page. . . .

Till suddenly the darkness swept moaning over the Chiapas country and the pages lay smashed and torn and stained with blood.

(And this is the end of Malcom Maudslay's saga.)

L'ENVOI

George Buxworth came down the steps of a Chelsea house, lighted his pipe, and turned westwards along the lamp-lit Embankment. He had passed the last six hours in Domina Maudslay's flat, in the helpless capacity of Malcom's friend and Stuart Isham's messenger.

God, what hours! What a night!

He took off his hat and wiped his forehead. Jane never had a time like that. . . . She'd be glad about the baby.

A son for Malcom. . . .

He stopped and yawned and knocked his pipe against the Embankment parapet. He felt very tired. He glanced at his wristwatch and then at the sky. The darkness was thinning.

Already in the air there was a smell of morning.